girl
crushed

girl crushed

KATIE HEANEY

EMBER

Text copyright © 2020 by Katie Heaney
Cover art and interior illustrations copyright © 2020 by Josephine Rais

All rights reserved. Published in the United States by Ember, an imprint of Random House Children's Books, a division of Penguin Random House LLC, New York. Originally published in hardcover in the United States by Alfred A. Knopf, an imprint of Random House Children's Books, a division of Penguin Random House LLC, New York, in 2020.

Ember and the E colophon are registered trademarks of Penguin Random House LLC.

Visit us on the Web! GetUnderlined.com

Educators and librarians, for a variety of teaching tools, visit us at RHTeachersLibrarians.com

Library of Congress Cataloging-in-Publication Data is available upon request.
ISBN 978-1-9848-9734-3 (trade) — ISBN 978-1-9848-9735-0 (lib. bdg.) — ISBN 978-1-9848-9736-7 (ebook) —ISBN 978-1-9848-9737-4 (pbk.)

Printed in the United States of America
10 9 8 7 6 5 4 3 2 1
First Ember Edition 2021

For Lydia

One

The way I saw it, I had two options.

One: I could walk into school acting how I felt—i.e., sewage seeping out of a gutter.

Two: I could walk into school acting how I wanted Jamie to think I felt—i.e., happily single, carefree, and one hundred percent over her.

I could pretend it no longer bothered me that she'd dumped me a month before we started our senior year, thus destroying all the elaborate—forgive me—promposals I'd already started thinking up, and the love letter I'd started drafting for her yearbook. Never mind how many hours I'd wasted mapping the perfect road trip course between NYU (where she'd be next fall) and the University of North Carolina (where I'd be), the perfect plan to keep us together even in the face of medium-long distance. Jamie would never have to know I'd begun the initial research on a surprise fall-break trip to Washington, DC, the natural halfway point between our colleges, because Jamie talked about it like it was Disneyland. She wanted to be the third woman president—third, specifically, because it would be pathetic and disgusting if there weren't at least two other women presidents before she was old enough to run herself. Her words.

I looked at the dashboard and realized I'd been gripping the wheel of my parked truck in the student lot for eleven full minutes. And I was still too early. For the first time since I'd gotten my driver's license, Jamie hadn't ridden with me to school. After she dumped me, she texted me to say she thought it would be best if she caught a ride with Alexis for a while instead. I hadn't thought that far ahead yet, hadn't imagined all the things we did together that I'd have to start doing without her. It made me wonder how long she'd been thinking about breaking up with me before she did it.

Fine with me, I'd texted back. **You're pretty out of the way.**

(Obviously, that was before I'd decided to be cool and mature and happy, honestly, about this whole thing.)

The upside to driving to school alone was that I could listen to any kind of music I wanted, and no one could complain, or ask me to play some horrible new indie band's EP instead. The downside was that, so far, I'd used my newfound freedom to blast my *Tragic Lesbian Breakup* playlist sixty-four times in a row. A sampling: "One More Hour" by Sleater-Kinney, "Where

Does the Good Go?" by Tegan and Sara, "Cliff's Edge" by Hayley Kiyoko, "Give Me One Reason" by Tracy Chapman, "My Heart Will Go On" by Céline Dion. Maybe Céline Dion wasn't gay (*allegedly*), but whatever. The song broke my heart in exactly the way I wanted my heart to be broken.

I thought about giving it one last listen before I left the truck, but I didn't want to be the girl caught cry-mouthing *whereverrrrr you aaaaahhhhh* in the parking lot at 7:32 in the morning on the first day of school. Instead I closed my eyes and repeated in my head: *I am happy. I am carefree. I am totally over Jamie.* We were just going to be friends now, and someday, if not today, I would be completely cool with that, because I had promised her I could be. Of course, being friends was her idea. This was part of her very practical reason for breaking up with me. Jamie had told me that romantic relationships always ended, and most of them ended badly, and if eventually we were going to break up (and we would), we might as well do it early. Damage control, she called it. This way, she said, we could more likely stay in each other's lives indefinitely. As friends.

Imagine being told the reason your girlfriend can't date you anymore is that she likes you too much. It's very confusing. I asked and I asked but she could never explain it in a way I understood. So eventually I had to stop asking.

And of course, a part of me had wanted to refuse, to tell her through tears that *I don't know how to be just friends with you anymore*, because maybe if I could borrow a line from a TV show it would feel like a TV show instead of my actual life. After she'd left my house I'd paced around the living room, working up the nerve to call her and tell her. But every time I tried to imagine *not* talking to her, I couldn't. It was like my brain didn't have the right files. *Does not compute*. And anyway, it didn't really feel like a choice. If I admitted I couldn't be friends with her, I lost, even more than I already had. I'd have to be the one to sit somewhere else at lunch. I'd be the one who had to stay home when Jamie and our other friends hung out. I'd lost my girlfriend, and that was already more than I could take.

So we would be friends, and it would be fine. One day I wouldn't dread walking into the class I knew we had together—a now-unwanted miracle, really, since Jamie was always in AP everything and I was not. One day I'd be able to sit down to lunch with her and Ronni and Alexis without worrying exactly where I sat, because the spot next to her wasn't safe, and neither was the one directly across from her. One day I'd again be happy instead of furious that our lockers, thanks to the goddamn alphabet, were separated only by the locker assigned to Alex Ruiz, who, historically, didn't seem to make much use of it. He was popular, and the popular boys never seemed to carry books or folders or anything, really, around school with them. It was like they were here for something else altogether. I once asked my straight friends (Ronni and Alexis) to look into this issue for me, but they shrugged it off. Alexis said, "Who knows why they do anything the way they do?" *They* being boys, in general.

At home, and in the safety of my truck, I still ached when I thought about that last conversation with Jamie. I still held back tears multiple times a day. But I knew I couldn't be that version of me in school if I wanted to make it through the year. It was bad enough knowing in my bones that everyone at school had already heard that the only out queer couple in Westville's incoming senior class had broken up, and worse, that I was the dumpee—Alexis had surely been briefed by Jamie, which meant it was only a matter of time until people three school districts away found out. If I started my senior year as the tragic spinster lesbian, that would be how everyone remembered me. At our ten-year reunion, instead of asking me what it was like playing for the U.S. women's national soccer team, or how many free shoes I got as a result of my Adidas sponsorship, or if they could go for a ride in my Aston Martin, my former classmates would ask me if I still kept in touch with Jamie (who would be too busy in the Senate to attend), and from their expressions I would know they were *really* asking if I'd ever gotten over her.

I couldn't let that happen. Everything I felt had to stay here, in the truck, with Céline. I slung my backpack and soccer bag over my shoulders, and by the time I'd crossed the parking lot I really did feel like a new person, almost.

* * *

I thought I saw Jamie about a dozen times before I actually did. In the hallways, between classes, I kept seeing girls with dark hair, and my throat would go hot with panic. Then I'd get another look and realize they didn't look like Jamie at all. It was embarrassing, and draining, and by lunch I was almost eager to see her, just to get it over with. Our first post-breakup encounter had to happen sometime; this way, at least, I was prepared for it.

I spotted Ronni sitting at our usual table, alone so far and completely unembarrassed by it. Even though I'd seen her last weekend, at the last club tournament of the year, I rushed toward her like it had been months. When Ronni saw me, she cupped a hand around her mouth and yelled "RYAN!" at the same time as I yelled "DAVIS!"

Ronni Davis was my first real best friend, long before I ever met Jamie. We met in sixth grade, when I finally made the Surf Club's premier soccer team after spending two years stuck on the Triple-A team. Ronni had made the premier team from the start, way back in fourth grade, and when I moved up, she was the only girl who said hi to me on the first day of practice. Everyone else ignored me, laughing too loud at their dumb, private middle-school jokes, throwing me and my floppy boy's bowl cut the occasional skeptical glare. After a week or two I was one of them, having proved I was good enough to be there, but at the time, it felt like earning their approval took years. If it hadn't been for Ronni, I might have quit, or begged to be put back on my old team, where at least I was the very best player on the medium-good team. We were inseparable, until I met Jamie. Jamie eclipsed everyone and everything, for me.

Oh God, I thought. *Keep it together, Ryan.*

As I reached our lunch table, I dipped into a subservient bow before Ronni. "My liege."

Ronni shook her head. "You are *so* corny."

At the end of our junior year, Ronni had been elected captain of our high school team over me, and I was devastated. I'd expected her to be chosen as club captain, which she also was, but I'd hoped somehow that I could be captain at school. Being captain didn't mean much of anything as far as college recruiters cared, but I wanted it anyway. I had never been the head of anything. I wanted the word *captain* printed below my name in the yearbook as a matter of public record: I meant something.

Now all my short-term hopes and dreams rested on being named the United Soccer Coaches National Player of the Year, or Gatorade Player of the Year, like Ashlyn Harris, UNC alum and butch style icon, who earned both when she was in high school.

In the end, of course, I wanted to be Megan Rapinoe: World Cup champion, Golden Boot *and* Golden Ball winner, the best and most beloved player in the world. I wanted my name on jerseys and my face on girls' walls. There was still time.

In any case, I got over the lost election after a week or so. For one thing, it quickly became obvious that Ronni would be a better captain than I ever could have been. Unlike me, she wasn't afraid of our coach, even though Coach was objectively terrifying. At our last few school-season games as juniors, when she was captain-elect if not yet captain in practice, she stood next to Coach on the sidelines on the rare occasion she wasn't playing, and together they assessed the rest of us with their arms crossed. Ronni looked so grown-up and official, exactly in the right place. Besides, the captain couldn't be everyone's best friend, just like a boss could never be real friends with her employees. Free of the responsibility to critique my teammates when they messed up a play, I could instead be the one who cheered them up after.

I unwrapped my sandwich and took a bite, hoping food would soothe the anxiety humming in my chest. Now that I was sitting down, I felt trapped—and paranoid. I couldn't keep my eyes off the cafeteria doors. Ronni smacked a hand on the table.

"I thought we agreed: no liverwurst!"

"It's the first day of school!" I protested. "It's a special occasion!"

Ronni made a face. "Fine, but I don't want to smell that smell again before your birthday."

"What about *your* birthday?" I countered, and it was at that moment that I saw Jamie out of the corner of my eye. She'd just walked in with Alexis. I swallowed fast, too fast, and tried to obscure my small coughing fit in the crook of my elbow.

"You okay?" said Jamie.

How dare *you,* I thought. Ronni clapped me on the back, which only made me cough more. So far, this was going extremely well.

"Do you need the Heimlich? I'm still certified from my Red Cross babysitter training . . . ," offered Alexis.

"Someone who actually needs the Heimlich isn't gonna be like, 'Yes, thanks, that would be great,' " said Jamie.

"I'm fine," I rasped.

"You sure?" asked Jamie.

It was clear from the way she asked that Jamie wasn't just wondering whether or not I was done choking in front of her. Maybe she was trying to be nice, but as far as I was concerned, she could pluck those pity eyes right out of her head. I couldn't make her un-break up with me, but I could certainly deny her the pleasure of knowing how much it still hurt. I could be friend*ly,* but she couldn't rush me right into unloaded friendship, either. I nodded quickly and changed the subject.

"Alexis," I said, "give us the goods. What have you heard so far?"

Alexis was our school's own *Us Weekly.* If anyone in our

class hooked up with anyone, or got in a fight with anyone, or got detention, or got wasted over the weekend, Alexis knew about it, and she would relay the episode to us in more detail than anyone needed, and often more than anyone wanted. She had sources in every social group. People told her things because she had a small mouth and huge, understanding blue eyes, but also because she told them things in return. People only pretended to care when their secrets got out. We all knew that to get the best gossip you also had to give it. And there was no day better for the very best gossip than the first day back after summer break.

"Well," said Alexis, eyes gleaming. She leaned over the table conspiratorially, and I breathed in relief. For as long as Alexis talked, I would be safe: I wouldn't have to look at Jamie, or think of what to say to her, or notice Ronni and Alexis watching us interact, trying to judge whether or not we were "okay" yet. What would that look like, anyway? We weren't together anymore, but we were both here. I wasn't yelling and I wasn't crying. If they expected more from me than that, I'd go sit somewhere else. No—they could sit somewhere else. No, wait—that would leave just me and Jamie. *Ugh.*

"—*and,* Ruby and Mikey broke up," Alexis was saying. "A few weeks ago, apparently."

"Wait," I said. "What?" Jamie and I made eye contact for only an instant, but it was long enough to know we'd both had the same exact thought: Ruby Ocampo, number one on the list of Straight Girls We Wish Weren't. I hadn't thought about that list in a year.

Alexis misinterpreted my confusion as shock and clapped her hands in delight. "I *know*!"

"What about Sweets?" Jamie asked.

"Who broke up with who?" I asked.

Sweets was the name of a band composed of four Westville seniors: Mikey Vingiano on bass, Ben Cooper on drums, David Tovar on guitar, and Ruby Ocampo on vocals. Like many of our classmates, Jamie was obsessed with them. She'd sent me links to their SoundCloud page about a dozen times before I actually clicked on one, and even then I only lasted about twenty seconds. Ruby had a nice voice, but calling the noise underneath it a "song" felt generous. Jamie had told me I had to see them live to *get* it, but I often had soccer games when they had shows, and the rest of the time I invented menstrual cramps. They played most of their shows at the Six-Pack, which was the idiotic name given to the dilapidated old house in which Mikey's older brother lived with three other college sophomores. Jamie said it wasn't so bad, but when I pictured it I saw a dark and sweaty basement overflowing with smelly boys nodding to the music and drinking flat beer. I'd asked her if that sounded right and she agreed: it was more or less just like that. So, no thank you.

"Ruby broke up with Mikey," said Alexis. "And Sweets is fine, for now . . . but apparently Mikey revoked use of his brother's house as, like, punishment for the breakup, I guess. So they need a new venue."

"What a little bitch," said Ronni. We didn't have to ask—we knew she meant Mikey.

"I wonder if they could play at Triple Moon," said Jamie.

"Ha!" I laughed. "Right. I'm sure those guys would love to play at a lesbian coffee shop."

"Why *not*?!" Alexis nearly shouted. Alexis was *very* offended on Jamie's and my behalf whenever someone did or said something vaguely homophobic. Because Jamie was Jewish and Ronni was black, Alexis also took anti-Semitism and racism very personally. Needless to say, she found most things sexist. Her backpack was covered in pins that read STRAIGHT BUT NOT NARROW and COEXIST and WHO RUN THE WORLD? GIRLS and BLACK LIVES MATTER, the last of which Ronni gave her to replace one that read ONE RACE: HUMAN.

"They need somewhere to play, don't they? And Triple Moon has shows," said Jamie.

"Yeah, like . . . spoken-word shows."

"I dunno," said Jamie. "I think Dee and Gaby would be down. A lot of people like Sweets. It'd be good for business."

"I'm sure *they'd* be fine with it. I just think those guys would sooner play a Panera Bread than Triple Moon."

"Maybe a break will be good for them," said Ronni. "You

know, take some lessons . . . learn to read music . . ." (Fine: I'd sent Ronni the link I'd listened to.)

I cracked up. Jamie looked annoyed. "They *know* how to *play.* You guys just don't get it."

"You got me there." Ronni shrugged.

"I *get* it," I argued. Suddenly I was mad. "I just don't like it."

"The one song you listened to?"

"One was enough."

My heart hammered against my ribs, and I saw Ronni and Alexis exchange a quick look, just like I knew they would. We were making them uncomfortable, which was the last thing I wanted. No matter how stupid Jamie had made me feel, I had to be cordial. I didn't want to give them the opportunity to pick sides unless I knew for sure they'd take mine.

"I'm sorry," I said. "Triple Moon isn't a bad idea."

Jamie stared at me for a moment. It took everything I had not to look away before she muttered, "Thanks."

Under the table Ronni grabbed my wrist and squeezed it. I couldn't look at her or I'd cry, so instead I slid an Oreo into my mouth and focused on chewing that instead.

The good thing about not having Civil Liberties until last period was that I got a break from seeing Jamie for two hours. The bad thing about having Civil Liberties last period was that I spent those two hours dreading seeing Jamie. She shouldn't have even *been* in Civil Liberties, which was, for most people, a civics graduation requirement taken at the last possible second. Jamie, however, had already taken AP Government junior year, and was taking Civil Liberties for "fun," which to me felt a little like a billionaire choosing to take the bus.

At passing time I stepped into a stall in the girls' bathroom and waited the remaining four minutes out, not wanting to get there before she did. When the warning bell rang I checked my teeth in the mirror and pulled and poked at pieces of my hair until it looked almost normal, and then I walked into class. And for a moment—just a moment—I considered walking right back out.

There was only one open seat left: the one closest to Mr. Haggerty's desk. Sitting in the seat directly behind that one was Jamie.

"You've *got* to be kidding me," I muttered to myself.

I dropped my bag alongside the desk, and Jamie gave me a bashful, closed-mouth smile.

For the first time in my life, I prayed to be given a seating chart. And I prayed it would put me as far away from Jamie Rudawski as possible.

Mr. Haggerty introduced himself and took roll call, pausing to make notes when someone corrected his pronunciation or specified a nickname. We could have done the whole routine collectively, on each other's behalf, so many times had we heard each other's names read aloud over the last three years.

I stared at the surface of my desk, imagining I felt Jamie's eyes boring into my brain. *Don't let her catch you thinking about her,* I thought. *Ah, I mean—shit.*

Then Mr. Haggerty called out, "Ruby Ocampo," and I looked up.

Two

You know those people who were a little too good-looking as fifth graders? Like, so good-looking that you knew, as a fifth grader yourself, that something deeply and biologically unfair was afoot? Before fifth grade, my classmates and I were on pretty equal footing, looks-wise—all of us barefaced and missing teeth, wearing braids and ponytails that hung loose and weird by the end of each day. Back then the only person fit for a crush was my teacher, Ms. Urlacher, who had a bottle-blond newscaster blowout and wore blue mascara and Britney Spears perfume. (I knew this because she kept a bottle on her desk, and once I'd pretended to leave something behind so I could run back and sniff it.)

Then fifth grade started, and a few of the girls I *thought* I knew came back to school so pretty it embarrassed me to look at them. That was when I learned two very important things: one, that I was *super* gay, and two, that life wasn't fair.

Ruby didn't go to my elementary school, or my middle school for that matter, but I knew, I just *knew* she'd been one of those fifth-grade girls. You could see it in her face, in the way she sat in her chair: the mind-numbing boredom of life-long beauty.

When Mr. Haggerty called Ruby's name, she didn't say anything. She just lifted the hand she'd been using to hold her head up. She was seated across the room from me, so it was easy to get away with looking at her, which I felt like I hadn't done in forever. When Jamie and I were together, other girls stopped existing to me. But way, way back *before* Jamie and I got together, I had a not-so-tiny crush on Ruby. So did Jamie. Once we figured out we both liked girls, but before we figured out we liked each other, we spent a gleeful afternoon listing all the girls we thought were prettiest at school. All of them were straight, just like everyone we knew. And lo, the Straight Girls We Wish Weren't list was born. It was a joke, obviously, and I'd fully forgotten at least five of the fifteen or so names we'd written. I no longer knew where the physical list *was*, and I kind of hoped I'd never find it. But I would never forget writing Ruby's name in the number-one spot. She still belonged there. That much, at least, hadn't changed.

Ruby was—how to put this?—so hot I wanted to die. Her

hair was incredible: long, shiny, and black, the tips currently dyed emerald green. This was one of her signatures. In fact, I had a theory that Beauty Supply Warehouse based its Manic Panic stocking decisions on the color of Ruby's tips. When she showed up to school with a new shade, it was like a pandemic: at first there would be one alt-girl copycat with a streak in the same color, and then there were three, and suddenly there were twelve. Ruby had the kind of hair you'd naively bring a picture of to your salon, as if there were any way a mere mortal could turn the mess on your head into *that*.

Ruby also had high cheekbones, straight teeth, a sharp jaw. All the desirable adjectives, correctly applied. Back in freshman year, the unconfirmed rumor (circulated thanks to Alexis) was that her bra size was 32E. I hadn't known such a size existed.

I was for *sure* staring, I realized. I returned my attention to the front of the room, but the problem was that nothing there was hot *or* interesting. Slowly my eyes crept back. While I was sure my newfound singleness was as visibly disfiguring as a horn growing out of my forehead, Ruby looked refreshed, light, happy. For her, anyway. She wasn't a big smiler, so it was hard to say. Maybe I was reading too much into nothing because of what Alexis had told us. Maybe it wasn't even true. But every time I looked at Ruby during class (and it was a lot of times), I felt a tiny but inarguable fluttering in my chest.

The first time she caught me staring at her I looked away

quickly, giving the notes scrawled on the whiteboard an unfocused once-over. My chest burned, and I felt Jamie's presence behind me, mocking me. *You're kidding, right?* I heard her say. *You stood a better chance with Ms. Urlacher.*

But what, romantically speaking, did I have left to lose? Not one thing. So the second time Ruby caught me, I kept looking. She held my gaze for two full seconds, which—in every bad lesbian movie I've seen, anyway—is usually all it takes.

When the bell rang, everyone leapt from their seats, and I grabbed Jamie by the backpack before she could escape down the hall. I pulled her close enough to hear me whisper, ignoring the flip in my stomach, "You should tell her about Triple Moon."

"What, now?"

"Yeah, why not?"

"I mean, so many reasons . . ."

"I'll go with you."

Jamie threw her arms up in the air. "Oh, well, *then.*"

"If you won't, I will." I gave her a second to reconsider, and when she didn't, I booked it out the door, searching the hallway for the back of Ruby's head. I found it ducking into the restroom I'd hidden in before class, and, as casually as possible, I followed her inside. Two of the three stalls were occupied, and Ruby walked into the third, a favored graffiti spot so thick with layer upon layer of rust-colored paint the door barely shut.

I washed my hands until I heard a flush, and when the person that joined me at the sinks wasn't Ruby, I kept washing. My heart pounded in my chest, but I couldn't just walk out. I couldn't have needlessly washed my hands all that time for nothing. Somehow I'd committed myself entirely to a bathroom ambush, and I wouldn't leave until I did what I went in there to do.

When Ruby emerged, I pounced, casually.

"Hey," I said.

This was the second time we'd ever spoken. The first was sophomore year, in 2-D Art, when I leaned over to ask if I could borrow her eraser. She'd handed it to me wordlessly.

"Hey." She looked neither especially happy to see me nor confused as to why I was talking to her, which I took as a win.

"This is kinda random," I continued, "but I heard you might be looking for a new space for shows."

Ruby frowned, shaking her hands dry over the sink. "That's a thing people are talking about?"

"Well, your fans are concerned."

She smirked. "Is that so?"

"Anyway, I only mention it because I know a cool place that might be into having you guys. It's called Triple Moon?"

"Isn't that a bookstore?"

"It's more of a coffee shop, but they sell some books, yeah."

"They do live music?"

"Sometimes." *Please don't ask me for examples,* I thought.

"Huh. Cool. Guess I'll look into it."

"I know the owners, if you want me to put you in touch." I held back a grimace. Surely there was a cooler way to say what I'd just said.

Ruby hesitated, and for a long, terrible moment I worried she'd say something devastating, like *no thanks,* or *that's okay.*

"Um, sure," she said. "Should I give you my number, or email, or . . . ?"

Both, I wanted to say. *All of it.*

"Number works," I said.

I pulled out my phone and handed it to her, and just a few seconds later, I had Ruby's number. It was crazy, and a little terrifying, how quickly things could change. For almost a year I'd been Jamie's girlfriend and then one day I wasn't. For a full month I'd been sad and lonely and absolutely without-a-doubt certain I'd never feel good again. And while what I felt in that moment didn't quite qualify as *good,* exactly, it was something in the vicinity. A little spark of hope, maybe, for the first time in what felt like forever.

"I gotta get going, but talk to you later," said Ruby.

"Yeah," I said. "Later." I hung back for a minute after she left, and then I sprinted for the locker room, barely suppressing a full-blown grin.

That night after soccer practice I got a text from Jamie.

Soooo . . . did you talk to Ruby

I stared at the screen for two minutes before texting her back: **Yep.**

I watched the three little typing dots flicker and disappear and flicker again. I waited.

Two minutes later: **And?**

I could have kissed my phone. So rarely was I the one making someone else wait around for my response. Especially with Jamie. For more than two years every text I got from her had felt like a ticking time bomb I could only defuse by replying within seconds. I'd been desperate to give her the go-ahead to text me again. *Desperate and Pathetic: The Quinn Ryan Story.*

I took my time tapping out a response, imagining Jamie on the other end, forced to watch my infuriating bubble. I hit send, and heard the whoosh, and I thought, *This is what drugs must feel like.* I wrote: **Well, I have her number now. A master-piece. My finest work.**

Then the dots appeared, and I held my breath, and then they disappeared, and I let out an aggravated sigh. There I was, waiting for Jamie's words again. The bubble reappeared and I inhaled. It was a reflex I'd have to unlearn. At a later date.

Wow, she wrote. **#1 straight girl. Congrats.**

You didn't have to know Jamie as well as I did to know

that *congrats* followed by a period was essentially equivalent to *how embarrassing for you*. But I did know Jamie that well, and I could tell that *congrats* was a front, and that I'd gotten to her. And that made it pinch a little less.

I didn't say I was trying to date her, I wrote, regretting it instantly. *Defensive. Not good.*

You can date whoever you want, Jamie wrote.

"Oh, *reallyyyyy?"* I said in a high-pitched whine. I was furiously typing a reply when she texted again.

Sorry. Patronizing. I meant, you don't have to explain yourself to me.

A pause, and then: **But she is straight.**

Ugh. As if I needed reminding.

Yeah, as of two years ago, I wrote.

Lol, she replied.

Was that the last time she registered?

I accidentally laughed, even though I was furious.

That's when we made the list.

I know. I was jk

Well– I started.

Look, she wrote.

We both waited. I watched her bubble flash and disappear four times at least.

It's none of my business, she wrote finally. *That's it?* I thought.

There were a dozen angry texts I wanted to sling at

Jamie like arrows. I typed and deleted **I get to decide if it's your business or not,** which I wasn't even sure made sense. Telling Jamie I'd gotten Ruby's number hadn't felt as good as I'd expected, but I also hadn't really thought it through. What else was there for her to say at this point? I had a hot (straight) girl's phone number, but I hadn't done anything with it. Jamie clearly didn't believe in me. So maybe I'd have to make her.

But in the meantime, I wanted peace, and I needed a friend. Specifically, my gay friend, still the only one I knew. God bless Ronni and Alexis, truly the two best straight people I knew after my mom, but there were things they'd never understand the way Jamie did. She wasn't my girlfriend anymore, but what if I still needed her to be everything else?

Evidently I'd waited too long to compose a reply because Jamie texted again.

Is this always going to be weird?

It was like she'd been reading my mind long-distance. Only it was different coming from the person who'd made it weird by doing the dumping.

You don't get to ask me that.

OK. That's fair.

I blinked back surprise tears and took a deep breath. I didn't want things between us to be weird forever, either. So I offered her an out. I wrote: **Sorry. You know how emotional first days make me.**

Haha. I do.

I remembered our first day of sophomore year, when Jamie's mom dropped us off outside, and how I'd teared up on the curb, thinking about how serious life was about to become now that we were no longer freshmen. We didn't even have drivers' licenses yet, but we still felt so grown up. Everything up until that point had just been practice; sophomore year was when high school *really* began. Jamie had had to pull me toward the door by the arm. Somehow I knew she was picturing the same first day I was. I felt my heart grow two degrees warmer. Maybe we really would be okay.

Do you wanna go to Triple Moon on Saturday? Do homework? I wrote, surprising myself.

Are you sure?

Yeah, I texted. **Gotta start somewhere.**

It wouldn't be easy, I knew, to go back there. Triple Moon had been our place. But Triple Moon was also *my* favorite place in the world, and I couldn't stay away forever. Two weeks earlier I'd gotten a concerned email from Dee asking where we'd been, and I'd had to tell her that Jamie and I broke up. Her reply was brief, but so gentle and kind it made me cry. I wanted to see her again, and Gaby, too. And as much as it might hurt to go back there with Jamie, I couldn't imagine being there without her.

* * *

Jamie was the one who found Triple Moon, obviously. When she told me about it freshman year, I didn't know this would become our dynamic: Jamie told me what we should do, or where we should go, and I followed.

We met in Algebra I, though we only sat next to each other for a week and a half before it became clear to our teacher that Jamie did not belong there. He arranged to transfer her to Algebra 2/Trigonometry, the students of which called it "Squeeze" for short, because as geniuses, they were far too busy to say the whole name. Jamie and I were devastated. We acted like she'd been conscripted into the army. I had other friends, from soccer and middle school, but the thought of getting through the day without seeing this girl I'd only just met was unbearable. Jamie told me she'd flunk out on purpose, that she'd be back in Algebra I in no time. I held out hope until the semester ended.

In the meantime, we texted and slipped notes into each other's lockers. We wrote about our favorite movies and TV shows and books. We wrote about our families, Jamie's overbearing parents and my divorced ones. Because Jamie had gone to a different middle school, I filled her in on the first- and second-tier popular kids in our grade, and who was dating whom. One day I opened one of her notes—always neon-blue or purple writing on black paper, folded into a triangle—and read: *Who've you gone out with?*

I still had the note. It was faded gray, pressed flat between the pages of *The Return of the King*.

When I read it, I knew. We'd been dancing around the inevitable for weeks by that point—some abstract point of connection between us, some fundamental recognition that we had something essential and rare in common. Jamie was asking me without asking me if I liked girls. And I was pretty sure that because she was asking, she already knew the answer, because she liked girls too.

So I came out to her, and she came out to me. We were afraid to put it in writing, so we made plans to meet one Saturday morning, at a coffee shop Jamie had been waiting for a reason to go into: Triple Moon, which I'd seen but never really *noticed*. We got our moms to drop us off at noon and told them to pick us up at two. At one we texted them to say **actually, make it 3:00.** At two-thirty we said **actually, make it 4:00. Wait—4:30.**

Triple Moon was the first place I ever felt safe being fully myself. It was where I first said the words *I'm gay* out loud. It was where I found so many books that changed my life: *Rubyfruit Jungle, Keeping You a Secret, Summer Sisters, Annie on My Mind, Women, The Miseducation of Cameron Post*. The owners, Dee and Gaby, kept two giant mismatched bookshelves crammed full of dog-eared, marked-up LGBTQ books left there by customers. Taped to the top shelf was a handwritten note outlining the books' honor system: you could borrow whatever you wanted, up to two at a time, so long as you brought them back in readable condition when you were done. And if you bought a new queer book, from their small selection or somewhere else, you were encouraged to leave it on their shelves when you were done, for someone else to discover.

Triple Moon was also where Jamie and I fell in love, though it took nearly two years for us to notice. *Before we were girlfriends we were friends,* I reminded myself. *Somewhere inside we must still know how.*

Three

On Saturday morning I texted Jamie to ask if she wanted a ride, but she said she wanted to bike, even though the shop was at least five miles away from her house. It stung a little, and I wondered what she thought was going to happen if she got in my truck. Did she think that being side by side in such a confined space would make me cry, or beg for her back? I would have been offended, except I was a little afraid of the same thing. When we were apart I could believe I'd reached acceptance, but my body still reacted to her presence in a way I couldn't seem to shut off.

I was too nervous to listen to music on the drive over, so I called Ronni on the speaker's Bluetooth instead. She answered after three rings.

"What's up."

"Nothing much," I said. "Just headed to Triple Moon to meet Jamie."

I could pretty much hear Ronni close her eyes, pinching the bridge of her nose.

"I actually think it'll be really good," I added.

"You're a masochist, you know that?"

"I don't know who that is," I said, only half joking.

"What are you gonna do?"

"Homework." Silence. I strained my ears. "Ronni?"

"Yeah, I'm gonna give you a chance to come up with something more believable."

I laughed. "I'm serious! I brought my books and everything."

"Just don't cry," said Ronni. "Even I can't help you come back from that."

"I'm not going to *cry*," I said, which made me feel a little like crying.

"Okay, well, I was about to go for a run," she said. "But you can text me after."

"You're running today? Now I feel guilty."

"Just go later."

"Okay, I will," I said. We both knew I wouldn't.

"Gotta go."

"Okay, byeeeee, I love youuuuuu!" I sang, and Ronni hung up.

The coffee shop was mostly empty when I arrived, so when I walked in the door Dee saw me right away.

"Q!" she said, throwing her hands up in the air. "Come here!"

I grinned and rushed over to give her a hug across the cafe counter.

"How've you been?" I asked.

"Good, good. Happy to see you." She gave me a concerned-mom look. I recognized it not from my own mother, who had treated me like an adult since I was six years old, but from TV. "How you holding up?"

"Much better," I chirped, lying. "Jamie's meeting me here."

"Oh, girl." Dee sighed.

"What? God! We're just gonna do homework!"

"All right." She shook her head. "Just don't do the endless-processing thing, okay? A dyke can lose years off her life that way."

Dyke. I still got a little thrill whenever she said it. To Dee and Gaby, Jamie and I were baby dykes. To us, according to them, they were dusty dykes, old-fashioned and just plain old. To hear them tell it, you'd think no one had ever been gay before their generation showed up. As they often reminded us, they were our foremothers in dismantling the hetero-patriarchy, and so they said the word *dyke* as readily as they said our names, with a kind of defiant urgency. As a word, I liked it so much better than *lesbian*—the hardness of it, the single middle-finger syllable.

Of course, it depended who said it. Coming from Dee or

Gaby or Jamie, it was like a secret handshake. Coming from that blond girl on the Valhalla soccer team sophomore year, after I stole the ball and she tripped over my leg, it was like being spit at.

"We're not processing," I promised. "It's over." A lump formed at the base of my throat, and I thought of Ronni, frowning at me. I had to change the subject fast. "Where's Gaby?"

"Hungover," she said, rolling her eyes. "She'll be in in a bit." Gaby was the shop's co-owner, and also Dee's ex-girlfriend, though they both cringed if you reminded them. *That was two hundred years ago,* Dee would say. The queer library had been Gaby's idea, as was the shop's early adoption of every new nut- and plant-based milk, and she organized every event they hosted. She was vegan and spacey and liked going to protests and decorating boxes and mirrors with sea glass she plucked off the beach. It was hard to imagine that she'd ever been in love with Dee, and vice versa. Dee loved meat and the WNBA and her dogs and that was about it.

"Good," I said. "I want to tell her about this band that wants to play here."

Dee adopted Gaby's airy, earnest tone. "Are they aligned with the queer anti-capitalist intersectional feminist cause?"

I considered. "I don't think they're *against* it," I offered.

"Good luck with that."

The bell over the door rang, and I turned to see Jamie walk in, helmet in hand.

"Jamie!" Dee cried, and the tiniest bit of jealousy prickled the back of my neck.

Jamie waved and ran a hand through her curls, wild as ever even after her bike ride.

"Hey, Dee. How's it going?" she asked. To me, she added, "You have a table?"

"You pick," I said.

Dee gave me a look as Jamie unpacked her bag, and I grinned. "Better get to work, I guess."

"What do you guys want to drink?"

"Two iced vanilla lattes," I said.

"Just iced coffee for me," Jamie interjected.

"What?" We *always* got iced vanilla lattes at Triple Moon. They tasted like milkshakes.

"Sit down, Q. I'll bring them over."

Dee waved away my cash, so I dropped a five in the tip jar when she wasn't looking and crossed the room to take the seat across from Jamie's. In just moments she had the whole spread assembled: laptop open, notebook out, planner with to-do list ready to be crossed off, favorite pen, favorite backup pen. In my bag I had my physics textbook and *Frankenstein* by Mary Shelley, of which I needed to read fifty pages by Wednesday. Still, I hadn't actually planned to read it *now*. I sighed and pulled it out of my bag.

"It's good," said Jamie, eyeing the cover.

"Oh yeah? When'd you read it, fourth grade?"

She grinned. "Last year." Jamie was in AP Lit. AP everything, really. AP Dumping. Ha.

Dee moseyed over with the drinks. "Iced vanilla, iced coffee. Make space, Jame."

Jamie reluctantly moved her planner. "Thanks."

"Yeah, thanks."

"You're welcome."

"Any updates on Gaby's ETA?" I asked.

Dee snorted as she walked away.

"You're going to ask her about Sweets," said Jamie. It wasn't a question; she always, always knew what I was up to. It was incredibly annoying.

I shrugged. "I thought I might mention it, as long as we're here."

"Right."

"Unless you want to? Since it was your idea?"

"Nah," said Jamie. "I'm good."

"You sure? Am I going to find out you're mad about this in three to six months?"

I knew Jamie very well too.

"I just want Sweets to still exist, as a band," she said. "I don't care how that's accomplished." She took a sip of her coffee and made a small, almost imperceptible face.

"Miss the vanilla?"

"No," she lied.

I looked over at Dee behind the counter to find her looking at me. *Processing,* she mouthed.

Jamie sat up straight, assuming her Serious Student position, so I opened *Frankenstein* and started reading:

> *I am by birth a Genevese, and my family is one of the most distinguished of that republic. My ancestors had been for many years counsellors and syndics, and my father had filled several public situations with honour and reputation. He was respected by all who knew him for his integrity and indefatigable—*

I set the book down. Jamie eyed me over the top of her computer screen.

"What are you working on?" I asked.

"A paper."

"What's it about?"

"Frankenstein."

"Funny."

I opened the book and tried again:

> *—indefatigable attention to public business. He passed his younger days perpetually occupied by the affairs of his country; a variety of circumstances had prevented his marrying early, nor was it until*

the decline of life that he became a husband and the
father of a family.

"Oh my *God*," I muttered.

"It gets better."

"It would have to."

I thought about trying again, but the bell chimed behind me, and I turned to see Gaby walk in. Her bob, dyed orangey-red, appeared freshly and unevenly cut, and she was missing the usual ring of turquoise eyeliner. She seemed vaguely clammy, and it looked like she'd spent the morning throwing up. Seeing me and Jamie, though, her whole face lit up.

"Sisters!" she cried.

"Hey, Gaby."

"Finally," said Dee.

Gaby's face fell, and Dee looked instantly regretful. Even when her reasons were entirely legitimate, and her tone light, she hated to make Gaby feel bad. Not for the first time, I wondered how many breakups they'd had before it stuck.

"I'm *sooorryyyy*," Gaby whined. "It's these drops I'm taking. They're like tranquilizers."

What none of us said, but what we all thought, was *Sure, "the drops."* I didn't know the full extent of Gaby's drinking, but I knew she drank more when she was stuck on an art project, and I knew from her tortured Instagram posts that she'd been stuck on the latest for weeks.

I got up from the table to meet Gaby in the office, where she dropped off her bag and threw a stinky tinfoil-wrapped lunch in the tiny refrigerator where they kept bottles of wine cold for events.

"I have a question for you," I announced.

Gaby pulled her blue pencil and a hand mirror out of her bag and began lining her eyes. "What's that?"

"What's the event schedule like over the next few weeks?"

Gaby paused. "Well, we've got the Womyn's Collective Poetry Series on Sunday evenings, obviously—"

"Right."

"—and on, I think it's the eighteenth, we have this amazing young performer who does these totally wrenching pieces accompanied by recordings of, like, famous wartime speeches"— I made a mental note not to come to Triple Moon on the eighteenth—"and I want to say there's a poster-making party on the twenty-fourth for the march next month," she finished.

"What march?"

It was rare for Gaby to make prolonged eye contact with a person, so when she fixed her eyes on you it was deeply unsettling.

"You baby gays are *un*believable." Then, just as soon as I'd disappointed her, she was over it. She resumed her eye lining. "Ask Jamie," she added.

"I will," I said. "But the reason I asked is because there's this band."

I told Gaby about Sweets, and how popular they were with people my age in our area. I promised her the band would handle the marketing to make sure people turned up (I assumed this would work itself out) and assured her they could easily charge a five-dollar cover to defray the setup costs. Gaby frowned at the idea of a fee, but I knew Dee could convince her. Probably she'd tell her it was actually feminist for a queer-run organization like theirs to take money from a bunch of straight people, teenagers or not.

"This is supposed to be a safe space," said Gaby. "Are all these kids going to honor that?"

I promised her they would and prayed they'd prove me right.

"Why don't you and Jamie do those gay-club meetings here anymore?"

I sighed. Gaby had asked me this at least once a month for a year.

"The Westville Gay-Straight Alliance is no more. Still."

"Remind me why?"

(This, the inevitable follow-up. I knew she remembered why. I knew the interrogation was meant mostly to guilt us for insufficient tenacity.)

"Too many straight people."

Toward the end of our freshman year, a few months after Jamie and I came out to each other, and then to our friends, and then, indirectly, to the rest of the school, Jamie decided she wanted to start a club—mainly because it would be good for her college application, which she was already thinking about, even then, but also because being gay was all we could talk or think about, and we wanted as many outlets as possible. And, as the only out queer people in our class, Jamie said, we had a responsibility to be a beacon of kindness and tolerance for our peers. I did anything Jamie wanted me to, so I agreed to be her vice president. We registered our group with Westville's indifferent administration and put up posters around the school. By then we'd been to Triple Moon enough times to have a new but friendly rapport with Dee and Gaby, and when we asked if we could host our bimonthly club meetings there, they gladly accepted—Dee because it would mean new customers, and Gaby because it would mean being able to witness *young queer community organizing.*

Then the day of the first meeting arrived, and Jamie and I presided over a meeting of six straight people. We knew they were straight because whenever they raised their hands to contribute something to our discussion (which, that week, was about a movie about a gay boy played by—you'll never guess—a straight one), they started all their sentences with "I'm straight, but." At the next meeting, four of those same straight people showed up. At the third, there were three. After each meeting, Jamie and I went home drained and annoyed, feeling more like someone's pets than anyone's leaders. So we dissolved the group, telling each other we'd restart it later on in high school, when there were more queer kids around to join us. But as far as we could tell, there were never more than a handful, and the idea of starting a club got less and less appealing as time went on. To start a club as a junior seemed unimaginably embarrassing. And then we were seniors, which was as good as graduated, and there was no point.

"Well," said Gaby. "Can't argue with that."

"So will you think about having Sweets?"

"I'll think about it," she agreed.

"And you'll talk to Dee, too?"

"I'll talk to Dee."

"When do you think you might know by?"

"Quinn."

"Okay, okay. Thank you."

Gaby shooed me out of the office and I returned to the table, where Jamie was still tapping away at her keyboard. She didn't ask me what Gaby and I had talked about, which I found infuriating, if unsurprising. Jamie rarely asked for details because she rarely needed to. Usually, details came to her. When she ignored me, I would do almost anything for her attention.

But Jamie's attention was something I had to learn to live without. So I picked up *Frankenstein* and read for as long as I could, and then I got up to look through the bookshelf, hoping to find something I could take home and care for.

Four

I got my good news a little over a very long week later. I was sitting at the kitchen table in my sweaty soccer practice shorts and a sports bra, eating around the still-semi-frozen center of a chicken pot pie, when my mom abruptly announced that I'd gotten some mail from my dad. She tossed me an envelope, business standard white with my name written in slanty blue ink across the front: *Quinn Y. Ryan.* He always included that middle initial, *Y* for Yvette, his mother's name, a name so preposterously femme it felt incorrect when applied to me. Yvette sounded like roller curls and red lipstick, and the few pictures I'd seen of her as a young woman suggested she fit the name exactly. By the time I met her, just a handful of times when I was a kid, she was old and mean, especially to my mom, who uncharacteristically never talked back, and who told me afterward how hard Yvette's life had been.

I tamped down my excitement, not wanting my mom to see me open the envelope too eagerly. My dad wrote me letters every few months, and he always sent a few twenty-dollar bills along with them. The first time he sent me money, when I started high school, I made the mistake of telling my mom, and she said, "Oh great, forty dollars. Guess we're even." I stopped showing her what he sent me after that. He'd left her ten years ago, when I was eight. Sometimes I wondered how many more decades it would be before she could hear his name or say *your dad* without the corners of her mouth curling down in disapproval. I was sure she didn't know she was doing it; she'd always encouraged me to maintain a relationship with him as long as I wanted one, and it was important to her, at least conceptually, that I form my own opinion of him. Which was a weird way to think about your parents.

Anyway, the letter was not the good news. Or it was good news, but the better news was the email I got from Gaby minutes later, arriving in my inbox with a whoosh. I'd kept my phone volume on at home ever since Jamie broke up with me, just in case. I slid my finger across the screen and read:

Sweets OK w/ me & D. Calendar w/ avail dates attached. –Gaby

"YES!" I exclaimed.

"What?"

"Dee and Gaby are gonna let this band I like play at Triple

Moon." Band I like, girl I kinda like, same difference. *Did* I like Ruby? I didn't think my heart had relearned that emotion yet, but when I imagined giving Ruby the good news, I felt the faintest stirring where liking someone used to go. And then an even bigger thrill when I imagined Jamie finding out.

"What band?"

"They're called Sweets?"

"Never heard of them."

"Well, they're my age, so."

"Oh, rock on."

"*Mom.*"

She grinned. "What have you got going tonight?"

"Eh, not much," I said. "A little reading and a little math homework. What about you?"

"Mmm, I've gotta file by eleven," she sighed. My mom was a crime reporter at the *Union-Tribune*, had been for twenty years, which meant I'd gotten the grisliest details on every murder trial and car wreck that happened in the greater metropolitan area since I was old enough to listen, which by her estimation was second grade. She was my own personal afterschool special, warning me against the dangers of drinking and driving, texting and driving, using drugs, and befriending troublemakers. On several occasions she'd half jokingly, maybe quarter jokingly, told me she was glad I was gay if only because it meant no boyfriend or husband of mine would ever murder me. What a relief.

"What's the story?" I asked.

"Money laundering," she said. "Totally boring."

"Good luck," I said.

"Clean up after yourself, okay?"

"I will."

She hovered in the doorway.

"What?"

"Are you feeling a little better?"

I knew she was asking about Jamie, and I knew she knew I wasn't yet *good*. But I told my mom I felt better, a lot better, in fact, because in that moment, I did. Later, when I was in bed with the lights off and my phone was in my hand and both were slid under the cool side of my pillowcase, I would feel a little worse again. I was always surprised when I felt better, and I was always surprised when it didn't last.

When I heard the door to my mom's room close upstairs, I ripped open the letter from my dad. I unfolded the standard sheet of loose-leaf paper and found sixty dollars, which I slipped between my phone and its case.

In my dad's all-caps handwritten scrawl, the letter, which was really more of a note, read:

HEY QUINNIE [ugh],

I'M WAITING FOR THE PEST CONTROL GUY TO COME TO MY APT. MOTHS ARE BACK IN FULL FORCE—YESTERDAY WHEN I WENT TO MAKE OATMEAL I FOUND THREE MIXED IN WITH THE OATS.

PRETTY SICK. THE GUY SAID I CAN'T BE HERE WHEN HE SPRAYS SO I THOUGHT I MIGHT HEAD TO RUDY'S FOR A PANCAKE. NOT AS GOOD AS MANTEQUILLA BUT THEY'RE ALL RIGHT. SPEAKING OF—WAS THINKING I MIGHT COME TO TOWN IN A FEW WEEKS TO VISIT A COUPLE FRIENDS. MAYBE WE CAN DO SUNDAY BREAKFAST. PEST GUY'S HERE SO MORE LATER.

LOVE,

DAD

I had to laugh. My dad always wrote his letters to me mid-errand, or under some arbitrary time constraint, as if he couldn't just stop writing partway through and return to it later, without my ever knowing he'd paused. It made his letters feel like *dispatches*, like he was away at sea, when really he was home in Durham with, as far as I knew, a working phone. But I didn't mind. Letters felt old-fashioned and meaningful. Even the ones that were mostly about moths. They might not have been the most efficient way to communicate, but they did give me something to keep.

And then there was his super-casual suggestion of breakfast, as if we had seen each other more recently than a year and ten months ago (not that I was keeping track). My dad was terrified of flying, though in his words he just really, really hated it. I wondered if he was planning to drive all the way from North Carolina like last time, and if not, which friends were worth getting on an airplane for.

I sent him a text: **Got your letter. Thanks for the $. Let me know when you have dates for your trip. Love you too.**

I sat on my Triple Moon news for a few days, trying to decide how to deliver it. A text would be easier, for several reasons: one, I wouldn't be face to face with Ruby, who seemed to get prettier and prettier every time I saw her, even though you'd think that sort of thing would have a ceiling; two, I could fine-tune my wording, thereby avoiding the possibility of sounding like an awkward freak; three, by texting her, I would set a precedent for texting as a thing we did, and maybe eventually we would text about something other than venues for her band.

But one day, at the end of Civil Liberties, just after Jamie had booked it out of the classroom, waving goodbye over her shoulder, I saw Ruby pause in the hallway to look at her phone, and I found myself walking—no, *gliding*—over to her, and saying her name.

She looked up, and smiled.

"Hey, Quinn," she said.

"Hey, um," I said. In my defense, I had not been prepared for her to greet me by name. On top of the smiling it was just too much.

"Hi . . ."

"Yeah, so, you know that coffee shop I told you about? I

told the owners about you and they'd love to have you guys come do a show," I said. "Or, multiple shows, I think."

"Really?" She grabbed my arm. "That was so nice of you."

Keep it together! I screamed in my head. *Ignore the electricity coursing into your shoulders!*

"Ah, well," I said. "I'm glad they went for it."

"Should I email . . . someone? Should I stop by to meet them?"

Until then, my plan, insofar as I had one, had been to simply send her Gaby's calendar, and mediate from there until a date was set. But going there in person was a *much* better idea.

"Yeah, maybe you should meet them and, like, see the space," I said. "If you want, I could go with you? Just, since I know them."

"Oh! Sure," said Ruby. "Yeah, that would be cool."

It occurred to me then that this was a lot of attention being paid and a lot of effort being put into preserving a band whose music I did not, historically, enjoy. Not that Ruby knew that. But if my sudden enthusiasm felt like it *should* seem weird to Ruby, it didn't seem like it actually did. Perhaps she was on the receiving end of this sort of eager desire to help and please all the time. *Her life must be so fun.*

"Maybe Saturday?" I suggested. "I have soccer tonight, so."

"I thought you guys played in the winter."

"We do," I said, feeling strangely touched she knew. "This is my club team."

"So you play *all* the time."

"Kinda, yeah," I said. It was true: between club soccer and school soccer, there was virtually no down season, except a week or two here and there for holidays. Soccer was the reason I couldn't have a part-time job, which meant soccer was keeping me broke until it made me rich.

"Okay, well, let's do Saturday, then," said Ruby.

"What time?" I was trying not to sound desperate, but she wasn't really giving me a lot to work with, detail-wise.

". . . Three o'clock?" she guessed.

"Yeah, three works."

"Well, I've gotta get to class."

We smiled at each other, each of us (I assumed) surprised to have formed an actual plan with the other. "Well," she went on, "I gotta go meet my ride."

"I could give you a ride," I said. For some reason.

Ruby seemed as surprised and confused as I was. But also—maybe—a little charmed.

"Thanks, but—"

"Yeah, that would be rude," I interjected. She laughed.

"Exactly."

"You don't have a car?" I asked. Ruby's family obviously had money, and in Southern California, no one who had any money didn't have their own car. I was curious, but more saliently, I was stalling. I didn't want her to walk away.

"I do, but," started Ruby, sighing. "My parents have a lot of rules."

"They're still together?" I asked. She nodded, and I nodded. "Classic divorce trade-off."

She laughed. Again my chest twinged with that long-lost crushy feeling. The warning bell rang, and Ruby smiled, and I smiled, and we took off running in opposite directions.

I spent all of soccer practice thinking about Ruby and most of it trying to talk to Ronni about her, running over to fill her in in thirty-second installments every time-out and every water break. After five or six of these she grew exasperated. "Oh my *God*," she yelled. "Can this PLEASE wait until after?"

But it honestly didn't feel like it could. For the first time in ages, I felt something other than heartbroken. When Jamie broke up with me I knew I'd never love anyone like I loved her. Maybe this was true. But other loves were still possible. Or at least other likes. Other girls existed. And that felt revelatory and huge and exciting. I was still very aware that the public record didn't show much (any) evidence that Ruby had any romantic interest in girls. But the way she smiled at me made me think it was possible. How could I explain all that to Ronni?

Someone was yelling my name. I came out of it just in time to see the ball flying my way. I trapped it, pivoted my body toward the net, and kicked it, hard, just over Halle's out-stretched hands. The rest of my squad cheered. Ronni, even though she was on the other side, ran up and smacked my butt hard. "Lucky shot."

"I know." Even though I'd scored, I was embarrassed, having narrowly escaped a whiff. I wished I could turn off my brain to everything but soccer when I got on the field—when girls got in my head, it tended to throw off my game. And if I wanted to play for UNC (and I *had* to play for UNC), I pretty much had to have a flawless season. I hadn't heard from their recruiter since last year, and I was starting to get nervous about what that meant. This time last year, I'd been so confident it would come easily, like it always had. For my whole life I'd been great at this one thing, and my biggest fear was that, one day, I'd only be good. And then what?

 *Five*

On Saturday I woke up gasping, my upper body damp with sweat. I flung my comforter to the foot of the bed and pulled up my ratty practice T-shirt to wipe my chest and neck. Like so many nights over the past two months, I'd dreamed about Jamie. We were at some outdoor party, or some unspecified holiday barbecue, and she was wearing a light blue dress. I kept trying to talk to her, but every time I got near her, she'd disappear. Then I'd look around, and she'd be standing twenty feet away, talking to some other girl instead of me. Finally I shouted her name, and everyone turned to look at me but Jamie.

Not very subtle, brain, I thought.

I looked at the clock on my nightstand; it was only 7:46. That meant I had seven hours and fourteen minutes to kill until I could pick up Ruby. I wondered at what time I could reasonably text her for her address without seeming like she was the first thing I'd thought of when I woke up. Noon?

There was a crazy part of me that wanted to text Jamie right now, to describe to her my dream. I wanted her to tell me she'd never ignore me like that. I wanted her to tell me she dreamed about me sometimes too. But Jamie wasn't the type to make bold, impossible promises, and she definitely wasn't the type to admit to having feelings. It had taken her months to admit that she liked me as more than a friend.

Things between us changed in the spring of our sophomore year. She was sleeping over at my house, like she did almost every Saturday that year, the way we told ourselves all best friends did. We were watching a movie in the usual position: her lying on the floor beneath me lying on the couch. It hadn't always been that way. The first few times she came over, she sat on the couch with me, like a normal person, but at some point she started insisting she liked the floor better. That way we could both stretch out. I didn't protest because I liked taking up the whole couch, but also because I liked the way my elevated position let me look at her without her knowing. At the time, the slight tilting of her head, her hand reaching for the bowl of popcorn, her feet rubbing against each other, one sliding over the other until her socks slipped off—it was enough to keep me occupied during the boring parts of whatever movie she'd picked out for us.

I don't know what it was about that warm, late-May night

that made me do it. I still don't know what made me so brave. We were watching our favorite *Lord of the Rings* movie, *The Return of the King,* for the fifth or maybe the twentieth time. Gandalf had placed the crown on Aragorn's head, and tears were streaming down my face. And then, before I could think about what it would change between us, I reached down and took Jamie's hand in mine.

We stayed that way for the rest of the movie, and when it was done, she rolled onto her back to look at me. I could barely make out her face in the dark, but it felt like I could feel her heartbeat in my chest too. I slipped off the couch and onto the floor next to her, and then I kissed her.

She kissed me back for what felt like hours but was probably only thirty seconds before pulling away. She said it was too weird.

I could feel the crush of it even now, reliving it. Kissing Jamie had not been weird for me. It had felt like—*finally.* It had put me into my body, in control of it, my hips pressed into hers and my hand on her waist. The few times I'd kissed boys, in hallway enclaves outside middle school dances when the chaperones weren't looking, I'd felt so far away from myself. Even with Brian, the eighth-grade boyfriend who was so cute and so nice and so patient with me, kissing had felt like the warm-up to a game I'd never get good at. There was such an enormous gap between what my friends described kissing boys to be like and what I actually felt when I did it, I wondered for a while if some key sensory ending was missing from my mouth. Even when I knew for sure that I liked girls more than I'd ever like boys, I worried.

Then I kissed Jamie.

And then Jamie told me kissing me was too weird. We hardly spoke that whole summer, and it wasn't until three months later that I got to kiss her again. But then I got to kiss her for eleven months straight. Even after we started sleeping together, kissing her was still my favorite part. It would have been enough for me if that was all there was. Maybe I knew, from the start, that our time was limited, and that's why I kissed her every chance I got. It all felt too lucky to last.

It was annoying to me now, how grateful I'd felt. Three months was nothing. I would've waited for her forever.

I didn't say any of this when Jamie came over to my house and broke up with me. I said, *Okay.* I said, *If that's what you want.* I said, *If you're done, I should really go study.* She cried and, for once in my blubbery life, I didn't. Not until she was gone and I was upstairs, knocking on my mom's bedroom door because I realized I didn't know what else to do. The only person I really wanted to talk to about something as monumental as being dumped by Jamie was Jamie.

I needed to be stronger, and thicker-skinned. I remembered the letter from my dad, now stacked atop its predecessors in my old soccer bag in the closet, and I knew what he'd tell me if I saw him next month, when I told him I didn't have a girlfriend anymore—the same thing he'd said to me anytime I told him I was sick, or had done badly on a test, or lost a soccer game: "Tough times don't last. Tough people do." Then he'd tell me the same long story about his war-hero grandfather, my great-grandfather, who, in his telling, was the tallest, strongest man who ever lived to be two hundred years old. (In my mom's telling, he was just "a grade-A asshole.") He died well before I was born, but I'd seen pictures of him looking handsome in his uniform, and on my thirteenth birthday my dad gave me his worn silver army bracelet.

I went to my dresser and pulled the bracelet from the velvet-lined box I stored it in, and slipped it onto my wrist. I didn't know if it was good luck or not, because I'd always been too afraid to wear it out of the house. Today seemed like a good day to change that.

I knew Ruby's family had money because she'd gone to the most expensive K-8 in the county and had the kind of smooth, shiny hair even good genes can't account for. But I hadn't given the *amount* of money a lot of thought until I found myself on the way to La Jolla to pick her up—and not just La Jolla, but prime, multimillion, oceanfront La Jolla. Like, the part of the neighborhood where there was a house on the bluff with an elevator that descended to the person's private beach. Where Bruce Wayne would live, if he lived in San Diego.

I took the curving streets slowly the closer I got, not wanting to be too exactly on time, but when I pulled up to Ruby's
house she was sitting on the front step already, waiting. I
waved, and she started the long journey down the driveway
to my truck.

"Nice house," I said when she opened the door.

"*I* didn't have anything to do with it."

"I know. . . ."

She gave me a look. "It was a joke."

"Oh. Right. Ha."

"Thanks for picking me up."

"No problem."

We were quiet as we wound our way back to the highway,
Ruby looking out the window while I tried my best to look
at Ruby and the road at the same time. She was wearing jean
shorts and high-top Chucks and a giant Nirvana T-shirt with
the sleeves rolled up. If an outfit could have a sexuality, I
thought, hers would be bi at *least*.

After another five seconds the silence started seeming
weird, and ominous, like if I didn't say something *right now*
she might realize where she was and who she was with and
ask me to turn the car around.

"So how come you're not playing at your normal place anymore?"

(I pretended not to know the name.)

"Because my ex is a baby moron."

I laughed in surprise, and after a moment she did too.

"Is that, like, only slightly a moron?"

"Major moron, major baby," she clarified.

"Got it." My hands felt sweaty on the steering wheel. I hadn't expected for us to land on this topic so quickly. I couldn't blow it. I couldn't say *have you thought about dating a girl instead,* for instance. "Is it nosy of me to ask what happened?"

I looked her way once, and then again. Finally she looked back, eyebrows arched in mock offense taken.

"It's *super* nosy."

"Okay, just checking." I waited a beat. "What happened?"

Ruby laughed. "I dunno. We were fighting a lot. We've broken up, like, six times."

"Really?"

"Yeah, at least."

"Do you think this one's for good?"

"Do you care?" she asked.

I looked at her. She wasn't mad—she was teasing me. Maybe. I turned up the music a little, worried she could hear my heartbeat. "I'm a concerned citizen."

"Right."

"You didn't answer."

"Yes, I think it's really over. I hope so, anyway."

"Well, good thing you have a say in the matter."

"So people keep telling me."

I realized I wasn't sure who the people she referred to might be. Excluding her three bandmates, Ruby didn't seem to have a lot of friends, at least not that went to our school. And yet she was considered cool by everyone—even, I was sure, by the also-rich, boring-beautiful, too-tan, water polo–playing popular crowd, though they pretended to be above admiring anyone.

I was disappointed when, a minute later, Triple Moon came into view through my windshield. Our conversation was *just* getting somewhere, and I knew it would deflate as soon as we opened the truck's doors.

We parked and went inside to find the shop overheated and completely empty except for Dee, who was wearing a bandanna and fanning herself with a newspaper. When she saw me she waved. "AC's broken," she explained.

"It's like ninety degrees out," I said.

"I realize that, thank you."

I could see her noticing Ruby behind me, assessing the situation, so I cut her off before she could say something embarrassing.

"Dee, this is Ruby," I said. "She's in that band that's going to do a show here?"

"Of course. Nice to meet you. The AC will be fixed by then."

"Oh, I wasn't worried," said Ruby.

"*I* was," I said. "Can I get an iced . . . coffee?" Around Ruby, suddenly, a drink with flavored syrup in it seemed childish.

Dee gave me a look but filled a glass with ice without saying anything about my usual order, *thank God.* "Ruby, can I get you anything?"

"Iced tea is great, thank you."

I watched Ruby take a lap around the shop, presumably inspecting it for music-person concerns I wouldn't understand. Dee set our drinks on the counter, and when I picked them up she gave me a look that I knew meant something like *You're in trouble with this one.* Which of course I knew.

Dee yelled for Gaby, and a moment later she emerged from the back.

"This is Ruby, from Sweets, that band," I said.

"Oh, hi! I'm Gaby. I'll give you a proper tour."

I trailed along after them as Gaby showed Ruby where they usually set up the stage, and where they could plug in their amps, and explained how the sound system worked. They talked through Dee's proposed cover charge, and Ruby agreed that five dollars a head (two for the band and three for the shop) seemed fair. Then Gaby started giving Ruby a mini lecture on women-centered safe spaces, and I started to worry we were losing her. "Our doors are open to all identities at Triple Moon, but cis men are sort of . . . low on the priority list," she said. "I hope the young men in your band will be respectful of the fact that they're only here because you're here, and because I trust Quinn's judgment. Their voices are secondary."

"Oh, don't worry," said Ruby. "I never let them forget that."

Gaby smiled, which made me beam. I had nothing to worry about. Ruby fit in here, just like I knew she would.

The show date was set for two Saturdays away, and when Ruby and I got back in my truck we were giddy and triumphant.

"Two dollars a head!" I exclaimed. "If fifty people come, that's a hundred bucks!"

Ruby smiled patiently. "And divide that by four . . ."

"Oh, yeah. Well, it's not about the money, really. Right?"

"Right," said Ruby. "That part can wait."

Oh no, I worried inwardly. *Does she think Sweets is going to, like . . . make it big?*

"So you think you guys'll stay together after graduation?"

She shrugged. "I hope so. I feel like we've finally figured out our sound—"

"Totally." I nodded.

"—but David wants to go to school in New York, and Ben thinks we should focus on Portland, so we'll see."

"What about you?"

She sighed. "Stanford." She said it so boredly, and definitively, like she was already in.

"Oh. Wow. Are you . . . did you . . ."

"I'm pretty sure. My parents went there, and they donated, like . . . a building," she explained. "Part of a building? I don't remember."

"Oh sure," I said, like I had also donated several buildings myself. "My friend Ronni is going there too," I added proudly, a little jealously.

"Soccer?"

I nodded. "I heard you got a perfect SAT."

Her mouth dropped open. "You *heard* that? From who?"

"Alexis," I said.

"That bitch knows everything," she said admiringly.

"I know."

So it was true. Ruby was rich and beautiful *and* brilliant. And straight. What was I doing here again?

"You don't seem very excited," I said. "You know Stanford is kind of a good school, right?"

She smirked. "Yeah, I think I've heard that. No, I mean. It'll be fine. I would have preferred to go to school in LA, but my parents pretty much told me I'd ruin their lives if I didn't go to Stanford, so, whatever. It's four years."

"And it's Stanford."

"You think I'm a brat."

"No," I said. "A little."

I looked over to make sure she wasn't mad at me, once and then again. I could get used to her sitting there, I thought. I could survive off the intermittent eye contact alone.

"Fine," she said. "Where do you want to go, then?"

"The University of North Carolina," I said—definitively, though I still hadn't heard anything more from their recruiter, and had not yet gotten around to actually applying. But I would, and I had to.

Ruby's eyebrow lifted disdainfully. "What's . . . there?"

"Uh, the best women's soccer program in the country." I knew I sounded defensive, but I didn't want her to think UNC was some shitty country-kid school just because it wasn't an Ivy League, or in a big city. It wasn't easy to get into, either. Unlike Ruby, I did not have perfect test scores, or even close. Everything I had to show for my academic capability was average. If I didn't have soccer, I knew, there was no way I'd get in.

Ruby's face softened. "Oh right, soccer. Okay. That makes more sense."

"Do you know who Tobin Heath is?"

She stared blankly.

"Crystal Dunn? Ashlyn Harris? *Mia Hamm?*"

"I'm gonna guess . . . soccer players?"

"Soccer *stars.*"

"My mistake."

"Anyway. They all went to UNC, was my point."

"You want to play professionally?"

I nodded. I'd wanted to play for the U.S. women's national soccer team since I was five. I "tried out" for my first team the next year, not that you could really be cut from a team when you were in kindergarten. My dad drove me to the park where the tryouts were held, having purchased a high-tech collapsible lawn chair with its own canopy just for the occasion. (That way, he explained, he could watch me from the sidelines without having to sit on a hot metal bleacher, or talk to the other parents.) After every drill we ran that first day, I'd look to him for reassurance, and every time I glanced over he'd moved a little closer to the sideline. Eventually he stood up. And then it was clear, by the look on his face: all of a sudden, I was special, in a way I hadn't been the day before.

When my parents got divorced, my dad moved to Durham for a job, and he started the hard sell on UNC. Not that I needed much convincing, especially once I got a little older and started following college soccer. UNC was my favorite team to watch, and often the actual best, and playing for them would mean my dad could come to all my games.

Ruby frowned. "I don't think I've ever actually been to a soccer game. Can that be right?"

"You should come to one of mine," I said. I glanced over, and when she looked at me I grinned. "You kind of owe me now."

Oh my God, that was flirty, I thought. Right? Hopefully she could tell, unless it didn't work, in which case I hoped she couldn't.

"Oh, I do?"

(She could tell. It worked.)

"Yeah, pretty sure you do."

We grinned at each other like twin idiots.

"Okay, maybe I will," said Ruby. "A high school sporting event. How quaint."

My cheeks burned a little. "Okay, I mean, you don't *have* to come."

"No, I want to. You can't stop me."

"Okay, fine," I said. My head felt like it was filling up with sparkles. I turned onto Ruby's street and realized I hadn't paid any real, conscious attention to the road since I left the Triple Moon parking lot. Somehow we were already there, far too soon. I parked in front of her house and blurted out, "What are you doing now?" Ruby looked at me, seeming surprised, or something. "Just wondering," I hurriedly added. "I've got plans with my friend Jamie?"

No such plan existed, though now I wished it did.

"I thought she was your girlfriend," said Ruby.

Even though Jamie and I had been very much out as a couple at school, this stunned me. I'd assumed there was a rung on the social ladder above which nobody knew or cared what my relationship status was, and Ruby hovered in the stratosphere above it. But maybe not.

"She, uh—she was," I stammered. "We broke up."

"Ah. I'm sorry."

"It's okay," I said. "We're friends."

Ruby gave me a tight-lipped smile. "Yeah, I know how that goes."

"No, it's—not like that. At all," I said. Suddenly it was crucial that she know that Jamie and I weren't like her and Mikey. I didn't want her to think I was anything but available, and I couldn't afford to let myself think like that either. "We might not even do anything. We haven't texted about it," I added, but I knew it was too late to reverse course.

"Okay," said Ruby. "Well, I should probably go practice with the guys, now that we have a show to prepare for."

"Right. No time to waste."

She smiled at me a little quizzically. "You're funny. Thanks for doing this."

Then she leaned over and hugged me, one-armed, across the console. Her hand on my shoulder blade felt electric, and her hair smelled salty-sweet and expensive. I put my hand on her back and let it slide the tiniest bit lower, not wanting to seem too platonic but not wanting to creep her out, either. Every day at school I watched straight girls cling to their friends like they were long-lost lovers, but I worried those girls thought it was different when I did it.

Ruby pulled back, opened the door, and hopped out. "This was fun."

"Agreed," I said. "See you Monday?"

"Don't remind me." She waved and then began the long trip back up her driveway, and I fought the urge to honk my horn, just to get her to look at me one more time.

Six

On Sunday I woke up to the beach calling my name through the window. It was that kind of morning, where you can sense it before your eyes are all the way open, in the way the sunlight filters through the blinds and in the salty-clean smell of the breeze. It was perfect, and I knew that toward the end of September, it would be one of the last (if not *the* last) tolerable ocean temperature days of the year, sans wet suit. As I lay in bed scrolling through everything that had happened on my phone overnight, I briefly considered asking Ruby to go to the beach with me. But seeing her two days in a row would be pushing it, for someone I had no relationship with until this week. Not that we were in a relationship. Plus, I didn't want her to think I had no one else to hang out with, even if it was true. Ronni could never hang out on Sundays because of church and the extended family get-togethers that followed, and Alexis didn't "do" beaches because she didn't like being hot, sweating, or getting sand in her shoes.

Technically, this left me with one final option.

Before I could overthink it, I texted Jamie, because if I pretended to be at the stage at which asking Jamie to hang out was habitual, and emotionally unloaded, maybe I would trick my brain into actually moving into that stage. *In fact,* I thought, *why not go a step further and offer to make us a picnic?* Picnics didn't *have* to be romantic. Two best friends could share a platonic picnic, no problem.

It took Jamie seven minutes to respond, during which time I weighed the pros and cons of moving to Romania to start a new life. But then, finally:

Sure

I sighed. During our relationship I'd repeatedly begged Jamie to use punctuation—exclamation marks, specifically—in her text messages so I'd know she didn't hate me. She tried a few times, but soon reverted to habit, and when I brought it up again she said I should know she didn't hate me because we were girlfriends, and we saw each other every day. Which is exactly what someone who will eventually break up with you would say.

Friends, fortunately, didn't care about punctuation. So I got up and got dressed, and walked downstairs to the kitchen, where my mom sat at the table drinking at least her third cup of coffee and reading an Ann Rule book over a box of half- and three-quarters-eaten Sunny Donuts. One might think she'd get sick of crime, given the day job, but in the seventeen years and counting I'd been around, she hadn't. Every weekend was the same: on Saturdays she took an eight-mile hike with her middle-aged lady hiking friends, and on Sundays she read about murder. Early on in high school I used to ask her once every few weeks if she had any dates coming up, but eventually she asked me if I really wanted to come downstairs in the morning to find some strange man sitting at the table with her, eating our doughnuts, and I'd been forced to concede she had a point.

"Good morning," she said. "Nice day. You should go to the beach."

"I'm going to," I said. "I'm meeting Jamie."

My mom peered at me over the rim of her coffee cup and said nothing.

"What?" I snapped. "We're friends."

She held up a hand in defense. "Okay! It just seems soon."

"Well, it's not," I said. "I see her every day, and the sooner it's normal, the better."

"If I were you, I'd still be mad," she said, poking the doughnut carcasses. She picked up a piece of powdered sugar and took a bite, leaving white residue on the corner of her mouth. "The anger stage is the best part of the grief cycle."

I brushed the corner of my mouth so my mom would wipe

hers. *Ten years since the divorce, and you're still in it,* I thought. I felt guilty immediately. "Wouldn't that be acceptance?"

My mom scrunched up her face as if thinking it over. "Nah."

I laughed, which made her smile. She returned to her book, and I began assembling twin turkey-tomato-mustard-provolone sandwiches. I threw them into a bag with chips and cookies and two giant water bottles left over from soccer seasons past.

"Okay, Mom," I said. "I'm headed out."

"Hey, Quinn?"

"Yeah?"

"Speaking of your dad. You know he's coming into town, right?"

"Yeah," I said cautiously. I didn't know *she* knew, actually. I was never really sure how transparent to be with either of them about the other. "I think we're going to get breakfast or something." I knew we were, really, but I didn't want my mom to think I was too eager.

"You know why, right?"

"He said he's visiting a friend?"

She sighed. "He's got a job interview."

"A job . . . here?" I asked dumbly.

"Yeah."

She peered at me again, trying to see how I felt, which meant I had to work out how I felt and then keep it from showing on my face. Mainly I was confused.

"It's not a sure thing," my mom added. "They might not make an offer, and even if they do he might not take it. I think he's content where he is."

Only then did it hit me. "What about UNC?"

"*If* he took the job, and if UNC is where you end up—"

"It will be," I interjected, now fully annoyed. I couldn't believe this. Any of it.

"Okay, well," my mom sighed. "We'll cross those bridges when we come to them."

My mom watched me stew for a few moments, until I remembered that the polite thing to do was to not make this all about me.

"How would you feel about it?" I asked. "If he moved here again."

"Eh." She shrugged. "I don't expect it to change anything for me. I don't see him."

I nodded, not entirely sure whether I believed her. My parents' divorce was not amicable, though they communicated about me via oddly abbreviated text message when necessary. Which must have been how my dad had informed her of the job interview. I wondered why he hadn't yet told me. Maybe he didn't want me to freak out before he knew for sure. Or maybe he was just waiting for our breakfast, so he could freak me out in person. He did love a big reveal. I'd have to pretend Mom hadn't already told me so he wouldn't be mad at her for ruining it.

I leaned over to kiss her on the cheek, and she hugged me around the neck, still propping her book open with her other hand. "I don't think it will change much for me, either," I said, both reassuring her and trying to convince myself.

"I hope not."

"Yeah. Okay." I slung my beach bag over my shoulder, suddenly desperate to get away. "I really have to go."

"Be safe. And say hi to Jamie for me."

"I will."

Despite what she'd said, my mom *loved* Jamie, a fact about which my feelings had changed at least seventeen times. I had been relieved, and jealous, and happy, and proud, and surprised. Lately I hovered somewhere between sad and touched. She'd been good enough about hiding her personal disappointment when we broke up, but I knew she felt that she, too, had been in some way dumped. The affection was mutual: she and Jamie had been on a semiregular texting basis with each other, and they'd even hung out without me a few times. Sure, it was mostly in the context of attending my soccer games—sitting together in the bleachers, stopping for drive-through In-N-Out milkshakes on the way to one of my away games—but still. Jamie never said so, but it was clear she viewed my mom as a sort of second mother, more supportive than her own. Jamie's mom hadn't spoken to her for almost three months after learning she was gay, which only made my mom love her harder, and which made me jealous. And yet I was incapable of being as straightforwardly kind to her as Jamie was. I still kept so much to myself. I hadn't explicitly told my mom Jamie and I were dating until three months in, and then I'd found out she knew almost to the day when things had changed. She never pried. She never asked me if I was sure this was what I wanted. I knew I should be grateful. And I was. It was not impossible for a person to be deeply grateful and profoundly annoyed at the same time.

When I pulled my truck into Jamie's driveway, I realized that the last time I'd been there, we'd been together. I wondered, not for the first time, how long I'd have to keep having these before-and-after epiphanies: the first night I went to bed without calling her to say good night; the first Friday night she wasn't my built-in plan; the first time I watched one of our movies alone. At first it was devastating, and then it became soothing in its devastatingness: for a while, all I'd wanted was to keep crying. I came to know my most reliable triggers and I pulled them again and again. But they stopped working, or else my body decided it had had enough. Now that the glamorous part of the suffering was over, I hoped someday soon I might order my life around some other major event. Or person.

It was early enough when we got there that the beach wasn't yet swarmed, and Jamie and I trudged through hot sand to get to our usual spot, perfect for being equidistant between the ocean, the outdoor bathrooms (Jamie refused to pee in the ocean, not wanting to harm any fish), and the pier, which we'd walk under when we needed shade and a breeze, and which we'd climb the stairs to when we needed shaved ice. When the beach was available to you every day, almost year-round, people tended to get lazy, showing up midday, squeezing themselves into four-foot spaces between other towels, applying sunscreen upon arrival. But I took the beach seriously. Being there was often the highlight of my week, and I thought it only fair to give it the attention to detail it deserved.

While Jamie stripped off her T-shirt and shorts, I twisted my umbrella down into the sand and tried not to stare. When I sat down next to her, she held out the tube of sunscreen, somewhat apologetically. "Can you get my back? I tried, but . . ."

It was funny, or maybe awful, that after a certain point in our relationship, I'd stopped noticing her body so much. Her strong swimmer's shoulders, the dimples at the small of her back, the curve of her waist, even her breasts, which for a time had been virtually all I could think about—these things faded into the background of her role in my life. It wasn't fair, how something stopped feeling so special once you were used to it. I hadn't meant to stop feeling that I was lucky just to touch her. I hadn't meant to forget that I might not always get to.

I rubbed the sunscreen between my hands to warm it up first, but Jamie still arched in shock when I pressed them to her skin. Her back was fair and freckled, and I told myself it was only her safety I had in mind when I slipped my hands under the straps of her bikini to make sure no skin went uncovered. I wiped the extra lotion down her arms and then my own.

"Do you need me to do yours?"

I quickly shook my head, even though I wanted her to. "I put it on at home." I'd worried in advance about the erotic potential of sunscreen application and decided it was best to limit it as much as possible.

Instead I unpacked our lunches, though it was barely eleven o'clock. Being on the beach, even for a minute, made me ravenous. We chewed our sandwiches silently, watching people arrive all around us. At the far end of the beach the last surfer holdouts were coming out of the water in their glittering wet suits, done until the late afternoon, when the rest of us would start packing up to leave.

"How do you make such good sandwiches?"

I laughed. "Me?"

"Yeah. Whenever I make one, even if it has the same exact ingredients, it tastes like shit."

"That's because you made it for yourself," I said. "Food always tastes better made by someone else."

"I think it's specific to you, though," said Jamie. A warmth entirely unrelated to the sun spread across my chest. "I mean, my mom's food tastes like shit too," she added.

I grinned. "It really does."

Jamie elbowed me in the ribs. "Only *I'm* allowed to say that." I winced from her touch but smiled through it. It was a nice but complicated feeling for her to tease me now, especially for something no one else knew me well enough to joke about. While Jamie could tolerate criticism of the people she loved—especially of her mom, especially during those few months of post-coming out silent treatment—I could not, even and maybe especially when I knew it was fair. One of my and Jamie's biggest fights as a couple had started because Jamie had agreed when I said my mom seemed lonely. I'd stormed out of the restaurant where we were eating late-night tacos, gotten in my truck, and driven away. I came back for her a minute later, but still. It had not gone over well.

"Do you wanna go in?" I stood up fast, and bread crumbs fell from my board shorts to the towel below.

Jamie squinted up at me. "You *just* ate."

"That rule isn't real."

"Yes, it is."

"Maybe for, like, babies."

Jamie rolled her eyes. "I'll stay with our stuff."

Then it was my turn for an eye roll. Jamie was always worried some stealthy preteen thief was going to make off with our beach bags in broad daylight. And *then* we'd be destitute, out a whole twenty bucks and a half-punched taco-shop loyalty card between us.

"Suit yourself," I said, and took off jogging toward the

water. I never got sick of that feeling: the way my adrenaline kicked up and my sun-roasted sleepiness fell away in anticipation of plunging myself into cool, salty water. I loved the moment the sand switched over from hot and dry to cool and damp. Sometimes, when there weren't too many people in the water to see me do it, I ran that last stretch with my eyes closed, leaving it to my feet to sense when I was almost there. When I felt water slap against my calves I was awake.

I dove under the water and resurfaced where the water came up to my chest. I smoothed my hair back and turned to look at the beach. Jamie waved and I waved back. Then I did something I knew she'd kind of hate me for, but which I also knew would work: I started yelling.

"COME ON IN, JAMIE!" I hollered. "THE WATER'S FINE!"

I watched her glance casually around, pretending to search for whoever this Jamie person was.

"YEAH, YOU! GIRL UNDER THE BLUE UMBRELLA!"

I could see her scowl from forty yards out. *Oh, she is going to straight-up* murder *me*, I thought. But she'd have to come into the water to get to me first.

Slowly she stood up, and slowly she strode into the water, trying to make it clear to me and anyone watching that she'd just happened to decide, independently, that she was ready to swim after all. She dipped gracefully underwater, and moments later, when I saw her gliding directly at me, still underwater, I screamed. There was nowhere to hide; Jamie looped her arms around my legs and took me under.

Water rushed into my ears, and I was on my back, looking up through water into blue sky. Jamie let go of me right away, and I wasn't hurt, and I didn't expect to be so mad, but I was, and I wasn't sure why. I shot to the surface and flicked the wet hair from my face.

"What the fuck, dude?"

"*'Dude'*?"

We squinted at each other, blinking back saltwater tears.

"You're stronger than you think. That hurt." I was lying, sort of.

"Oh, I know I'm strong," she smirked.

"Oh, well, then, great."

"Relax. You survived. And anyway, you kind of asked for it."

I didn't know how to argue with that, so I turned my head and spit, trying to get the salt out of my mouth. I *hated* being told to relax. *Everybody* hated being told to relax. It was, like, the one thing you could say to guarantee a reaction opposite to its supposed intention. So I changed the subject.

"Sweets is gonna play Triple Moon."

Jamie didn't react. She didn't even look at me. She slowed her treading until she was hardly moving at all. She dipped the back of her head into the water and asked the sky, "When?"

"Two weeks," I said. "Less than."

"So they already talked to Gaby?"

"And Dee." I could have left it there but I didn't. "I went with her, actually."

"What do you mean?"

"Ruby and I went over there yesterday. Together."

I watched her face, desperate for any indication that she was unsettled, or jealous, but there was nothing. She stayed on her back, apparently singularly focused on staying afloat.

"How was that?" she asked.

"Fun. She's cool."

"That seems to be the general consensus."

Ugh. Like she hadn't ranted and raved over how amazing and stylish and pretty she was when we put her first on our wishful-thinking list in the first place.

"Aren't you excited?"

"Sure. I mean, I'll be happy to see them live again."

"And at our favorite place!"

"Yeah," she said. She swept her arms up and down across the water in short strokes, like she was making a very skinny snow angel. "I don't know. I'm kind of surprised Gaby went for it."

"I'm not. It'll be good for business."

"Maybe, but she doesn't care about making money."

"Well, maybe she should."

I thought back on the last few times we'd been to Triple Moon, and how quiet it had been. It had never been especially *hopping* (it was a lesbian feminist coffee shop that served mediocre coffee), but I was sure that even a year ago it had been busier on the whole.

"Well, I'm glad your grand idea for saving a band you don't even like worked out."

"You know I didn't do it for the band," I spit.

Jamie stopped floating, and for just a second, I thought I had the upper hand. But then she looked right at me and said, "Oh, right, the straight girl."

Once again I was infuriated, powerless to prove her wrong. All I had were my tiny, stupid, inconsequential clues, which could have gone either way, and which would probably go nowhere. Suddenly my previous confidence was embarrassing: Even if Ruby *did* have the capacity to like girls, why would I think I'd be one of them?

"You thought you were straight once too," I muttered.

"Oh, I know," said Jamie. "I was eight."

I slapped the water in frustration. I was *not* going to argue about sexual fluidity in the middle of the ocean. I needed enough energy to swim back to shore. "You're not allowed to be like this!" I exclaimed.

"Like what?"

"Mean because I like someone else."

Jamie stopped floating then. She let her feet sink and looked at the water for what felt like a full minute before speaking, and it still wasn't enough time to prepare me for what she said.

"You're right."

Wait. "What?"

"I'm being weird," she said. "I'm sorry." She smiled sheepishly.

"You're freaking me out right now."

She rolled her eyes, and that, at least, was familiar.

"I apologized. Accept it. I won't do it again."

"Okay," I said. "I accept."

But my brain was running in overdrive in a thousand different directions. Was she admitting that my being into Ruby bothered her? Had she already known I liked Ruby before I said it? I wasn't completely sure *I'd* realized it before I said it, so how could she? And if it did bother her, what did that mean? Could she really be over me if she still got jealous? Did I want her to be jealous, and if I did—let's be clear: I definitely did—did that mean I still wanted to be with her?

Stop, I thought. *Just stop.* I dipped underwater, hoping all these unwelcome and unproductive thoughts would somehow slip out of my ears and nose and mouth and into the ocean and stay there.

I knew what I had to do to move on. To chin up. To *get my head back on*, like Robyn sang in one of my favorite songs from the *Moving On—I Mean It This Time* playlist I'd made recently.

I had to go home and have a good final cry. Yes, I'd had other "final" cries. But those other times didn't count. This time was different. I was reborn in the ocean that day, baptized, not heartbroken but a heartbreaker. I wasn't going to spend my senior year moping over Jamie. I was going to spend it winning over Ruby.

Which was why the second thing I had to do when I got home was text her.

Seven

In retrospect, **what are you up to** wasn't the ingeniously, slyly seductive message I thought it was when I sent it at 10:48. On a Sunday night. Probably the answer was **sleeping,** or **going to bed soon,** or something similarly unlikely to lead to a flirtatious back-and-forth. But we had to start our text rapport somewhere, and everything else I'd thought of was even stupider. For longer than I'd like to admit, I'd entertained the idea of texting her my favorite picture of Ashlyn Harris, in which she's sitting with her teammate and partner Ali Krieger on the pitch, her hand on Ali's shoulder—I guess as a way to be, like, *See anything here that interests you?*

Ordinarily I'd have been devastated that Ruby didn't text me back within two and then five and then ten hours, but luckily I'd become a very laid-back person over the weekend. And then, presumably as an award for my unprecedented chillness, my phone buzzed on the table at lunchtime the next day. Just thirteen hours later. I felt all eight of our eyes on my phone until I picked it up.

"Who's texting you? We're your only friends," said Ronni.

I was too excited to come up with a retort. *Ruby* was texting me. That was who.

Sensing potential gossip, Alexis perked up. "Wait, who is it?"

I ignored her and reread Ruby's message, again and again: **hey, sorry, just saw this.**

It wasn't Shakespeare, but it was a response. It was an acknowledgment that I'd texted her, that texting her was an okay thing for me to do. As I watched the screen, the typing bubble appeared, and I gasped.

"Wait. Really, though," said Alexis. "Like—"

"It's Ruby," said Jamie.

That snapped me out of it. I locked eyes with Jamie, and hers narrowed, daring me to deny it. So I decided to put Alexis out of her misery, and I nodded.

"Omigod," she said, not altogether surprised by my confirmation. *Interesting,* I thought. I hadn't talked to Alexis about my crush on Ruby at all, and if I knew Ronni, it had never even occurred to her to relay that information to anyone either. Which meant Jamie must have said something to Alexis. "What did she say?"

I looked at the screen but the bubble was gone.

"Nothing, honestly," I said.

"Let me see." Alexis reached for my phone, and I swatted her hand away.

"Really, it's nothing. Last night I asked her what she was up to, and she just responded now."

"*Interesting*," said Alexis. She drummed her fingers together like a mad fortune-teller.

"Not really," I lied. I risked another peek at Jamie, but she'd returned to her salad. She scraped the bottom of the Tupperware with her plastic fork, which made a horrible noise she knew I couldn't stand.

"What are you going to write back?" Alexis continued. "I can help you if you want."

If she'd had it her way, Alexis would have drafted every email, text, and Instagram caption the rest of us ever posted. It wasn't that she thought we were incapable of communicating. She just thought everyone could afford to communicate a bit more like her. She had a *lot* of feelings about punctuation and emojis.

"I don't think I should text her again right now," I said. "But thanks." I gave the screen another quick glance—no bubble—silenced the phone, and threw it in my backpack. If Ruby did text me again, I wanted to keep it to myself.

"Smart," she said. "Give it a few hours."

"So are you guys, like . . . ?" said Ronni. She glanced at

Jamie, unsure what was kosher to say in front of the person who really shouldn't get to have any opinion on the matter, if you asked me. But Jamie didn't look up. She just scraped. *Ksss click kssssss.*

"We're just friends," I said. And then, unable to resist, I added, "For now."

"Yeahhhh. That's what I thought," Ronni said, grinning. She gave me a captain-ish clap on the back. Across from me, Alexis clutched her hands and wiggled her shoulders in delight.

My face was fire-truck red. I could feel it. *I shouldn't have said anything in front of Alexis,* I thought. I didn't want it getting out that I thought I was capable of seducing Ruby Ocampo. I only wanted everyone to know when it had already happened.

Jamie threw her plastic container back in her backpack and got up.

"Quinn, you ready?" she asked.

"Oh! Uh. Yes. Yeah, I should go." I shoved the remaining quarter of my sandwich into my mouth and hoisted my backpack over my shoulder. "Bye, you guys." Ronni waved, and Alexis mouthed, *Text me later.*

Once we were out of earshot I muttered my thanks to Jamie for helping me escape before Alexis could keep interrogating me.

She shrugged. "They were being annoying."

"Agreed."

We walked without talking until our routes to class diverged, and then we saw each other off with a nod. I loved Ronni a lot, and Alexis, too, but even now I felt more comfortable around Jamie in the tensest silence than I did around my other friends. I wondered if I'd ever feel that at ease around anyone else, friend or more. It was almost impossible to get to that place with someone, and when it did happen, it took such a long time. And even then, cruelly, there was no guarantee you'd both stay there.

After practice, I pulled out my phone and saw I finally had a text from Ruby. It took everything I had not to yelp.

It said: **Wanna help me make posters for the show?**

She'd sent it twenty minutes earlier. I hoped I hadn't missed my window, that she hadn't already changed her mind.

Yes!! I wrote. *No*, I thought. *WAY too much.* Delete.

Sure! I sent it quickly, before I could find something wrong with that, too. I knew from past experience that I could lose hours of my life this way.

Your place? I added. I wondered what her bedroom looked like. I pictured band posters and clothes everywhere. Maybe one of those big white vanities girls in movies had just for putting on lipstick and spritzing perfume on their wrists. I imagined her sitting there in a silky black robe, awash in golden light, and zoned out until Ronni shouted my name and I realized I was sitting alone.

Ruby still hadn't replied, so I threw on my bag and dragged myself out to the parking lot, trailing behind the rest of the team. I waved goodbye to everyone and climbed into my truck, where I sat very still and stared at my phone until it lit up.

Eh.

Yours?

Ugh. Why did exactly zero of the rich people I knew ever want to spend any time in their own beautiful houses? If I lived in a house like that, I'd make everyone come to me. Wasn't that the point?

I thought it over. My mom definitely wasn't home from work yet, but would be soon. She was weird, but she was also busy, and would probably say hello and head right for her office. We didn't have a lot to offer, snacks-wise, but if I remembered correctly there were ice cream sandwiches in the freezer. My room was fairly clean, and I'd taken down all the pictures of Jamie and me weeks ago. Despite its modest size and the general anxiety associated with letting someone like Ruby into it, my house was . . . fine. For a minute I thought about suggesting neutral territory—Triple Moon?—but that felt somehow disrespectful to Jamie. That my instinct was still to protect her feelings, to do anything to avoid offending her, annoyed me. But not enough to change my mind and risk it.

Sure, I wrote. **Do you need a ride?**

Shockingly, I've been cleared to drive. What's your address?

I took a breath and texted it to her, both embarrassed and grateful that the name of my street would let her know not to expect much.

I raced home, shoveling drive-through tacos into my mouth on the way. I took the world's fastest shower and then tried to survey the setting from an outsider's perspective: the tiled entryway, in need of a sweep; the laundry room straight ahead, piled with dirty clothing (I shut the door); the papers and books scattered across the kitchen table, which I stacked in neat piles and then arranged slightly askew for a more natural effect. I hated the way the staircase overhung the entrance to the living room, and I especially hated the spaces between the steps, which had terrified me as a kid, and which sometimes still scared me if I thought too hard about getting my foot stuck in one of them. But there was nothing I could do about that in the next ten minutes or so. So instead I turned on various combinations of lamps and overhead lights until the room felt glowy and warm, and folded our most presentable blanket over the back of the couch. Then I swept the floor and dusted the TV and searched the pantry for a snack I could put out, clapping victoriously when I found a mostly full bag of kettle corn. I dumped it into a bowl and put it on the coffee table and then I sat down to wait.

Ten minutes passed, then twenty, then forty: three-quarters of the way into an episode of *Chopped* I'd already seen twice. At the forty-five-minute mark I sent Ruby a text.

Hey, are you on the way?

Then I felt bad for having texted her while she was in the car, because what if she got in a car crash and died, and the last thing the police found on her phone was a half-typed response to me? I had seen a commercial about this very thing happening once and it haunted me. I quickly typed another message.

Don't text me back

If you're driving, I mean

My phone buzzed anyway. She wrote: **Almost there!**

When the doorbell rang, another thirty minutes had gone by, and I'd dozed off to the dulcet drone of Ted Allen naming ingredients. I jumped up and slapped myself a couple times on the cheeks before answering the door.

I'd started to get a little annoyed with Ruby by then, but when I opened the door and I saw her I wasn't mad anymore. Her hair was wet and her eyes were puffy. She was wearing a hoodie, the front pocket lumpy with markers and pens, and she held a small stack of brightly colored paper under her arm. I took these from her and set them on the table.

"What's wrong?" I asked.

She looked up at me, seemingly surprised and grateful all

at once. Maybe I wasn't supposed to be able to tell that she'd been crying. But it was pretty obvious.

"Is it weird if I ask for a hug?" she said.

I didn't answer. I just stepped closer and put my arms around her shoulders. She moved closer still, looping her arms around my lower back and resting her head gently against my collarbone. My body felt less solid where hers touched it, like a bubble that might burst if she pressed any harder. I wanted her to press harder anyway. I wanted us both to hold on for dear life.

"Tell me," I said. We separated and sat on the couch, and I wished I had something to offer her besides popcorn, which now seemed irredeemably dorky.

"It's stupid," said Ruby. "I don't know why I cried. I think I have PMS or something." She rubbed at her eyes, leaving little shadows of mascara beneath them.

"I'm sure it's not stupid," I said. "At least, I'm pretty sure."

"Thanks a lot," she laughed.

"Boy problems?" I guessed.

She looked at me then, so intently I blushed. She shrugged. So I was right.

"Mikey?"

"Yeah, kind of."

"What happened?"

"Just him being a dick, as usual."

I wanted badly to agree but it seemed wiser to wait.

She sighed. "I talked to the guys about the show, and everyone seemed fine with it, and into it, and then a few hours ago Mikey texted me to say he wasn't sure he was up for it after all, and it turned into a whole thing."

"Do you think he meant it?"

"Of course not!" she scoffed. "He would never miss an opportunity to be adored."

"Then what is he doing?"

"Getting back at me, I guess?"

"Boys are *such* drama queens," I said. "Everyone acts like girls are the emotional ones, but have you ever seen a girl punch a locker? No." *I sound like Jamie,* I thought.

"It's true," Ruby sniffed.

I paused. "Is it really *that* important to have a bass player?"

Ruby laughed spitefully. "Unfortunately, yes," she said. "And he's really good."

"I feel like I could learn."

"You have two weeks."

"Okay, how about this: if I'm *somehow* not ready by then, Mikey can play."

"So he's your alternate?"

"Mm, I prefer the term 'understudy'?"

There was that laugh again. We smiled at each other until we remembered why Ruby was in my house in the first place. The posters and markers were on the coffee table three inches away, but neither of us moved to touch them. As for me, I didn't want to break the spell. As for her, I couldn't tell yet. But there was something.

"You're so lucky you're not attracted to them," she said finally.

"Who, bassists?" I said. She smiled patiently at my joke.

My heart thrummed in my chest. Obviously Ruby knew I was gay (everyone did), but something about the way she was bringing it up now felt loaded. There was always that moment when it came up with someone for the first time, not as an abstract concept having to do with one's values but specifically about *me*, when I reflexively held my breath, waiting to see where they wanted to take me: the long-held questions they might have, which I was expected to answer as a representative of my people; the stories about the other gay person they knew, and how genuinely thrilled they were when said person came out; the soft-eyed affection that told me they were a Good Person who also, incidentally, thought of me as something entertaining and cute, not unlike a puppy.

Unless, of course, the person talking to me about my queerness was queer too. Then we could both be normal.

"Sorry," said Ruby, rolling her eyes at herself. "That was not a woke thing to say."

I shook my head. "No. I *am* lucky. Every time I meet a boy, I feel lucky."

She laughed, and the tension broke, which was the goal.

I was okay with being the joke so long as I was the one who made it.

I could have asked her then if she had ever liked a girl, or thought she ever could, but I wasn't ready to know. At that moment, it felt possible, and I wanted to preserve that hope in amber. So I grabbed a poster and a marker and asked Ruby what she wanted the posters to say.

"We're calling it the Rock Your Fucking Face Off tour."

I paused. "I don't think you can write the f-word on posters for school."

Ruby laughed. " 'The f-word'? That's adorable."

I cleared my throat in an attempt to distract her from my reddening face. "I don't know why I said it like that. I have said 'fuck' before."

"Congratulations," she smirked. "For the posters, we can censor it with asterisks and dollar signs."

"Oh, yeah. That makes sense." I held my marker close to the paper and paused. "You're doing promo on Instagram and stuff too, right . . . ?"

"Of course. But posters are so classic."

Ruby watched me start to write a giant *S* on my poster and then stop again. "You're making me nervous," I said.

"Thank you," she said. "For listening, I mean."

"Oh. You're welcome."

"You're sweet."

Again with the *fucking* blushing.

"Where's your bathroom?"

"Around that corner there." I pointed over my shoulder, and then Ruby put her hand on my leg to hoist herself off the floor, and I almost passed out. It was there and then it was gone, not a squeeze or anything, but—given the alternative options she'd have available: the couch and coffee table—not nothing, either. She didn't look at me, didn't act like it meant anything in particular, but why do something like that unless it did? When I heard the bathroom door close I put my hand on the spot where hers had been, just above my right knee, and I held it. I actually held my own knee because a girl's hand had briefly been there. That's how far gone I was.

I heard the garage door creak open, and I leapt up like I'd been caught masturbating. My mom was home, at exactly the worst time. Not that the sex trajectory leaps directly from knee grazing to making out, but now it *definitely* wasn't going to happen.

Ruby emerged from the bathroom at the same time my mom came through the side door, creating a brief yet torturous standoff.

"Hi, Mom. This is Ruby. Ruby, this is my mom . . . Ms. Antoniak . . . ?" Most of my friends called my mom by her first name, but it had been a while since anyone new had come over and I wanted to be polite. Instead, I feared I sounded like I didn't know my own mother's name.

"Um, no. Call me Nadine," said my mom. "Nice to meet you, Ruby."

"Nice to meet you too, Nadine," said Ruby. "I love your name."

"Really? It's so old-fashioned."

"That's why it's cool."

"Ha. Enjoy that association while it lasts."

"Just say thank you, Mom." Sometimes she could be so cynical and so self-righteous I wanted to scream. When I was younger I loved the way she treated the two of us as a team the world was out to get, but the older I got, the more exhausting I found it. Not every compliment was backhanded. Not everyone who seemed nice turned out to only want something from you. Not everything that was good had to go sour.

"Thank you," my mom sighed. "I'm sorry, it's been a long day."

"Vintner?" I asked. For the last few weeks my mom had been the main reporter on a sexual harassment case involving our young, handsome, and very well-liked mayor. It was obvious that she was excited to be covering it, but I could tell she was running low on steam; her face was pallid and puffy, and I was pretty sure she'd worn that shirt two days in a row at least.

She nodded. "Another intern came forward."

"What a dick," said Ruby. "I never trusted him. With that hair?"

My mom raised her eyebrows, and she smiled. "Indeed."

I tried to contain my pride by shoving a handful of popcorn into my mouth.

"Well, I'll leave you girls to your . . . arts and crafts?"

"We're making posters for Ruby's show."

"Oh, *right*, you're the rock star."

It was amazing, really, how quickly embarrassment could replace every other feeling.

Ruby grinned. "You could say that."

"Sick," said my mom.

"Bye, Mom!"

She headed upstairs, waving and calling out, "Bye! Love you! Don't stay up too late! Don't forget to brush your teeth! I'll leave your night-light on for you!"

"She's kidding," I clarified.

Ruby smirked. "Funny." I couldn't quite tell if she meant it, but there was no way I was going to ask. Instead we both checked our phones, or I pretended to while sneakily watching Ruby frown at hers.

"How is it almost ten?"

"How is this all I've accomplished?" I held up my poster, which read *SV.* Not even a full *W.*

Ruby laughed. "It's okay. Let's just knock out a bunch right now. And then I should probably go."

I felt like Prince Charming, desperate for time to stand still so Cinderella could stay. But that's not how it works, and when we'd made a reasonably decent thirteen posters, Ruby got up, and I walked her to the door, where she pulled me into a one-armed hug, the other holding her new advertising. Which made three times she'd touched me in one night. At that moment it didn't feel possible I could get any luckier.

Eight

On the day of the Sweets show I woke at six for the ninety-minute drive to San Juan Capistrano, where we had a meet. Even then, the air was thick and soupy, and I sweat through my jersey by halftime in the first game. That left two and a half games to go, and only one backup jersey in my bag, and by the time I got home I was ready to trade the rest of my life for a long, cool shower. We'd won two of three, and I'd scored three times, which was the best I'd done in a while. I wanted to email UNC with a recap, but of course that wasn't how things were done. With a radio silence as long as the one between me and UNC, you had to let them come to you.

After my shower I tried on eight hundred T-shirts before settling on a plain white one, and then I slicked my hair back with wax and put some black eyeliner inside my lower lid, hoping the overall effect was Kristen Stewart dirty and not just dirty dirty. I didn't usually wear makeup, but Jamie had once called my eyes beautiful when I was wearing eyeliner, and I hoped Ruby would think the same. Downstairs I inhaled some reheated pizza and a Red Bull, and after yelling *good night* to my mom I rushed out. On the drive over I listened to my newest inspirational playlist, entitled *You Can Do This*. (It featured a lot of Taylor Swift.)

Jamie and I had made plans to meet at Triple Moon at eight-thirty that night, technically thirty minutes after the show began. There was an opening act, these kids who went to Torrey Pines and called themselves Pineapple Under the Sea, like from *SpongeBob* but ironic. Jamie said they were okay, which meant they were awful, so I proposed getting there a little late, hoping we'd miss at least half their set, and wanting to seem to Ruby like I had a life outside her.

I beamed when I pulled into the parking lot and found it mostly full for the first time in . . . maybe ever. People had come, just like I'd promised Dee and Gaby they would. And it was still early: despite my best efforts to wait, I arrived at 8:16. The sun had set by 7:00, taking all the day's earlier heat with it. I wished I'd brought the jean jacket I'd eagerly dug out of my closet a week before school started. Though San Diego was still very warm throughout October, the nights could finally feel a little like fall.

When I pushed open the shop's door I was met with velociraptor-esque shrieking and piercing guitar. It took everything I had not to clap my hands over my ears. Instead I made my way to the counter and took the stool that seemed farthest from the noise. Nobody else was seated at the bar; people were mostly huddled together close to the stage, incurring hearing damage. I counted thirty-five people in attendance, and every few minutes another pair or group came through the door and joined the herd. I hoped Jamie would arrive soon—I didn't want to be seen sitting alone for too long. Not for the first time, I cursed Ronni and Alexis under my breath for having other plans: Ronni, visiting her brother at college, and Alexis, on a first date with some boy who went to her church. (She was texting our group thread updates so frequently she couldn't possibly have any time left to talk to her date.)

I felt a jab in my shoulder and turned to find Dee, eyes wide in a mixture of alarm and possibly regret.

"What do you think?" I shouted. She held up rock hands and stuck out her tongue, and I laughed. It was too loud to have a proper conversation, or else I would have asked her for advice on what to do or say to Ruby after the show so she'd fall in love with me. For an older person, Dee was a stud, and I'd seen her charm a dozen or more twentysomething customers since I started coming here. They'd giggle, and sometimes leave her their numbers, and then they'd come back two days later, and again a few days after that, hoping to be asked out. Which Dee almost never did. Her favorite joke was that she'd rather get a root canal than go on a first date. Jamie liked to pretend Dee was still in love with Gaby, but I didn't think that was it. Dee just liked dogs more than she liked people. She had three of her own, all of them rescues, plus a foster or two at all times. I'd once convinced her to get Instagram just for dog content alone, and now she posted like four dog pictures a day.

"Where's Gaby?" I yelled.

"Hiding," said Dee. I nodded. That meant Gaby was in the tiny office across from the bathroom down the hall. I crossed my fingers and wished for her to be happy with how the night went, and then I tacked on the same wish for Dee, and Ruby, and me.

Dee pointed to the espresso machine by way of asking me if I wanted a drink, and I nodded, more because my mouth was dry than anything else. I'd have preferred a beer or a wine or anything even remotely alcoholic, but no matter how much Dee liked me, she wasn't going to give me anything like that. When she set my coffee in front of me I swallowed half of it in one go, I guess so that instead of being slightly tired with a dry mouth, I'd be sweaty and insane. Immediately I wanted to text Ruby, again, but I'd promised myself I'd give her a break while she got ready for her show. This was turning out to be easier said than done: we had been texting more and more since our poster-making session, Ruby's response times shorten- ing from double-digit hours to single-digit to ten or twenty minutes. Which, don't get me wrong, still felt like an eternity. But the point was, I told myself, she always responded. A few times she'd even been the one to text me first. As a result, I'd spent the better part of two weeks clutching my phone anytime I wasn't in class or asleep. Though sometimes I also held it while I slept. Each interaction felt monumental, though whenever I scrolled up to reread them I found mostly trivia: Ruby's favorite candy was blue Laffy Taffy, her favorite color was orange, her favorite band was . . . one I'd never heard of, and couldn't actually recall the name of at the moment, but if I scrolled back far enough in our text history I would find it. She hated coffee and she still loved wine coolers, even though they were for freshmen. She slept with a small, worn stuffed elephant her grandma had given her when she was born, but she hid it under her bed every morning in case anyone came over unexpectedly. This last one, especially, felt significant: it told me that she trusted me.

I wanted to send her something now about the coffee, something to the effect that she was right and I'd rather be drinking a wine cooler, even if it wasn't totally true. I got as far as opening our conversation on my phone. But I'd texted her good luck an hour earlier, and she hadn't responded, so I re-placed it, facedown, on the counter and took another big gulp of my sugary latte. And checked my phone one more time, very quickly, and put it back.

A particularly loud group of people pushed through the door, and I spotted Jamie at the back, seemingly arriving with them. Band kids, I realized, not without a little nausea. As first-chair clarinet, Jamie was the one who played the tuning note before the conductor waved his wand and the band started playing, and this made her some sort of god. For the most part, Jamie's social interaction with the other band kids was limited to summer camp, and weekends when Ronni and I had soccer and Alexis was busy, so it was weird to see her with them now, here, when she'd implied she would be meeting me. Especially unsettling was the girl she walked in next to: Natalie Reid.

How to describe Natalie Reid? She was my nemesis, a wolf in first-chair flautist's clothing, and number three on the Straight Girls We Wish Weren't list. When Jamie and I were dating and Jamie had plans with band friends, I spent hours at home alone, worrying about Natalie Reid. I was always ten percent convinced Jamie was in love with her, and I was *certain* Natalie Reid was in love with Jamie, straight though she claimed to be. Natalie Reid was always touching Jamie on the arm, and flinging herself into Jamie's side, and calling her "Jame." Whenever I half teased, half prodded her about it, Jamie told me she found Natalie annoying more than anything else. Jamie told me she loved me and no one else. But still, I knew Natalie Reid was Jamie's *type,* more than I would ever be: she was cute and vaguely emo and wore vintage sweaters and giant blue-framed glasses that suited her dark brown eyes perfectly, and, today, a neon orange beanie that should have looked hideous but didn't. She matched every TV character Jamie had a crush on: a tiny, smart hipster who was pretty enough to be popular but somehow too cool to be. I'd hated her freaking guts ever since Jamie put her third on our list. I hadn't thought of her once in the months since Jamie broke up with me, and now I wondered how I could have been so stupid.

I saw Jamie see me, and I waved. I watched her cup a hand to Natalie's ear, and I held my breath, watching Natalie giggle. Then they separated, and I exhaled. Natalie led the rest of the band kids closer to the stage, and Jamie weaved through the crowd toward me. Even from across the room I recognized the glint of the earrings I'd given her for her seventeenth birthday. They spelled *shut up* in tiny gold script, one word per ear. She hadn't worn them since we broke up, at least around me. I didn't know how to interpret this, but I'd spent nearly fifty dollars of my own hoarded birthday money on them, so, in a purely financial sense, it was good to know she was still getting use out of them. When she appeared at the edge of the crowd as Pineapple Under the Sea wailed to a pained-sounding end, I gave her a one-armed hug, and she slid onto the stool next to mine. She looked pretty: she was wearing the faded-nearly-white overall shorts that I loved, and her cheeks were flushed, her eyelids sparkly. She leaned over to yell in my ear, and I smelled her cinnamon gum.

"Are they done?"

"I really hope so."

Dee slid down the counter to greet Jamie and asked her what she wanted to drink.

"Wine?"

"How's an iced tea?"

Jamie sighed. "Just water. Thank you."

On closer inspection, Jamie's flush extended down her neck, and her pupils were wide and glossy. "Are you drunk?" I asked.

Jamie, uncharacteristically, giggled.

"Did you pregame with your band friends?"

She rolled her eyes. "You can just call them my friends."

"Since when?"

"It makes them sound less important to me."

They are, I thought. Jamie herself had said as much. But defensive positivity was one of her many annoying qualities. *She* could say one of her friends was bugging her, but if I so much as suggested the same thing, she'd insist she'd never been annoyed at all, and in fact was the opposite, and nobody had ever been a better, more important friend to her than that person had. It was easier just to let her have it.

She was quiet for a moment, perhaps ruminating on her close and unfaltering friendships with the entire wind-instrument section. As soon as it became evident she wasn't going to offer up any additional details voluntarily, I tried another approach.

"How are they?"

"Who?"

"Your friends."

"Like, collectively?"

I could feel steam pressing against my skull, threatening to pour out my ears at any moment. I took a few relaxing breaths, as inconspicuous as possible: in through the nose, deep in my diaphragm, out through the mouth, the way my post-divorce therapist, Jennifer, had shown me when I was younger.

"Sure," I said. "All of them."

"They're good."

"And Natalie?"

I studied Jamie's expression, but her eyes stayed fixed on the stage. Only her eyebrows rose a little: a facial shrug. "She's good," she said, sounding like someone who wanted to sound ambivalent.

My insides roiled, which made me furious. Why did my body have to take it so hard when my head and I both knew she hadn't said anything meaningful? And even if she had, what then? We weren't together. We had been broken up for two months. Nine months from now, we'd have been broken up for exactly as long as we were together. And then, for every day after that, we'd be exes for longer than we were ever girlfriends. It was weird the way that worked. Anyone who became your ex stayed your ex forever, no matter how long ago they broke your heart, or you broke theirs.

I knew I was straining hard against the point at which I could reasonably say that we'd "just" broken up. I knew it wasn't my right, anymore, to feel betrayed by the prospect of another girl. Much earlier, it would have been too soon. But at some point very recently, what would once have been cruel had shifted imperceptibly to fair. Maybe it had happened that day at the beach, when I told Jamie that Ruby and I had come here, to our spot, without her.

Speaking of—when in the name of Xena, Warrior Princess, was Ruby going to come onstage? Never in my life had I been so eager to hear a high school band play. If anyone could drown me out, Sweets could. But Pineapple Under the Sea was still ambling around, picking things up and setting things down, and Dee had turned the lights back on so people could buy something to drink between bands. Or that was the idea, though not many people seemed all that eager to buy iced coffees at nine p.m. Looking around, I had a sudden suspicion as to why.

"Is everyone here drunk but me?" I asked Jamie.

Jamie laughed, a single honking *ha!* "Sucks to be you."

She gave me a sidelong glance and, seeing my bewildered

expression, burst into laughter. My shoulders dropped, releasing tension I hadn't realized I'd been holding, and I laughed too.

"I'm sorry," Jamie croaked. "That was beneath me."

"I don't think I've heard anyone say 'sucks to be you' since fourth grade."

"I'm bringing it back."

"Please don't."

She shrugged and took a big gulp of water, and for a minute we both scanned the room. Now that it was almost time for the lead act, Triple Moon was as packed as I'd seen it in months, if not years. I couldn't wait to find out how much money Dee and Gaby had made, and to see how happy with me they were. Maybe they'd let us—well, them—have another show or three here. Maybe I could convince them to give me a dollar commission for every cover charge they collected. Or even fifty cents. It looked like there were probably sixty people here, which would translate to thirty dollars a show. Which wasn't a lot, but after five shows, it would be enough for . . . one college textbook. Hm. Maybe we could compromise and do seventy-five cents a head.

I looked for and found Natalie Reid, easy to spot in her stupid neon beanie. She appeared fully engaged in conversation with Justin (trombone) and Becca (flute—why did I know this?), and I breathed relief in and out. It truly hadn't occurred to me that anyone from band would be here, least of all Natalie. I imagined her as more of a gentle indie girl. Songs with ukuleles, and people who murmured more than they sang, so you couldn't really tell if they had good voices or not. Then again, I was here. There could be other motives for coming here. Mine was a girl. I hoped Natalie's was anything else.

Natalie Reid aside, everyone else I could see was more or less whom I'd expected: the burnout boys, helmed by Sam Perpich and Nick Weiss; Lara Hammond and Kaela Brown, the otherwise straitlaced popular girls whose interest in MDMA necessitated their friendship with Sam and Nick; the nervous-looking sceney sophomore boys, wearing lots of hair product and cologne, and the goth-lite girls they were trying to impress; a cluster of freshman and sophomore girls who were one hundred percent going to cry the second Sweets took the stage. As if reading my mind, Dee leaned over the counter between Jamie's shoulder and mine and muttered, "I've never seen so many heteros in here at once."

"You don't know they're all straight," Jamie scolded.

I looked at her in disbelief, but evidently she was too tipsy to notice her hypocrisy. Now that Natalie was here, we weren't supposed to assume anything about anyone. How interesting.

Dee squinted. "Mmm. Yeah. I do."

I tried to distract myself, watching as some skinny freshman who looked about twelve in his dad's jean jacket bustled onto the stage from behind the drop cloth hanging from the rafters and began arranging the instruments. I wondered if

Sweets paid him part of their earnings for his services. Or, I thought, maybe he was planning to put this on his college application as volunteer work. *Assisted local artists in presenting their work to the community.* Or, maybe more likely, he was in love with Ruby too.

"Is she still dating that guy?" I asked suddenly. I knew, of course, that Natalie Reid's college boyfriend, Ian, had dumped her in our junior year, just as I knew Jamie knew I knew. Just as I knew she knew who exactly I meant. All the many associated implications hung between us like cobwebs, and as a favor to each other we tried our best to ignore them.

"Who?" said Jamie.

"Natalie Reid," I said.

"Oh," she said. "No. They broke up last year." A pause. She couldn't help herself. "Remember?"

I pulled my best perplexed face. "Huh. No."

Jamie nodded, eyes firmly fixed to the stage. Again I tried to focus: the twelve-year-old, disappearing behind the curtain, the crowd perking up in response. You could feel it—the specific, restless energy of waiting for your favorite band to show themselves. One of Sam's friends tried to start a slow clap, presumably ironically, but only a couple of others picked it up, and it died off, embarrassingly, within thirty seconds. Without the cue of dimming lights, it was hard to know when to start making noise. A girl shrieked, "WE LOVE YOU, DAVID," and everyone else at her table immediately hunched over giggling.

My heart thrummed with excitement. I was, quite literally, on the edge of my seat. I couldn't wait to see Ruby. I couldn't stop asking Jamie questions I didn't want her to answer.

"Who's she dating now?" I said, sounding as bored as I could manage.

"Natalie?"

I ground my teeth into dust so I wouldn't scream. "Yeah."

"She's not," said Jamie. I waited, and finally she glanced my way. "She was seeing this girl at camp, but they broke up."

This is it, I thought. *This is what dying feels like.* I leaned an elbow onto the counter behind me to keep myself upright, but still the room tilted and swayed.

"What girl?" I asked.

"She goes to a different school," said Jamie.

"Sounds made-up," I said. I took a panicked slurp of my coffee, which was now mostly water, and raised my hand to my neck, surreptitiously feeling for my pulse.

"I mean, *I* know her," said Jamie. "Her name's Sami Lerner, if you wanna look her up." She nodded at my phone, faceup on the counter, and I flipped it facedown.

"What instrument does she play?" I asked, absurdly.

Jamie raised an eyebrow. "French horn . . . ?"

I nodded, like that explained everything. Jamie half laughed, half scoffed, and we returned to staring at everything but each other. I breathed in through my nose and out through my mouth, and jabbed at my neck with my middle and ring fingers until I was satisfied my heart wouldn't explode. *So Natalie Reid likes girls too*, I told myself. *This doesn't change anything for you, and it doesn't necessarily change anything for Jamie, either.* I was clutching my neck again, I realized. I wedged my hands into the crooks of my elbow, locking myself in place. Along with the hollowed-out-husk feeling spreading through my body, there arose a wrenching, not unpleasant satisfaction. *You called it.*

I sat up straighter, scanning the crowd for that telltale orange beanie, but Natalie was short, and the crowd was denser now, and I couldn't find her, which was just as well. Finally the curtain came to life, puffing out and retreating like a wave as people scrambled into place behind it. A few seconds later, the entity known as Sweets emerged from backstage to whooping applause. David led the pack: floppy brown hair, tight jeans, tight T-shirt, an illicit under-eighteen tattoo of what appeared to be a cheeseburger on the forearm he now used to tune his baby-pink electric guitar. I had to give it to the shrieker: he was, like, totally dreamy onstage.

But I didn't look at David for long. In fact, I hardly looked at him again for the rest of the show. As far as I was concerned, Sweets had no guitarist, no bassist, no drummer. They had only a singer.

Ruby's lips were painted a deep, vampy purple, and her silver hoop earrings nearly touched her shoulders. She wore baggy jeans over Timberlands and a red Mickey Mouse T-shirt she'd cropped at her belly button. Boy-style boxers peeked over the top of her waistband, which caused me to feel briefly dizzy, this time in a good way. Her hair was twisted into tight French braids, the tips freshly dyed emerald green. *She was texting me when she was applying that dye,* I thought with substantial satisfaction. I had previous and direct knowledge of that dye. Who else here could say that? Who could think of Natalie Reid when Ruby Ocampo was onstage? Certainly not me. Not very often, anyway.

I watched Ruby as she smiled at the crowd, took a drink from a water bottle, turned to say something to the guys. I felt Jamie look at me and quickly away but I couldn't and didn't take my eyes off Ruby. The palpable excitement in the crowd bordered on impatience. Someone in the audience shrieked, "SWEETS!" The boys stayed serious, focused on fiddling with their instruments, but Ruby smiled and blew the yeller a kiss. I searched the backs of their heads, trying to figure out who had been so lucky, and how much I should now hate them. But then Ruby took the mic in her hand as the drummer raised his sticks to count them off, and she had me captive all over again.

Their first song was, primarily, loud. I noticed Jamie's head bobbing in time to what I could only assume was the beat, and I followed suit. It was difficult to isolate any one instrument from the others: they all crashed into and over one another. But above it all, Ruby's voice soared. Most of the time her singing was clear and sweet, but on the choruses she broke into a Hayley-Williams-meets-Karen-O scream. These are not my words. I stole them from Jamie.

"She sounds a little like Hayley Williams," Jamie shouted in my ear. "And maybe a little like Karen O."

I nodded thoughtfully and shouted back: "I AGREE."

Ruby had a surprisingly commanding presence for someone who mostly stood still, occasionally pointing to someone in the crowd (I always looked), or thumping herself so hard on the heart I had to wonder if it hurt. She was wildly expressive, almost goofy, and if she hadn't been so obviously sure of herself (and so hot) it might have been hard to watch. But she was, so she was a rock star. As each song came to an end she dropped down into a squat and bounced there, bobbing to the beat of the next song starting up. She smiled at David and Ben and waved to people she knew in the audience, and I found myself craning my neck like I might intercept one of these gestures for myself. I was falling a little bit in love with her.

They finished another song and everyone clapped. "WOOOO!" I yelled.

"Thanks for coming out!" Ruby yelled back. This time she saw me. She broke into a huge, gorgeous smile. "We're SWEETS!" People screamed. I swooned.

The band started up a slightly slower song, and David sang in Ruby's place, plaintively mumbling with his mouth pressed up against the mic while the girls in the front lost their minds. *What a waste*, I thought. I watched Ruby sway back and forth and mouth the lyrics into open air. It wasn't fair, how cool some people got to be. But maybe she'd fall in love with me, and I would become that cool also. Sexually transmitted coolness. Oh my God, I was really losing it.

Impulsively I leaned over and cupped my hand around Jamie's ear. "She's been texting me for weeks."

The words left a semi-sour taste in my mouth. I was openly, pathetically bragging, and so soon after Jamie's big Natalie reveal. Surely she saw through me now more than ever. But I had *needed* to say it, I couldn't not; it was only a matter of when. The relief at having said it was instant, then gone, and then I just felt gross and strange. Surely I could have come up with a more natural segue. Almost anything beat suddenly shouting something like that in someone's ear. But it was done, I'd said it, and at least now, if something did happen between Jamie and Natalie, I could claim I'd been first to move on. And couldn't I be proud that Ruby, the person we were all here to see, wanted to spend her rare free time talking to me? So I couldn't help myself. So I bragged. Sue me. I just wanted Jamie to be happy for me. And maybe the littlest bit jealous, too. Or a lot jealous. A lot would actually be great.

The way Jamie actually responded, though, shocked me: she *squealed*. Not only that—she clasped her hands together, like an old lady whose daughter has informed her she's going to be a grandmother. She leaned in, grinning maniacally. Maybe she was drunker than I thought.

"Oh my God! Tell me everything."

"Seriously?"

"Yes!"

I squinted. "Alexis? Is that you?"

She deflated, relaxing back into herself. "Okay. That was over the top. But I mean it. I know I was weird about this . . . before, and I shouldn't have been. I'm trying to make up for it now, so let me, okay? It's exciting. She's . . . Ruby. Tell me everything."

But something clenched in my stomach, and in the face of her unexpected, wide-open encouragement, I found myself with nothing to say. *This is what you wanted,* I told myself. Jamie was happy for me, or at least supportive, which was the least she could be. There was no weird, painful tension, no snotty retort or disinterested nod. She cared. She wanted to know more. I should have been so much more relieved than I was.

"Nothing significant." I shrugged. That sounded unpromising, so I added, exaggerating, "But it's been a lot."

"Are you gonna hang out?"

"Well, technically we have."

Jamie's eyes widened. "What? When?"

"Just the other night. We made the posters for this." I swept my hand around the room, and glanced at the stage. The music was picking up now, and Ruby resumed her rightful place at the mic.

Jamie nodded, a small smile pulling at her face. "I thought that handwriting looked familiar."

"You *are* the foremost expert."

Jamie had once kept all the letters I'd written her in a Batman folder labeled WORLD STUDIES—for maximum discretion—beneath her bed. It was stuffed fat with my notes and printed emails, and I only found it a few weeks before we broke up. At the time, I had taken it as evidence she'd love me forever. I wanted to know if she still had it, but I really didn't want to know if she didn't. To keep myself from asking her I turned back to the stage, where the band was winding down. How was I going to tell Ruby which song I'd liked best when I kept missing them? I vowed to listen to the next one carefully—whatever it was, it would have to be my favorite. Ruby sidled up behind the mic stand like it was a person, pressing her body against it, and I felt my mouth go dry. Then she looked straight at me, again. She smiled at me, and I smiled back. Fireworks crackled in my chest.

"Thank you guys for coming out to see us," she said. "It's exciting to play somewhere new that, like, actually has room for people to stand."

Everyone laughed but Mikey, who glowered visibly at Ruby's words. It felt *so* good.

Ben lifted his arms and smacked his drumsticks together, and Ruby shouted, "We've been Sweets, and you can get our new EP, *Type Two*, after the show!"

"*Type Two*"? I whispered to Jamie. "Like, diabetes?"

"I know." She nodded, wincing a little. "It's their second one. Get it?"

"Mmm." *Shit,* I was supposed to be listening. "What's this one called again?"

"'If You Say So.'"

"Right." The track was one of their new ones and, judging by the crowd, an early favorite. It was catchy, and a little bit punk, and between verses Ruby jumped up and down to the beat, swinging her braids side to side. I even found myself shouting along to the chorus, or at least the half of it I could make out: "IF! YOU! SAY! SO! IF! YOU! SAY! SO!"

When it was over, the crowd whistled and clapped, and one of the girls up front flung a ninety-nine-cent grocery-store rose still wrapped in plastic onstage. It smacked into David's shin and fell to his feet. He ignored it in favor of pushing his hair back, and lifted the hem of his T-shirt to wipe his forehead, revealing four inches of scrawny boy stomach "by accident." Ruby bowed deeply, while Ben and Mikey gave little nods and waves and refused to smile. Together they hustled offstage, but they left all their instruments onstage, so it was clear they weren't really done. The crowd cheered and clapped and chanted, stretching the band's name into two syllables: "SWEE-EETS! SWEE-EETS!"

I leaned over to Jamie. "Is it really an encore if they make you do it?"

"I know," she yelled back. "It's like, guys . . . you're not fooling anyone."

"'Bye! We're definitely finished!'"

"'The only song we didn't play is your favorite, see ya!'"

Sure enough, the band came back, and Jamie and I turned to each other with our mouths hanging open in mock disbelief, which made us both crack up. Sweets launched into their crowd-pleasers, a couple of screamy, dancey jams that made Ruby seem so happy I was nearly lifted off my stool just watching her. Her face was red and shimmering, and she jumped up and down. I felt myself grinning, watching her, like a moron. Then I felt Jamie watching me and pulled myself together.

"You were right," I shouted. "I'm a fan now."

"I bet you are."

Ruby held her last note, and the crowd smothered the end of it in applause. Once again she bowed and sauntered offstage, the rest of the band trailing behind her. This time, they really were done. The lights lifted like magic, controlled by the still-invisible Gaby, our own (wo)man behind the curtain.

Dee came over to pick up our empty glasses and leaned over the counter to mutter, "They're no Le Tigre."

"Nobody knows who that is."

Dee pointed to Jamie. "She does."

"Thanks to you," said Jamie, and high-fived Dee's outstretched hand.

Dee and Jamie started chatting about their favorite all-womyn-with-a-*y*, gurl-with-a-*u* bands, and I fully tuned out, scanning the room for Ruby. The denim-jacket boy from before resurfaced, picking up instruments and waddling backstage with them one by one, and the lesser fans started filing out the door in pursuit of an after-party. I had no plans yet, which was why I had to grab Ruby before she left: so she could invite me to hers. I told Jamie I'd be right back and headed for the office. Right about now Gaby would be getting ready to clear out for a strict twenty minutes, during which time the office became a postshow greenroom for "the artists."

I made it only halfway down the hall before someone grabbed me around the waist, and I jumped and shrieked oddly. Something like this: "Yoweaagh!"

Ruby, her arms still around me, laughing just inches from my face. Pulling me into a hug and holding me close. My hand fell to the edge of her cropped T-shirt where her back was exposed. And a little sweaty. But I didn't care about that. Ruby was hugging me, in plain view of her bandmates, who came sauntering up behind her. Then she pulled back, smiled at me, and kissed me.

On the cheek. But still.

Over her shoulder, Mikey glared at me. *Say it,* I thought. *I dare you.*

But he said nothing. None of them did. Ruby released me, and the boys brushed past us, crowding into the office/

greenroom, where Gaby held the door open, trying her hardest not to look too displeased. We exchanged a look that meant: *Boys. Ugh.* Once they were inside she slipped discreetly past me toward the front, giving me a quick squeeze on the shoulder. I loved her so much at that moment, for making all of this possible and for knowing how important it was for me to stay right here, talking to nobody but Ruby.

"Thank you," said Ruby. "This was so much fun."

"You were amazing."

"Really?"

"Yeah. Best show I've ever been to." *One of the only, too,* I thought, but she didn't need to know that part.

Ruby clasped my wrist, setting it on fire. "That's really nice."

I shrugged. "What are you up to now?"

She looked over her shoulder, and my eyes followed hers—the boys were laughing and talking quietly, passing around a bagged forty-ounce beer they'd pulled out of thin air.

"We're probably just gonna go back to Ben's or something," Ruby sighed.

There was no invitation there. I knew that. But there was something about Ruby's expression that made me want to second-guess myself. I could still feel the spot on my cheek where she'd kissed me.

"Can I give you a ride?"

"Oh!" She smiled. "That's so nice. I'll probably just ride

with the guys, but thank you." I must have looked let down because she touched me again, this time higher up on my arm. "Seriously," she added.

"No problem," I said. "I guess I'll just . . ."

"Are you sure?"

"Yeah, I've got a thing." *(???????)*

"Sounds fun."

"Yeah. Okay. I'll see you soon?"

"Yes, please," said Ruby. I swooned so hard I almost felt seasick. Surely she was putting my health at risk.

"You know where to reach me," I said—lamely, but she laughed anyway. She gave me another quick hug, waved, and joined the guys in whatever it was they were going to do next. Before I walked away, I noticed that she had two open seats to choose from, and she chose the one next to Mikey.

When I returned to the main room, Jamie was gone, and so was Natalie Reid. Only a few stragglers remained, and Dee and Gaby eyed them warily from behind the counter. I ran out to the parking lot, hoping to catch a glimpse of Jamie and Natalie leaving separately, but I saw neither. I checked my phone, but Jamie hadn't so much as texted a goodbye. *It's late, for Jamie*, I thought. *I'm sure she just went home.* I was getting good at lying to myself. If I kept practicing like this, one day I might even believe it.

Nine

I forgot all about getting pancakes with my dad until an hour before I was supposed to meet him, at ten-thirty the next morning. My body woke me up, sweaty and panicked, and I checked my phone to find a reminder text from him, sent at five-fifteen a.m., which for him was sleeping in.

See u 10:30 @ Mantequilla—JR

My dad signed all his texts like I might forget who the DAD in my phone referred to otherwise. And still no mention of his apparently impending move. I texted him back (**Sounds good!**) and tapped my conversation with Ruby in case she'd texted me late last night when I was already asleep. Obviously that wasn't the case, but you could never be too careful. I really had missed a text message once. It was from my mom, not a girl, but it could happen. So a minute later I checked again.

I wasn't in the mood to see my dad, really, but I knew I

should be grateful for the distraction. It wasn't that I'd expected Ruby to text me, but what a relief it would have been if she had. Without it, I was left to my own horrible imagination of what she might have done with the rest of her night. She'd said she was done with Mikey, but couples like that were never really done. Brody Warshaw and Alina McCaskill had been on and off since *literally* the fifth grade. They were not good together, clearly, but no one knew what to do when they were apart. Once when they were broken up, the stock market crashed. It was all over the news. Sure, it was a coincidence, but then again . . . was it?

Ruby and Mikey felt a little like the alt Brody and Alina. I worried that if something more serious than a cheek kiss didn't happen soon, I would lose my chance for good. And then I would finish high school as single as I'd started it.

That said, the cheek kiss was pretty freaking great. I touched the spot on my face where it had happened and closed my eyes to replay it over and over, giving myself the good kind of chest pain every time.

I'd wanted to tell Jamie first thing. Had she still been there when I came out of the coffee shop, I knew *Ruby kissed me* would have been the first words out of my mouth. In the sharp morning light, I realized that might not have been the best idea, and I felt momentarily grateful she'd left, saving me from myself. But then I remembered Natalie Reid, and punched my pillow, and got up to get ready.

* * *

I was told (mostly by my dad) that Mantequilla was an institution. Though the food was delicious, this was somewhat difficult to accept, especially if you read some of the snottier reviews online. The cafe was situated in a strip mall between two constantly rotating storefronts—currently, an orthopedic-shoe outlet and a nail salon decorated to look like some middle-aged white lady's version of a Tibetan monastery. Mantequilla had a faded yellow awning and always sticky fake marble tables out front, which nobody sat at unless it was crowded. When I walked in at 10:32, I saw my dad sitting at our usual booth, if you could count a place we sat together every year or two "usual." His criteria for restaurant seating were as follows: (1) close to the windows, (2) within eyeshot of the bathroom, (3) as far as possible from the kitchen, and (4) highly observable by the server, whom he tended to flag down with special requests three or four times per meal. There was only one booth at Mantequilla that fulfilled all four requirements, so he made sure to arrive early to get it.

As I approached the booth he made a big show of checking his watch. "You're late."

"Two minutes doesn't count as late."

I slid onto the weirdly hard red vinyl seat across from him and took a calming sip of water from the glass waiting for me, peering at my father over the rim. He looked old, I thought.

· 125 ·

His eyebrows had an ombré effect, fading into white at the outer edges, and I could tell from his sunglasses-shaped tan line that he wasn't wearing sunscreen like I told him to. His belly pressed up against the edge of the table, so I assumed he hadn't cut back on his beer drinking, either. *Maybe I should get granola and lead by example,* I thought. But food wasn't really his problem, and no one went to Mantequilla for their granola.

"Three minutes, and yes it does," my dad sighed. "Thirty seconds counts."

"Maybe for old people."

A sly grin spread under my dad's mustache. This was one of the good things about him: he took shit as well as he gave it. With me, at least. My mom probably didn't see it that way.

Sara, the college-aged granddaughter of the cafe's owner, breezed by our booth, sliding two laminated menus onto the table without slowing down. Neither my dad nor I touched them: our orders never varied.

"So how's things?" he said, taking a big gulp of coffee.

"Good," I said. "Fine. You know."

"What's the status on UNC?"

I flushed. I'd emailed their recruiter, a woman named Paula, a few days earlier in a late-night existential panic, despite my promise to wait for them to come to me. I'd mentioned my recent two-goal club game, and asked if they were still sending out offers, and if I might expect to get one. She had written back the next morning, congratulating me on the win. They were still sending out offers, yes. As to whether I might receive one, she couldn't yet say. They were still making final decisions. It wasn't the worst news she could have sent, but it was far from the best. In some far, desolate corner of my brain there was a tiny pragmatist trying to manage my expectations, telling me that if UNC really, *really* wanted me, I would know by now. Most people knew before senior year started. Ronni had accepted her offer from Stanford last May. But I wouldn't give up until I got a definitive yes, or a definitive no.

In the meantime, I was on the wait list at UCLA, placed in purgatory while the players who'd been offered spots decided whether to accept them. I'd also gotten a full-ride scholarship offer from Baylor, a Baptist school in Texas that obviously hadn't gotten the memo that I was a full-blown queer, or—maybe worse—that was benevolently willing to overlook my queerness for the sake of their soccer rankings. When I'd first looked them up online I learned they'd only removed their policy banning "homosexual acts" in 2016. So that was going to be a no from me, thanks.

"Yeah," I said. "They're still finalizing offers. But UCLA looks good."

"Well, that's a decent backup."

This stung a little, though I thought of it that way myself. UCLA was just two hours north of where I lived. At least twenty kids from my school would go there too. And anyway, I was wait-listed. They weren't sure they wanted me, either.

I was saved by Sara, who reappeared with notebook in hand. "What can I get you?" she asked.

"I'll have the apple-cinnamon pancakes with a side of bacon, and she'll have the chocolate chip with a side of home fries and a small orange juice."

For some reason the thought of all that melted chocolate sticking to the roof of my mouth made me nauseous. "Actually, can I make that blueberry?" I interjected. It was the first other pancake variety I could think of.

My dad looked at me like I'd asked for, well, the granola. I shrugged.

"How's work?" I asked pointedly.

He didn't seem to notice, and launched into his latest grievances about the various "dumbasses" in his department. He ranted for nearly ten minutes straight, making two or three comments about his female coworkers' perceived intelligence. Jamie would have found what he said sexist, and maybe it was, though I maintained he thought every man *and* woman he worked with was stupid.

When Sara returned with our steaming pancakes and sides and he *still* hadn't mentioned moving home, I just about screamed. I glared at the mound of oozing blue-tinted pancakes in front of me, instantly full of regret. There should have been chocolate where those berries were.

"Want some of mine?" my dad asked.

"No, it's okay." I cut into the stack and ate a bite three layers high. "Dad," I started, hoping the pancake in my mouth would make me seem less invested in the answer to my question. "You have a job interview? Here?"

My dad's shoulders wilted, the ends of the fork and knife in his hands slumping until they tapped the table. "Your mom told you that?"

"Dad, you cannot be mad at her. You have had so much time to tell me."

"I was getting there."

"So when is it? Tomorrow?"

He speared a piece of bacon and held it aloft, examining the edges. "Yep. Nine-thirty."

"Do you want it?"

"I'm not sure yet," he said, so agonizingly casual and slow. As if this changed nothing, like I'd told my mom it would. "Depends on the offer. If they even make one."

For a minute or two we chewed in silence, staring over each other's shoulders.

"What about me?" I said finally.

My dad sighed and brushed his mustache with his knuckles. When he spoke he addressed his plate. "I know. This is not part of the plan. But it might not happen."

"What if it does?"

Finally he looked at me. "I'm gonna watch you play for UNC no matter what."

But I play now, too, I thought, *and you don't.*

He watched me take another bite, struggle to chew, and swallow.

"I won't take it if you don't want me to," he said.

I knew he thought this was the generous thing to say, but it wasn't what I wanted to hear.

"Let me know how it goes," I said. "I want you to try."

He smiled and took another bite. "Deal."

Mouth still full of pancake, he changed the subject. "How's Jamie?"

Oh yeah, I thought. He didn't know. I tried to avoid talking about girls with my father, which was easy enough to do over text. In person, though, I felt I had no choice.

"She's good, I think. We broke up, though."

"Really? What happened?"

I shrugged, like *no big deal.* "It just stopped working." I could feel my dad's eyes on me as I cut deeper into my pancakes. I couldn't tell him I'd been dumped. I just couldn't. I prayed to anyone listening that for once he would take my discomfort as a sign to stop asking questions.

"That happens," he said slowly. "You still friendly?"

"Yeah, mostly."

"Good. She's a smart girl."

I felt proud of her, even now. My dad did not hand that word out easily. I had to stop him before he said anything else good about her.

"I've sort of been talking to this other girl lately. Ruby."

My dad nodded, evaluating the name. "What's her deal?" he asked, by which I knew he meant: *Is she like you?*.

"I'm not sure yet," I admitted. "But she's cool. She's in a band."

"Good student?" My father was not impressed by extracurriculars and/or hobbies that did not directly lead to scholarships. Like rock bands.

"I think so, yeah. I don't have her transcript with me."

He gave me a look and took another bite, evaluating her as he chewed.

"Is she good-looking?"

Here we go, I thought. I knew, on some level, that his question was kind of (okay, fully) a creepy one. But I also knew to expect it. For him, good-looking and smart were the qualities that mattered in a woman. Though he'd never said so explicitly, I suspected he thought I could do better than Jamie—who, though striking, wasn't the kind of pretty everyone agreed on. I knew he thought he was looking out for me; I knew he believed people wouldn't give me as hard a time about dating girls if they were knockout beautiful, and popular, and decent students. And the thing was, I couldn't really say he was wrong. People probably *would* treat me better if I dated Ruby. So I answered honestly.

"She is very pretty, yes."

He grinned. "Good for you."

I felt proud and sick and sad and happy at the same time.

My stomach felt heavy with feelings, or else the lesser, non-chocolate pancakes. It was hard to be sure.

I gave my dad the rest of the bullet-point Quinn report: my soccer record so far, my grades so far, my best and worst teachers. He didn't ask any more about Mom, but I told him anyway that she was doing great. I didn't know if that was especially accurate, but I felt it was my duty to say it regardless. He accepted this information neutrally, like I was his doctor giving him his blood pressure reading. Not that he ever went to the doctor, now that Mom couldn't make him. How *was* his blood pressure? I wondered.

My dad put his card on the bill Sara dropped at our table, and then he pulled four twenties from his wallet and gave them to me. I pocketed them eagerly, already thinking of things I could use the money for. Homecoming, I realized, was a little under a month away. Was there a world in which Ruby went with me, and I spent this money on flowers for her wrist?

"Thank you," I said. He waved it off and signed the receipt, leaving his usual two-dollar tip on our twenty-four-dollar bill. When he got up to use the restroom, I removed a crumpled five from my pocket and tucked it under my plate. I met him at the front of the cafe, where we each took a crusty peppermint from the bowl on the register stand and popped them in our mouths.

"All right, Quinnie," he said. The candy clacked between his teeth.

"Thanks for breakfast. And the cash."

"You're welcome."

"So I'll see you . . . ?" *In a week? A month? And how often, after that?* I thought. I decided not to overwhelm him and left my question unfinished.

"Soon, I think," he said. He opened his arms to hug me, and I stepped in. He still smelled so good to me: the generic-brand woodsy body wash and the dryer sheets my mom wouldn't buy and Purell on his hands, applied religiously before and after every meal. We clapped each other on the back, and he squeezed me tighter before letting me go.

I vowed, when I got home, to go into the coming week with a renewed sense of purpose. I would ask Ruby to hang out, just the two of us, without homework or Sweets as a cover. I would catch up on my reading. I would even clean my room, maybe. And next Saturday, when our club team faced Albion, I would play the best soccer of my life, so good UNC would call me over the weekend to offer me a spot. Oh—there was an idea. I would invite Ruby to my soccer game. In my experience, watching me play soccer was the fastest way a girl could fall for me. At least, it had worked on Jamie, and she didn't even like sports. Once after a game she even told me I looked sexy (!). So yeah. That was my whole brilliant plan.

 *Ten*

I showed up for Wednesday night's practice having yet to ask Ruby to come to Saturday's game. Clearly, there was something wrong with me. But in my defense, I was in a real catch-22 (a term I only knew because Jamie had once explained it to me). The longer I waited, the less likely it was for Ruby to even be available to *consider* saying yes to something as dorkily mainstream as attending a sports function on a Saturday night, but it would *also* be uncool to ask her too many days in advance. I figured that formula worked out to make Thursday my best option. If Ruby already had plans, maybe she'd tell me she'd come to the next one. Even in the grand scheme of my triumphant, redemptive senior-year tour, I told myself, I could afford to delay the Ruby-seduction timeline by one week.

Until I couldn't.

At our halftime water break, Ronni appeared at my left

elbow, taking a seat on the bleachers behind me. I watched in confusion as she patted the spot next to her, the metal clanging a little beneath the gold rings I'd never seen her without on her forefinger. My heart rate picked up speed. Ronni was not the type to "goof off," as our club-team coach would call it, during practice. Believe me, I had tried. When the whistle blew she ran off the field, drank water, and ran back out, not-so-subtly encouraging the rest of us to follow her, no matter how many water-break minutes we technically had left. She did not just casually *sit down.* So I stayed standing, hoping I might freeze in place whatever bad news she wanted to give me.

"What's wrong?" I asked.

Again she patted the bench.

"Okay, stop doing that. You have the worst poker face on earth and I know you have something bad to tell me and me sitting down isn't going to make it any better."

"It's not bad, necessarily," she said unconvincingly.

"Just tell me."

She took a deep breath, and the worst sentence I'd ever heard rushed out of her mouth, too fast and way too loud. "Alexis-told-me-that-Jamie-and-Natalie-Reid-are-talking."

"Shhh!" I sat down. I felt like I might throw up.

Normally Ronni would have reminded me she'd told me to sit in the first place, but I must have looked upset, because she stayed quiet. I felt her examining me, and I sank my head into my hands to give my face some privacy. But that only made me look *more* upset, and soon I felt Ronni's hand on my back, so I leapt up again. I noticed our teammate Kate watching us over the lip of her water bottle, but when we made eye contact she looked away.

"Why couldn't you have told me this after practice?" I hissed.

Ronni gave me a patient, patronizing look. "If I'd told you after practice, you would have asked me why I didn't tell you sooner."

She was right, so I was silent. For a second.

"What kind of 'talking' are we talking about?"

Ronni looked away. "She didn't say."

"Alexis? I find that hard to believe."

Ronni glanced at me apologetically. "There may have been a suggestive tone."

That was the problem with *talking:* it could mean anything, or everything. I had spent a portion of every day since the Sweets show hoping and praying that what I'd seen was all there was to see. I kept telling myself they hadn't left together, and now that seemed idiotic, even puritanical. They were both single. They were both drinking. They were both, apparently, into girls. Of *course* something happened.

"When?" I said.

"I don't know," said Ronni.

"But something definitely happened?"

"I don't know."

I had seventy more follow-up questions, at least, but Coach Tara blew the whistle before I could ask any of them. Ronni stood, and I stood, and she gave me a supportive smack on the butt.

"It'll all work out, Q."

"Yeah, I know," I said, thinking: *How could anyone possibly know that?*

All I wanted was more information. But I knew there was something else I had to do first. So I ran to my bag and dug out my phone, ignoring my coach's increasingly irritated whistle blowing. When she saw my phone she dropped the whistle and barked my name, which meant I was about ten seconds from getting the lecture of a lifetime. "One sec!" I yelled, texting Ruby to ask her to the game on Saturday. I hit send, threw my phone back in my bag, and ran out to join my team. "Family stuff," I explained to Coach, the lie rolling easily off my tongue. She gave me a curt nod, and to make up for letting her down I played the best scrimmage of my life.

There was a reason I was especially mad about the prospect of Jamie talking to Natalie Reid. Beyond how much Natalie Reid sucked, I mean. And that reason had to do with what Jamie had told me when she dumped me.

She'd biked over on a weeknight, after texting me to ask if

she could stop by. I had no idea something was wrong until I kissed her in the doorway and she pulled away. After that, it was like watching someone else being dumped in slow motion—like I was floating above us, powerless to help the me below. I watched myself sit down and Jamie hover, then sit as far down at the other end of the couch as possible. I watched myself tilt my head, then pull my legs in to my chest. I could barely hear what she was saying to me, and at the time I wasn't sure how much it mattered. The gist was that it was all too much too fast, and she thought it better if we went back to being friends. Anyway, the end result was obvious. It was clear her mind was made up, and nobody convinces Jamie to change her mind.

But I remembered one thing she'd said with perfect clarity, now. I could hear her voice, her exact delivery: "I don't think anyone makes it through their freshman year together, and I don't want that to be us." The implication was that we would break up once college started, so we might as well break up now and save ourselves the time. The implication was that senior year was about *friendship*, about being single and unat-tached and free, savoring the easiest versions of everything and everyone you loved before you left them.

But if she really believed that, what was she doing with number-three, formerly presumed straight girl Natalie Reid? Was what she'd said just bullshit, meant only as it applied to me?

I spent all night thinking about it, always somewhere between asleep and awake, madder and madder the closer it got to morning. By the time my alarm went off I was practically radiating resentment. I grabbed my phone to silence it and saw that Ruby had texted me back overnight, a little after eleven-thirty, and I'd missed it. I read it and reread it, breathing in deeply and blowing air out. I didn't need to care so much about Jamie and Natalie. I had my own thing going on. Here she was, on my phone screen, having written **Yes! I'm there.** She liked me enough to come watch me play soccer on a Saturday night, and that wasn't nothing. I closed my eyes and held my phone to my chest, forcing the endless breakup replay out of my head, replacing it with Ruby with heart eyes, watching me score from the stands, shouting my name. I fell asleep that way, for eleven perfect minutes, until my mom knocked on my door and ruined it. I couldn't believe I still had to go to school under these conditions.

Frankly, I thought I deserved a medal for not interrogating Alexis about Jamie and Natalie the moment I saw her at lunch. It was excruciating to see her smile at me, knowing she knew something so relevant to my interests but wouldn't say it to my face. But I also knew there was no way she could have. We only had lunch together, and Jamie was always there. I could have texted Alexis about it, and I'd thought about it, but texts could be screenshotted and sent elsewhere, and the last thing I wanted was for Jamie to have physical, incontrovertible proof that I still cared. Alexis was my friend, but she was Jamie's friend first, the same way Ronni was mine. If I gave Alexis material she could pass on to Jamie, she'd do it immediately, reflexively, out of loyalty. It was probably agonizing for her to not tell me about Jamie and Natalie herself, but I had to imagine that Jamie had asked her not to. Which was probably why Alexis had told Ronni instead: so Ronni would tell me, and Alexis could remain technically innocent while satisfying her urge to spread information. She operated by a strict, if slightly confusing, ethical code.

So I waited. Somehow time kept passing—hours and even days. At lunch, whenever Jamie was focused on her sandwich or looking at her phone, I stared at her, trying to see through her, analyzing her expressions to see if they seemed like those of a person in love. But she was as stoic as ever. So either nothing was happening . . . or something was.

By game time Saturday I was both exhausted and jittery. We were playing Albion, most of whose players were eight feet tall and blond and went to private school. Instead of a huddle, they held a prayer circle, and whenever they beat us we took comfort in reminding each other they had God on their side. To make matters worse, they were all polite, modest winners, which made us feel terrible for celebrating when we beat them.

With fifteen minutes to go before kickoff, the field on the visitors' side of the bleachers was already packed with parents and friends wearing blue and white. Down below I spotted Hanna Ward, Albion's sacrilegiously beautiful lead midfield, who used to play for us before she moved in seventh grade. After she moved, it became a recurring fantasy of mine that she and I would fall into forbidden love, Romeo and Juliet style, and get found together in the locker room showers. She caught me looking, so I gave her a little wave, and she smiled tightly. *Progress.*

I turned around for the hundredth time to survey our own set of bleachers, which were still three-quarters empty and would likely stay that way. My mom always came to a handful of my off-season club games, but, encouraged by me, saved most of her momly duty for the school season, when attendance felt like more of a value judgment. And anyway, it made me nervous to have her there, and she got too worked up over what she perceived as bad referee calls, which were all the ones that favored the other team. Most of the time I had no one special to look for in the bleachers, and no reason to scan them. Which was fine, because the people I really wanted to impress were on the field with me. But I couldn't lie: I felt giddy scanning the bleachers for Ruby Ocampo.

Only I didn't see her.

I dug my phone out of my bag: four minutes until game time, and no explanatory text messages from Ruby.

But it was cool to be a little late. I wasn't happy about it, but it was.

Coach called us over for a pep talk, the usual stuff about playing our best and working together and remembering what we'd talked about in practice this week. We put our hands in and shouted the Surf Club chant, and then we dispersed to take final sips of water and stretch. I dipped a hand into my bag to check my phone again, but when I stood back up, Coach was right there.

"Ah!" I sort of shrieked.

"Do you need surgery?" Coach asked me, unsmiling.

"What?"

"To get that thing removed from your hand." She pointed to my phone, and I instantly dropped it into my bag.

"Oh. Ha. No. All better."

"You need to focus, Ryan," she said. I knew what she was thinking: *Is this how you plan to get off the wait list?*

Guilt rolled into a ball in my stomach. "I know. I will."

Coach gave me a stern-but-encouraging clap on the shoulder, and I ran onto the field.

I couldn't be sure when exactly Ruby arrived. I didn't have a chance to look in the first quarter—we were down a goal early, and I took Coach's scolding to heart, going after the ball like my whole future depended on it. Which, in a way, it did. Only when I scored the tying goal, and my teammates rushed to crush me in a hug, did I feel safe glancing at the bleachers.

And there she was, sitting at the very back, perfectly and *oh my God thank God* alone. She was leaning against the fence, and when she saw me looking, she sat up and lifted two thumbs high above her head. My whole body blushed and surged with adrenaline. It wasn't like I'd expected her to actually bail, but I must have very nearly lost hope without realizing it, because I was so happy, and so relieved, that I felt like I could fly if I took off running fast enough. Or else I really, really liked her.

Having Ruby in the stands wasn't like having my mom there, or even Jamie. With them I felt like I had something specific to live up to. They'd both been to enough of my games to know what I was capable of on my very best days, and to show them anything less felt like letting them down. But Ruby had never seen me play before. I was fairly certain she'd never been to a high school–level soccer game at all. She had no expectations, so it was easy to beat them. When Jamie was in the stands I felt her eyes on me with every step I took. Ruby's being there to see me was so improbable it felt made up, like a daydream I'd had as a freshman. My perpetual disbelief allowed me to forget she was there between time-outs, when I'd check to make sure she still was. As a result, I played better than I had in weeks. *If only UNC were here to see me now*, I thought. But then, of course, that would have ruined it.

Despite my best efforts, the teams remained tied until there were four minutes left. Then three. I was stuck in the corner trying to steal the ball from a furious Hanna Ward, when finally I got a foot past her and stole it. To my left I saw Ronni rushing the net, and I crossed the ball. The placement was perfect. She didn't even have to slow down. She kicked, and the ball sailed into the upper right corner of the net, just past the goalie's fingertips. My team erupted in cheers and we all ran toward Ronni in a mad leaping rush, burying her beneath a pile of our bodies.

After the obligatory interteam high-five lineup with Albion's very gracious losers—me trying desperately to make eye contact with Hanna Ward, who avoided it like her life depended on it—Ronni looped her arms around my waist and lifted me off the ground in a hug.

"*There* she is!" she yelled. "Classic Ryan!"

I laughed until she put me down. "That goal, though," I said. "Incredible."

Ronni shrugged, visibly pleased. Her eyes locked on the stands, and she half shouted, "Oh shit!" I turned to see Ruby descending the bleachers, and felt grateful to already be red and sweaty. "*Be cool,*" I hissed. Ronni nodded.

Ruby jumped smoothly off the last row of bleachers and sauntered over to us, speeding up at the last second to hug me with such force I was nearly knocked flat. I was slick with sweat, but she didn't seem to care.

"Wow, hello," I said.

"You were so good, dude!" At that last part, I winced a little, but I recovered before Ruby pulled back from our hug, and then it didn't matter. I couldn't be that close to her and *not* break into a huge, obnoxious smile. Ronni, a goddess among girls, excused herself without saying a word.

"I'm so glad you came," I told Ruby.

"Me too! I felt very, like, high school."

I laughed, blushing because I'd been thinking the same thing, though maybe not in the same way. I'd imagined this moment so many times when I was younger: me on the soccer field, after a game, being congratulated by the coolest girl in school, who showed up just to watch me play. In the fantasy version, it was the school season, and the bleachers were full of screaming fans wearing Westville green and white. In the fantasy version, I scored the winning goal, and in the fantasy version, the girl was wearing my letter jacket draped around her shoulders. But it was, like, seventy degrees out, and watching my best friend score felt just as good as if I had. And for Ruby to come to *this* game, off season, that she had no school-spirited or peer-pressured motive to attend—that was better than anything I could have dreamed up.

The fantasy ended abruptly, minutes after the game did, the girl and me still standing on the field. Even the outer limits of my imagination couldn't conjure a kiss. The girl's face was too blurry. She was more of a concept than a person. Here in real life, the girl standing in front of me didn't kiss me either, but she did speak, and that was better too.

"Should we go get burritos?"

Eleven

Half an hour later Ruby and I were seated at a table at La Posta, where she said she'd never been. Geographically, I understood: the restaurant was nondescript and cheap-looking, sitting in a strip mall on the other end of town from Ruby's family's neighborhood. It *was* cheap, and it was also responsible for the best and biggest burrito I'd ever had: four dollars and fifty cents for a tinfoil-wrapped mound the size of a human baby, tax included. Six if you got a horchata, which I insisted we do. Twelve dollars total. Ruby started digging for her debit card but I waved her off to grab us a table, handing over the second-to-last twenty from my dad. I wondered when I'd see him again, and not just because I was almost out of spending money. (Mom gave me a little cash here and there, too, but I didn't like to ask unless I was truly desperate.) He'd said he'd be here "soon," but coming from him, that could have meant just about anything. Including "never." Ruby was looking at her phone when I joined her, so I pulled mine out too and sent him a text: **When do you hear back?**

One of the chefs slid the tray with our food up to the serving window cut into the side of the dining room wall and shouted, "Ryan!" even though we were the only ones there. I jumped up to grab it and placed it gently in front of Ruby, who said "That looks *sooo* good" even though she was still looking at her phone. I unwrapped the top of my burrito and took a bite, *mmm*-ing loudly until she finally put it down.

"Sorry," she said. "Band drama." She took a sip of horchata, and her eyes widened. "Holy shit."

"I know."

"I'm gonna be here every day now."

"Cool, I'll drive."

She grinned and took a big bite of burrito, nodding approvingly. My shoulders instantly un-tensed.

"So what's going on with the band?" I asked.

She rolled her eyes. "Same shit as always."

"Oh, I see." I paused. "I don't actually know what that means."

"It means it's boring," she said. "Like, so boring I could cry."

Naturally, her saying that only made me desperate to know everything. But Ruby evidently didn't feel like sharing, and I figured I wouldn't become the kind of person she wanted to confide in by begging her to confide in me. And maybe it really *was* exhausting having everyone be permanently interested in your life. I couldn't imagine. In my daydreams of future soccer stardom practically all I did was give charming interview after charming interview on late-night talk shows. In some note-book somewhere I had notes for my *SNL* monologue already written. *I should really try to find those*, I thought.

"In that case, let's talk about me," I said. Ruby snickered. "I'm kidding."

"No, let's," she said. "Tell me everything. Who *is* Quinn Ryan?"

I laughed, if only to hide the fact that hearing her say my full name made my chest whirl and flutter. "Well," I started grandly. "It began with the forging of the Great Rings."

Ruby raised an eyebrow.

"Sorry. Um. That's from *The Fellowship of the Ring*." *Jamie would have laughed*, I thought. As if that had anything to do with anything.

She nodded. "Cool, so we know you're a nerd." But she wasn't making fun of me. Or if she was, there was affection behind it. I could see it in her eyes.

"I don't know," I said. "My parents are divorced. My mom works for the *Union-Tribune*. My dad is an accountant in North Carolina."

"That's your parents, not you."

"Well, my dad is moving back, supposedly. That's kind of about me."

"Kind of," she agreed.

Now that I had the spotlight I felt uncomfortable, unsure what was interesting enough to tell her, unsure what she wanted to hear. My solution was to eat the last bite of my burrito. And then I had a better idea.

"Want to go to Balboa Park?"

Second only to the ocean and any of its beaches, Balboa Park was my favorite place in California. Any time of year, any time of day or night, there was always something worth watching going on. Sometimes it was the foreign tourists posing in front of the parts of the park you least expected someone to want a picture with. Sometimes it was a couple making out or breaking up. Once I saw a woman in her twenties puke right off the carousel while her friends laughed and took pictures. Another time I watched a little boy wearing a tutu circle the pond, holding his mom's hand and touching a plastic wand to every flower they passed, as if he were the one responsible for making them grow. When I came alone I liked to loop in and out of the buildings' covered archways, vaguely imagining I was the handsome, bored duke who lived there. Then I'd make my way to the rose garden and find the prettiest, fullest flower there, ostensibly for my duchess. Or at least that was what I'd pretended I was doing when I was younger. Now finding the single best flower in the garden was just a habit.

I parked near the art museum, which, along with the rest of the indoor attractions, had been closed for hours. Daytime Balboa was for families and tourists, but nighttime was for locals and young people like us. The energy changed when the sun set, and I could feel it as soon as I stepped out of my truck: a boozeless buzz, relieved and anxious all at once. It felt like it had dropped ten degrees on the drive over, so I pulled an old team sweatshirt from my duffel bag and offered it to Ruby.

She hesitated. "You don't want it?"

"I'm still hot from the game," I lied. She considered, so I added, "It's clean."

"I wasn't worried about cooties," she smirked, pulling the sweatshirt over her head.

Even at the invocation of a word tangentially and childishly associated with kissing, I felt goose bumps form on my arms. That, and seeing her in my clothing. I shivered.

"See?!"

"No, no, I'm fine. That was an isolated incident."

"Good, because this is really comfy," she said.

"Other people's stuff always is."

"No. This is special," she said. She looked at me, and I got that tense, rubber-band-pulled-tight feeling in my chest, and I wondered if she felt it too. I used to assume that I could sense when something like that was shared, that I could tell when a moment loomed as large for someone else as it did for me. But

I didn't trust my instincts so much anymore. And it really was an exceptionally soft sweatshirt.

"Let's go this way," I said.

We walked into the park's main square, where a bunch of other high school kids were slung around the wrought-iron tables, eating ice cream and drinking cans of soda they tipped flasks of vodka into. I was disappointed not to recognize anyone; it would have been nice to have a witness.

"Do you want ice cream or anything?" I offered.

Ruby shrugged. "I'm okay. Do you?"

"Nah," I lied. Of course I wanted ice cream. But we kept walking. A group of thirteen- or fourteen-year-old boys was scootering back and forth under one of the archways, propelling themselves into the air and clattering back to the sidewalk while the rest of them hollered, "Sick!" They weren't really supposed to be there—skateboards and skates were banned, and scooters were implied—and they looked like they knew it was only a matter of time before they were asked to leave. I saw them see us, and I felt my shoulders creep up just slightly and pulled my hands from my pockets. Then one of the boys waved, calling, "Hi, Ruby!"

"Oh, hey, Elon!" Ruby waved. The boys standing around him immediately began elbowing him in the arms, murmuring their admiration.

"I used to babysit him," Ruby leaned over to explain. "His parents paid twenty-five bucks an hour."

"Wow."

"Still wasn't enough," she added. I laughed as if I agreed, like I wasn't wondering if Elon might still need a babysitter now.

We reached the end of the promenade, and without buildings on either side of us the breeze cut coldly across my shoulders. Ruby saw me shiver and looped her sweatshirt-covered arm through my bare one. I was afraid to look at her but I did it anyway. We were close enough that I could see twin freckles at her temple, which for some reason made me think of *Frankenstein,* which I still hadn't finished. I was supposed to be halfway into *Ceremony* by now.

"It's the least I can do," said Ruby.

"What is?"

With her free arm she pointed at the one wrapped around mine.

"Oh right. Thanks."

We crossed the bridge into the rose garden, which was lit only patchily, and therefore empty. I couldn't tell Ruby about the duke-and-duchess thing (obviously), but I wanted to play my game. I wanted to do whatever I could to make the night last. So I told Ruby the rules: find your favorite flower here, and I'll find mine. I started to walk away—I liked to start in a particular spot—but Ruby took my hand.

I froze, staring at our hands like I'd never seen anything like them and didn't know what to do next. But I didn't let go, and neither did Ruby.

"I'm scared," she said.

My heart was in my throat.

"It's dark," she continued.

Oh, that.

"Can't we find our favorite ones together?"

Technically speaking, that was against the rules. That sort of thing compromised the integrity of the individual's choice. But I figured I could make an exception, just this once.

"So tell me the deal with your dad," she said. Her hand was warm and small in mine. I wanted to look at it, lift our hands to my face, but then what? I couldn't risk alerting her to their togetherness. If she thought about it too much she might stop.

"What do you mean?"

"You said he's moving back from Virginia."

"Maybe moving back. From North Carolina."

"Same thing," she said, and we grinned at each other in the dark before she continued. "So would that be a good thing, if he came back? Or not?"

"Not if I'm going to be there for college," I said, surprising myself with that *if*. I needed to change the subject. "These are good ones," I said, using my free hand to point to the yolk-yellow roses labeled GOLDEN CELEBRATION. Ruby peered at them politely. "I'm worried you're not taking this seriously," I added. She laughed.

"I'm old-fashioned," she said. "I think roses should be red."

"Ah." I nodded. "Well, just wait for the Ingrid Bergmans."

"So which one of your parents filed for divorce?"

I was delighted by how blunt she could be. "Why, you a lawyer?"

"Sorry." She shrugged. "Sometimes I wonder which of my parents would be the one to file. Like, I think my mom loves my dad more than he loves her, but I also think he needs her more than she needs him. So I go back and forth."

"Dark," I said.

"I know." We walked in silence for a minute, dipping in and out of lamplight, passing the beach roses, the Gertrude Jekylls, the Sunsprites.

"It was my mom," I said finally. "But according to her, he basically forced her hand."

"You don't believe her?"

"No, I do," I said. "I don't know why I said it like that."

"You're still mad," explained Ruby, like it was the most obvious thing in the world. But I wasn't. I knew they shouldn't be together, and maybe never should have been. I was relieved when they'd told me. I'd always liked them better individually. But.

"I just didn't want him to move," I said. "But he's been gone so long I'm not sure I want him to come back."

"This one," said Ruby, stopping suddenly. She unclasped my hand and pointed to a full, blood-red bloom, lit from the lamppost above. I beamed, quickly cured of the devastation of not holding Ruby's hand by the all-encompassing pleasure of being right.

"Ingrid Bergmans," I said. "I told you."

"You get me."

My hand tingled where hers had touched mine. I didn't know what to do with it. What had I used this hand for before holding Ruby's? It hung at my side, useless and cold. And then, as if guided by a force I couldn't control, it lifted to the stem of Ruby's favorite rose, breaking it off in one clean snap.

Oh my God, I thought. *I am going to jail.* I offered the rose to Ruby, who looked as shocked as I felt. And, I thought, more than a little impressed.

"Wow," she said. "Thank you."

"You're welcome," I said. "Now we have to get out of here."

"What about yours?"

I looked around me, but there was no sign of the law, at least not yet. So I grabbed Ruby's free hand and pulled her into a run, making a break for the orangey-pink Louis de Funès roses. "There!" I whispered, pointing randomly as we flew past them, back over the bridge, laughing so hard we couldn't breathe.

On Saturday my night with Ruby felt like a dream come true. On Sunday it just felt like a dream—a rose garden? Really? By Monday I was starting to question my sanity: Had it happened the way I remembered it, or had I made the best parts up? My therapist, Jennifer, had once explained that my memory didn't work right when I experienced severe anxiety, but I hadn't been anxious that night, had I? I was nervous and excited, and sometimes that felt similar, but it wasn't the same. I was an anxious individual, but that did not mean I'd invented two (two!) separate instances of fairly prolonged hand-holding with the literal coolest girl at school.

What it meant, though, was still a mystery. History had taught me to be cautious of the casual girl-on-girl handhold. For some reason, straight-girl best friends did it *all the time,* and I was supposed to believe none of them wanted to kiss. Ruby knew I was an out, proud, capital-*L* Lesbian, and so it must have occurred to her that I might think it was more than friendly. But whenever I thought I knew anything about the things straight girls did, they moved the goalpost.

It didn't help that Ruby and I hadn't texted the rest of the weekend, leaving me without any sort of verbal confirmation. (What, did I want her to text me **Thanks for the romantic hand-holding in the Balboa Park rose garden, Quinn Ryan**? Yes, that would have been nice.) I was going to, but then I thought I should let her go first, seeing as the last move made was mine. But then she didn't go at all.

It did occur to me that she might be waiting for me the same way I was waiting for her. And then I thought: *Yeah, right.*

I'm not saying I'm psychic, but all Monday morning I *knew*

something horrible was about to happen. I texted my mom at work to make sure she was okay, and she was. I found Ronni in the hall between second and third period and asked her if *she* was okay, and she told me to get a grip. I raced into the cafeteria at lunch to make sure Jamie and Alexis were okay too, and when I saw them sitting there, apparently alive, I exhaled in relief.

But then I saw they weren't alone. Natalie freaking Reid was sitting next to Jamie, at *our* lunch table, and voilà: I'd found my something horrible.

I had three choices: One, I could make a break for the nurse's office, claiming sudden-onset flu. I probably wouldn't even have to fake it. I definitely felt like throwing up.

Two, I could sit with Kate and Janelle from my team and their assorted friends, and explain myself later.

Or three, I could sit in my normal spot, across from my best friend and my worst enemy, because I knew if I did anything else, all I would do was wonder what I'd missed. What I hadn't been there to see for myself.

I approached the table too fast, sat down too fast, said "Hey, guys" too fast, opened my lunch too fast. Ronni gently put her foot on top of mine, both a warning and a private show of support. "What's up?" she said in a tone that communicated *You are acting insane.*

I laughed. "Not much." I could feel Natalie's eyes on me, so I met them. "Hey, Natalie," I trilled. "How are you?"

Ronni pressed harder on my toes.

"Hey," said Natalie. "I'm . . . good. How . . . are you?"

"*Great*," I said. On Jamie's other side, Alexis radiated excitement, like a kid on Christmas morning. I wanted to yank the string cheese from her hand and hit her with it.

"You guys hear about Mr. Hughes?" Ronni half shouted. Everyone's shoulders dropped two inches, relieved to have something impersonal and uncontroversial to talk about: the skeevy tenth-grade biology teacher suspended for sexual harassment. Or, well, *an investigation regarding sexual harassment claims.* But calling it that was, for us, an irrelevant formality. Between the five of us only Ronni had had him for biology, but it didn't matter. Every girl in the school knew, whether they'd taken his class or not: he did it.

We took turns rehashing the rumors we'd collected since that morning, when he didn't show up for class.

"I guess his sub announced herself as the 'long-term substitute,'" said Jamie.

"She did," confirmed Alexis. "She said Hughes was out attending to 'personal matters.'"

"I wonder how he got caught," said Natalie freaking Reid.

"Emails," said Alexis.

"I heard there were pictures, too," said Ronni.

"Instagram screenshots, yes."

"Who's the girl?" I asked, just for something to say. "Or, girls."

Alexis leaned in confidentially. "Danea Traverso. Sopho-more. Obviously."

Natalie's eyebrows rose clear off her head.

"You know her?" said Ronni.

Natalie nodded. "She's my neighbor."

Alexis pounced. "Really? Do you talk to her? Apparently she didn't come today. Maybe you should check on her."

"We don't really talk anymore," said Natalie. "She's . . ." She trailed off, shrugging judgmentally. From her tone, and the look on her face, it was obvious that Natalie thought Danea was bad somehow. Maybe even deserving. I looked at Jamie, who was watching Natalie, realizing the same thing I was. I'd never met Danea Traverso, or even heard her name, but I felt certain then that I would kill for her.

"So you really don't know her, then," I said.

"Well—"

"Shouldn't we be focusing on Hughes?" Jamie interjected. "He's the grown man DM-ing teenagers on Instagram." Her eyes landed on mine for a millisecond before dropping to her lunch tray's half-eaten contents.

"Totally," said Alexis.

There ensued an awkward silence in which I worried every-one could hear my heart thumping angrily against my chest. I had to say *something*.

"So, Natalie," I said. "To what do we owe the pleasure?"

The bones in my toes crunched beneath Ronni's boot. Luckily, I no longer felt pain.

"What?" said Natalie.

"Because you don't normally sit with us," Jamie explained. No one else would have heard the exasperation in her voice, but I did.

"Oh!" Natalie giggled. "I was like, 'What?'"

"I wanted her to," Jamie cut in. This time it was me who had to feign interest in my food. Jamie and Natalie had band together before lunch, and now I pictured them leaving it together, walking here together, having so much to say to each other that they couldn't possibly separate for twenty-three minutes.

"Aw," said Natalie. I tried not to stare as she rested her head on Jamie's shoulder. I felt Ronni watching me. The warning bell rang, and I leapt up, my sandwich entirely untouched.

"I—forgot a book I need," I explained hurriedly. "See you guys later."

I held back tears all the way to my hiding spot, the weird two-stall bathroom at the far end of the hallway between the locker rooms and the gym. I allowed myself a brief cry while I ate my sandwich on the toilet, and when the second warning bell rang, I got up, splashed water on my face, and reentered the terrible world outside.

Twelve

That night, I decided something had to be done.

Jamie had tried extra hard to talk to me in Civil Liberties, and I had ignored her, pretending to be fully absorbed in the Fourth Amendment. I smiled once at Ruby across the room, and while she smiled back, it was pinched and joyless. After class I caught her in the hallway, but I had soccer to get to, and she had a ride to catch, and I didn't want to know who with, so we only talked for a minute. No acknowledgment of the rose garden or the mythical hand-holding was made. Ruby said she'd text me later, and I said, "Okay, I'll text you a reminder." This, at last, made her smile for real.

Here was my secret: I'd used that line before. And as soon as I said it to Ruby, all I could think about was the time I'd said it to Jamie. And then, for some reason, I pictured Jamie using it on Natalie.

It was then and there that I decided the reason I wasn't moving forward with Ruby was because Jamie kept dragging me backward. It wasn't even the real her, because the real her was clearly occupied with Natalie freaking Reid. It was last-year Jamie, last-summer Jamie, who was still squatting in my brain. I didn't want everything I did with Ruby to only be a shadow of something I'd already done with Jamie. If I was ever to be so lucky as to kiss Ruby, I didn't want to compare it to anything else.

So after I ate the dinner my mom had left out for me, and poked my head into her office so we could confirm we'd both lived through the day, I went into my room, closed the door, and removed the pieces of Jamie from their hiding spots one by one. I slipped the note from *The Return of the King* that changed everything. From under my mattress, I removed the photo-booth strip of us making faces and kissing. I surveyed the room like a crime scene, collecting every potential clue: the movie-ticket stubs; the hair ties she'd left behind; the books she'd lent me, her name and the year printed neatly inside each cover. Once all that was done, I could no longer pretend I wasn't avoiding the most incriminating evidence of all: the shoebox that held our letters, pushed deep under my bed.

The plan was not to reread them. The plan was to throw them away, or maybe even burn them. But I had never once cleaned my room without first examining every object I'd ever owned, no matter how many times I'd done so before. I studied the box from all angles, like a foreign object I'd only just dug up. On the lid I'd written BABY PICTURES, thinking, I guess, that this would seem less suspicious for me to store under my bed than an unlabeled shoebox. I lifted the corner of the box top with one finger, pretending for the benefit of no one that I was barely interested in what was inside. Somehow I felt that if I pulled each piece of paper out one by one, without ever removing the top, it didn't really count.

I tried skimming them, focusing on the spaces between the lines, and for some of them—the boring ones from early on, when we were so enamored that every point-by-point description of the other's day was Nobel-worthy poetry—it was almost easy. But toward the middle, and then the end, as the notes got less frequent, I got lost in them, looking for signs that she'd stopped loving me, or would soon. I'd done this before, right after it happened, and hadn't seen them. But I'd been raw then, in total denial. By now, I thought, I should be able to tell myself the truth about what I saw.

But I read, and I reread, and I still didn't see it. Not even in the ones I knew she'd written after we had a fight. And even though that didn't make it any easier to understand, it allowed me to unclench my jaw, and un-hunch my shoulders, and imagine a future in which I never really understood, and was okay anyway.

In order to get there, I knew I had to get rid of the letters. Everything was layered chronologically like sediment, and the line where our friendship turned into something else was clear. I excavated everything above that line and put it in a plastic grocery bag I retrieved from under the sink, and tied the handles into a knot. I dumped the rest of the box on the floor and sifted through the early notes, the fake tattoos we saved for who knows what, a small stack of flyers for our failed Gay-Straight Alliance. I picked up a tight paper football, realizing what it was before I even opened it: the Straight Girls We Wish Weren't list.

I could've sworn Jamie had the list, or that we'd long ago thrown it away. I unfolded it carefully, the paper worn thin from so many openings and refoldings and amendments. *Straight Girls We Wish Weren't (SGWWW)* was written at the top in Jamie's neat purple handwriting, and below it, Ruby Ocampo was number one.

Just like I remembered, Natalie Reid was number three.

I scanned the rest of the names, some of which I still felt the same way about, some of which I didn't. I imagined the revisions we'd make if Jamie were with me: we'd cross out Melissa Moore, who moved away, and replace her with some cute sophomore or junior. We'd have to cross out Indya Schoenberg, who'd taken a hard right, politically speaking, and no longer seemed as attractive as she once had. I'd add Erin Moss, who turned eighteen early and got four tattoos before senior year started, and if I knew Jamie, she'd add Ariel Park, who'd become a six-foot-tall volleyball superstar. For a minute

I considered drawing a line through Natalie's name, wondering if the list might work like a voodoo doll and make her disappear. Either way, she no longer belonged there.

But changing the list, especially alone, would ruin its sanctity. It felt a little eerie finding it now, with number one and number three so newly enmeshed in our lives. Neither of us had considered the list actionable, and yet here we were. And even though I still hated Natalie, and always would, I couldn't help feeling proud of Jamie and me. Our younger selves would be so impressed.

I tidied the mess of friendship mementos with the list on top. I tucked this stack—our revised and sanitized relationship history—back into the shoebox, and pushed it under my bed. Then I picked up the bag of love letters, carried it into the garage, and dropped it gently into the recycling can. I looked at the bag at the bottom of the can and imagined the garbage man opening it and reading them, and showing them to his garbage-collector friends. I imagined them taped up in some city-government employee lunchroom. I dove back into the can and retrieved the bag. *If I'm going to throw these letters away*, I thought, *I should really shred them first.*

I returned to my room, put the bag of letters as far under my bed as I could reach, and sat down at my desk. I opened my mostly empty UNC application, and this time I didn't let all that blank space—or my as-yet-unrecruited status—overwhelm me. I could be a walk-on. I could even still get the call. So I didn't get up until I hit submit and my future was safe in someone else's hands.

Friday's game was against FC Flash, currently the leading club team and our sworn archenemies. Where Albion girls were gracious, FC Flash ones were vicious. Legend had it their coach made them run five miles uphill every practice, and if someone failed to finish within thirty-five minutes, they had to do it again. I would have felt bad for them if they weren't also the biggest crybabies in history, faking fouls left and right like a professional men's team at the World Cup.

My mood going into the game was gloomy, and the only thing that seemed to help was spreading that gloom to others. As Janelle and I sat waiting in the stands I sighed deeply and said I had a bad feeling about this. When she got up to get a hair tie from her bag, I moved over to sit by Kate, and sighed again.

"I feel like we're going to lose," I half whispered.

She smiled sympathetically. "I always think that," she said. "But then we usually don't."

"But when we do, it's usually to them."

Concern dragged at the corners of Kate's mouth. "That's true."

"Ryan!" I looked up at Ronni, who I thought had just been deep in conversation with Coach. *How could she possibly have heard me?* I pretended not to know she was calling me over, and began retying my cleats as slowly as possible.

"QUINN!"

I sighed and got up, meeting Ronni on the field. I hung back while Ronni set the rest of the team off on a warm-up jog, yelling "let's go!" and patting everyone else's ass encouragingly.

When the other girls were out of earshot, Ronni turned to me, and I braced myself.

"What's your problem?" she said, more gently than I expected, which only made me crabbier. I deserved to be yelled at. I *wanted* to be yelled at. Coming from Coach or whoever was captain, I found being yelled at motivating. Someone needed to tell me I was the piece of shit I felt I was so I could convince myself to be better. Ronni knew that.

"Nothing," I muttered.

Ronni gave me a chance to go on, but I clenched my jaw.

"Okay, well, save it for after," she said finally. "But right now, you need to pull it together. Act like we're going to win, because we are."

But we didn't win. We lost, humiliatingly, 0–3. I tried, I really did, but after I missed the goal for the seven millionth time, Coach benched me for nearly the entire second half. I spent that whole time just trying not to cry because Coach found crying morally repellent.

After it was over we slumped our way back to the parking

lot, spread out instead of huddled close together, the way we were when we won. No one said much of anything, and I was sure they were all cursing me in their heads. It was clear we wouldn't be going out to dinner as a team like we usually did when we played there. Everyone just wanted to go home. I noticed Ronni hovering behind me, and considered making a break for my truck, but then she'd just be madder. Reluctantly I turned to face her.

"Let's get something to eat," she said.

All the tears I'd been pushing back for two hours rushed to the surface.

Ronni leapt forward to grab me by the shoulders. "Don't cry," she said, half empathy, half warning. Like I could just change my mind.

"I don't know what this is," I said. "It's just falling out of my face."

Ronni pulled me up by the arm and clapped me on the back. I sniffled the whole walk to our cars, which she politely ignored.

We went where we always went when one of us (usually me) needed to muffle her suffering with food: In-N-Out. We ordered burgers and fries and milkshakes (strawberry for Ronni, chocolate for me) and carried our trays to a table outside. The sun had set, and it was immediately twenty degrees cooler. I thought about my sweatshirt, and Ruby wearing it, and I realized she hadn't given it back.

As usual, Ronni and I ate more than half our food before we spoke. I inhaled my shake like oxygen, and when I started sucking actual air, Ronni gave me a look.

"You think you got it all?"

"Sorry."

"Is it Jamie or Ruby?"

"What?" My heart rate picked up just hearing their names. I reached for my milkshake again before I remembered it was gone. It was all gone. "What do you mean?"

"I mean, which one got in there before the game?" She pointed to her temple.

"Neither," I said. She cocked her head; she didn't believe me. But it was the truth, pretty much. "I just had an off day."

Ronni took a preparatory breath and I looked sadly, again, at my empty cup. "I say this with love, and with the acknowledgment that you are ordinarily a very good soccer player, but you've had kind of a lot of off days recently."

I felt the tears returning and pressed my palms to my eyes. "I know."

"I'm not trying to make you feel bad."

"I know."

"Although I would have preferred to win."

I laughed, and when I uncovered my eyes I saw Ronni grinning back at me.

"Halle played like shit too, you know," I said. "She should've stopped that last one."

"Oh, don't get me started."

I dragged a cold french fry back and forth through the sea of special sauce at the bottom of the paper tray.

"I don't know if I'm gonna get in," I said.

"UNC?"

I nodded.

"You haven't heard?"

I shook my head. "I sent in my application, finally, but . . . I don't know." The more time that passed, the more arrogant it seemed for me to think I could just show up and they'd let me play. Did I even want to play for a school that didn't want me?

"There's still some time," said Ronni, but it was obvious she barely believed herself.

"Not much, though."

"What about UCLA?"

"Still wait-listed," I said. "But even if they do end up wanting me . . ." I trailed off. It wasn't hard to imagine myself at UCLA, and maybe that was the problem. I could be a Bruin, and wear a blue-and-yellow jersey with my name on the back. Knowing I wasn't anyone's first choice.

"They have a great program!" Ronni added. "Sydney Leroux went there!"

I knew that, of course, and Ronni knew I knew. She also knew that Sydney Leroux had never been wait-listed, and that

Sydney Leroux would have been Sydney Leroux no matter where she went to college. If I didn't play for UNC, or Stanford (not that I'd ever been that delusional), or any other top-five team, I would just be . . . me.

I scraped at my empty cup with my thumbnail, refusing to meet Ronni's eyes. "I've wanted to go to UNC my whole life," I said.

"I know." She paused. "But."

"But what?"

"But it isn't only up to you."

She spoke softly, uncharacteristically so, but I still felt myself welling up. It didn't seem possible I had any moisture left in me.

Ronni took a deep breath and leaned in closer. "I have had a crush on Luke Bailey since *sixth grade.*"

That made me look up. Ronni *never* talked about boys at school.

"Him? Really?" Luke Bailey was the captain of the water polo team, and looked exactly like what you picture when given that information: tall, muscular, and tan, his skin and his hair the same shade of gold. Blue eyes. No brain.

"He's hot, okay?"

"So I'm told." From the way straight girls acted around him, it was obvious Ronni was far from alone in her opinion, and that's what made it so shocking. "Wow. Luke Bailey."

"I know," she said. "And for the longest time, probably into sophomore year, I kept hoping that someday, he might ask me out. And then I got tired of waiting, so I asked *him* out."

"WHAT?" I shouted, then clapped a hand over my mouth. "Does Alexis know about this?"

"No, and if you tell her I'll straight-up murder you."

"I won't," I said. "What happened? When was this?"

"May twelfth, sophomore year," sighed Ronni. "He and Kristen were on a break."

"Oh my God, that's right." I remembered the girls huddling in the hallway, the cryptic Instagrams, the widespread sense that Love Was Dead. "So what did you do?"

"I slid into the DMs," Ronni said.

"Wow," I breathed. Ronni Davis was the bravest girl in the world. "What did he say?"

She grinned. "Nothing."

"Nothing?"

"Nothing," she confirmed. "And I know he saw it, because it said 'seen.'"

She burst into laughter, which meant it was okay if I did too.

"What a dick," I said.

"Eh," she said. "He's all right."

"You'd still say yes, wouldn't you?"

"Oh, one hundred percent," she said, and we cracked up again.

"How can you not hate him after that?" I asked when I'd caught my breath.

Ronni shrugged, wiping the leaked mascara from under her eyes. "He didn't do anything wrong. He doesn't owe it to me to like me back."

"But he should," I said. "You're the best."

"I tend to agree." She grinned.

We sat in silence for a minute, and I thought about how unfair it all was, which I knew wasn't the point Ronni was trying to make. But she *was* the best: soccer captain, smart, loyal, beautiful, generous. Shouldn't someone like Luke be dying to be with her? And shouldn't it be easy for the program of my dreams to pick me, the second-best forward in Southern California after Ronni (at one point, anyway)? Shouldn't it count for something that I'd never once, in all my high school years, thought of any other school as mine?

"She likes you, you know," said Ronni. I looked up.

"You think?"

"Yeah," said Ronni. "It's obvious."

"We held hands," I said. Ronni's mouth fell open, and she whipped my arm with the back of her fingers. "Ow."

"When was this?!"

"Saturday," I said. I leaned back in self-defense. "After the game."

"Shut the fuck up."

"It's true. Two times, actually."

"WHAT?" Ronni exclaimed so loud that people at the other tables looked over to see what was so shocking. For once, I didn't care what they saw or heard. If even Ronni said Ruby liked me, it had to be true.

I texted her as soon as I got home. Since Monday, we'd texted a little every night. Not enough, in my opinion, but some.

Two things

1. I think you guys should have another show at Triple Moon

2. I think we should have a picnic at the beach

For the first time ever, she wrote back right away. Like maybe she'd been waiting all day for me to text her.

Deal.

Thirteen

Homecoming was now less than two weeks away, which meant people at school were starting to act insane. In the bathroom between classes I saw a junior being comforted by her friends and assumed the person she'd hoped to go with had asked someone else, but from the stall I overheard that he *had* asked her, just not creatively enough. It seemed he'd set a precedent the year before, filling her car up with balloons while she was at work at the mall, and now, she said, he could barely be bothered to ask her directly. "He just *assumed* I'd go with him," she whined. Her friends murmured sympathetically, rubbing her shoulders and petting her hair as I washed my hands and pretended I wasn't there.

Equally distressed was Alexis, who'd been dropping hints with no fewer than four different boys for weeks. She seemed to regard them like colleges: there was the reach (Anthony Millard, a second-tier but still popular water polo player she'd been friends with as a child), the targets (Eddie Soto, her chemistry lab partner, and Aaron Gray, the boy she let copy her Spanish homework), the safety (Jacob Ramos, who was gay and went to private school, where Alexis had gone to be *his* dance date on two separate occasions). Church boy—once a promising Plan Z—was eventually deemed inferior even to going alone. While all her options had initially expressed at least tentative interest in taking Alexis to homecoming, she worried she was "starting to lose them." The way she said it, it sounded like they were terminally ill.

"Jacob owes me, and he knows that," she said, catching me up after lunch one day. "But the other night he said he might have to go to a funeral."

"He *might* have to go? To a funeral?"

"I know," she said. "But what can I say to that?"

As for me, I still wanted to ask Ruby, obviously. Our picnic was set for Sunday, which felt twenty years away. I'd hoped for Saturday, but she was busy, and I had soccer every other night, and I knew if I met her afterward she'd be all I thought about during practice. For my team's sake, and especially for Ronni's sake, I was trying to keep girls and soccer separate.

So I would see her Sunday, and if it went well, maybe I'd ask her to homecoming then. It wasn't much notice, but Ruby didn't seem like the type of girl who'd need weeks to prepare. Though she also didn't seem like the type of girl who would go. So I'd feel it out when I saw her. I told myself I could always pretend I was asking as friends, but even the thought humiliated me. Everyone, but everyone, would see right through that. But then, what if she agreed as friends, and the dance itself changed things? As I considered and reconsidered every possible outcome, I began to sympathize with the crying girl in the bathroom. There really was so much that could go wrong. Maybe it was safer just to skip it after all.

But still: my last homecoming. One of my last high school dances. That meant something to me, even if I didn't want it to.

I was zoned out in Civil Liberties that afternoon when the first thing went wrong.

One moment, Mr. Haggerty was babbling on about discourse and debate, and the next, he ruined my month. I came to as he said the most hated phrase in the high school English language: "I'm going to have you count off."

This was unexpectedly formal from a teacher who'd never adopted a seating chart and who allowed us to choose freely to sit in slight variations from where we'd sat on the first day of class. Today, by evil, unfair chance, Jamie was seated two desks back, so that when Mr. Haggerty had us count off one or two, Jamie and I were both ones.

Guess what number Ruby was.

"Okay, so . . . now let's have you pick a partner in your number group," said Mr. Haggerty, who apparently hadn't really thought this through beforehand.

I made a show of pretending to scan my fellow ones for options before turning, inevitably, to Jamie.

"You wanna . . . ?"

She sighed. "Sure."

Our project was to choose one of six contemporary political debates, and to have the partners argue opposite sides using well-researched opinions. In front of the rest of the class. For five whole minutes—a decade in presentation years. The topics were first-come, first-served, and only three groups could argue each. The next thing I knew, Mr. Haggerty was taping the sign-up sheet to the whiteboard, and Jamie and I were racing toward it like we were taking back Helm's Deep in *The Two Towers*. Behind us, everyone began to rise slowly from their desks and mosey over.

"Can we do climate change?" Jamie asked.

"No," I said. I knew Jamie would get to argue the progressive side of any issue we took, and I did not want to be stuck pretending the earth wasn't obviously melting.

"Abortion?"

"Ehhhh."

"Guns?"

I made a face.

Jamie sighed, and wrote our names under *Federal Legalization of Marijuana*, the least awful of our many awful options. Then we stood back and watched the rest of the sheet fill up. Ruby and I exchanged eye rolls, and I felt Jamie notice. Ruby was partnered with Hailey Metcalfe, who was so excited about it she looked like she might levitate off the floor.

When everyone was signed up we returned to our seats, and Mr. Haggerty peeled the sheet off the whiteboard. He read off the groups and their corresponding presentation dates.

Guess which group Mr. Haggerty chose to go first, the next Tuesday. Here's a hint: after a two-second delay, the stoners groaned and sank into their seats. I could feel Jamie growing more and more smug behind me, until climate change was called dead last. When the bell rang and the luckier groups pranced out of the classroom, Jamie hovered by my desk as I packed up my things. I prepared for her *I told you so*. I'd tell her I preferred our competition to the try-hards who chose climate change. But I didn't end up needing to. All Jamie said was "When do you have time to work on this?" Knowing Jamie, I couldn't very well say what I wanted, which was *Monday night*.

"I could probably do tomorrow night," I said. "After practice."

"Triple Moon?"

I nodded.

By then we were standing alone together in the hallway, and there was nothing else to do but pretend I had to pee so I wouldn't have to walk next to her. We both knew there was nothing else safe for us to talk about.

I hadn't been to Triple Moon since the Sweets show, which was a long time for me. When Dee saw me walk through the door she crossed her arms in front of her chest so the script tattooed along her outer forearms looked like one long, menacing sentence.

"Who the hell are you?" she teased.

"I know," I said. I wanted to say *I missed you,* but I'd never said anything so explicitly affectionate to Dee before, and I didn't want to embarrass myself. So instead I said, "I missed it."

"Well, it missed you, clearly," she said, gesturing broadly at the all-but-empty coffee shop. Besides me, there was only one other customer, a college kid with a blue mullet I'd seen dozens of times in the exact position they were in now: one leg pulled up to rest against the table and the other bouncing against the seat, a graphic novel pressed almost flush against their face. Two glasses holding milky, melting ice sat on the table. *Two drinks is basically the same as two customers,* I thought. I wished I had more money so I could stuff a twenty-dollar bill or two into the tip jar when Dee wasn't looking, but

I had exactly eight dollars in my wallet, which was only enough to leave three.

"Iced vanilla?" Dee asked, and for a second I worried she'd been reading my mind. I nodded. Dee took my five-dollar bill without looking at me, and I stuffed my ones into the tip jar when she turned to the espresso machine. When she set my drink on the counter I looked at it instead of her and asked, "Are you guys doing okay?"

Dee paused for so long I was forced to look up. She leaned against the back counter and crossed her arms once again. But it was different this time, the script on her arms looking more like a lyric to the world's saddest song. I realized I'd never asked her what the tattoos actually said. They were in Latin, unreadable even on the rare occasions I got a good look at them.

"We're fine," Dee said finally. "We just had a slow summer."

"It's almost November."

"A slow summer and fall, then." She shrugged.

If Jamie had never said anything about it to me, I would have taken Dee at her word. But what I loved most about the coffee shop (its protective near emptiness, its free books, its often-free coffee) looked different to me now.

"Is there anything I can do?" I asked.

Dee pointed to my glass, perspiring on the counter. "You already did it."

"What do your arms say?"

Dee laughed, a single bark she directed at the ceiling. She held up one forearm and then the next. "This one means 'I'll never stop loving you,' and this one is, like, 'Even in death, love survives' or some shit."

"Wow, you were really serious."

"I was the first person in history to fall in love," Dee said, grinning.

"Gaby?"

"We broke up, like, a month later," she said, rolling her eyes. "Everyone told me not to get these and they were right."

"I like them," I said. "And anyway, you *do* still love her. It's just a different way."

Dee considered this. "You're a sharp one, Q," she said. "Except for the straight-girl thing. Not that I haven't been there. Several times."

I wanted to defend my honor and tell her Ruby really did like me, because we'd held hands, and because Ronni said so. But then Jamie walked in the door, and the subject had to be changed. Dee and Jamie exchanged warm hellos.

"Iced vanilla?" Dee asked.

Jamie glanced at me before she nodded, and I felt a tiny thrill of smugness.

"Hey," I said.

"Hi."

"What do you have in there?" I asked, pointing to the backpack dwarfing Jamie's body. "Actual pot?"

"What?" Dee yelled over the milk steamer.

"Kidding!" I shouted.

"I went to the library," Jamie explained.

I smiled. Of course she had. Jamie had never met a humanities assignment she didn't overprepare for by a thousand percent. Science was different (we both hated that), and math she seemed to know inherently, but if there was an opportunity to *research*, to borrow books and print academic papers and buy and organize color-coded note cards, Jamie took it and ran. She was going to be so good at college.

My backpack, meanwhile, contained my laptop, my Civil Liberties notebook, and about seventy-eight pens.

Jamie paid, and we carried our coffee over to our favorite table. I surreptitiously stared at her as we sat and arranged our things into serious homework mode around us. Between the end of the school day and now, she'd changed her outfit and put on mascara. A small, ridiculous part of me wondered if she'd done all that for me, but a much bigger part worried she was going to see Natalie after this, or that she already had, during the two hours I was at practice.

"What did you do today?" I asked casually.

Jamie looked at me like I was the hugest idiot in the world. Which, apparently, I was. "School," she said.

"Well. Yeah," I said.

"What's wrong with you?"

"Nothing," I said. *(Everything.)* "I'm just making conversation."

"Okay," said Jamie. "Well, let's converse about legalization."

I sighed, and Jamie passed me a book called *The Legalization of Drugs (For and Against)*. Then she pulled out another called *Weed the People*.

"Yours sounds a lot more interesting."

"Sorry." She didn't look up, just opened her book and ran her thumbnail along the binding, pressing the cover flat. Jamie treated her own books like a hot stovetop, touching them as little as possible, but with library books, she read the way she wanted to read: ruthlessly.

For what felt like at least an hour we read in silence, save for the soft scrape of a page being turned and Ani DiFranco warbling faintly overhead. I checked the time when the college student packed up and left, and I realized it had actually only been thirteen minutes.

I sighed, and looked around the empty shop.

Jamie peered up at me from her hunchbacked reading position. "Keep reading."

"It's boring."

"It's due Tuesday. Do you want to be doing this on the weekend?"

She flushed a little when she said it, and I realized she

knew about my date (question mark) with Ruby. Ronni must have told Alexis, who would have told Jamie. I felt both panicked and thrilled.

"No," I agreed. "I don't."

We resumed reading, and I took a few note cards off the top of Jamie's pile to write down the talking points I found in my book. (These were variants on *drugs are bad*, mainly, but expressed in many more and larger words.) I looked up a few academic studies online and wrote down facts and statistics from there, too. I didn't really agree with the point I'd be arguing, but the more I looked into it, the more determined I became to argue it well. The next time I checked the time on my phone, an hour and twelve minutes had gone by. The coffee shop was closing in less than twenty minutes. Jamie had headphones on, so I tapped on the page she was reading to get her attention.

"What?"

"It's almost eight."

"Really?" Jamie pressed her phone screen—to make sure I wasn't lying about the time, I guess. "Okay. I'm basically done anyway."

"Me too."

"Really?" I gave her a look. "Sorry."

"It's okay," I said. "I'm as surprised as you are."

"Do you think we'll need to meet again, then?" From the

tone of her voice, it was hard to tell whether this was some-thing Jamie wanted, or wanted to avoid.

"I don't think so," I said. "I can do the rest on my own. But thank you for getting these books."

"Sure."

"I'm gonna win, you know," I said.

Jamie laughed, which was the point. "We'll see about that."

We packed up our things and brought our empty glasses to the counter.

"Finally," said Dee. "I want to *go.*"

I remembered something. "Oh, hey—Sweets wants to do another show."

Dee looked from me to Jamie and then back to me. I could see the effort it took for her not to tease me about Ruby. "Do they," she said.

"Yeah."

"How's next Friday?"

"Um. I can ask, but that's homecoming weekend."

"Oh yeah," said Jamie. "Does that . . . matter?"

Does it matter to you? I thought. I felt myself go sweaty around the collar. I didn't want to know. "I dunno. I think that cuts into attendance a bit."

"Just remind me, and I'll send you the calendar," said Dee. "Actually, email Gaby too, will you? Pretend you're asking her first."

"Okay."

"How'd you guys do last time?" asked Jamie, and immediately I felt embarrassed for not having asked the same thing.

"Good," said Dee. "Better than average. It's just, you know." She shrugged.

"What?"

"The average is low."

She looked resigned when she said this, and I wondered just how dire their situation really was. Dee was proud, and she would never ask for help, especially from teenagers. I wished there were something I could do, but I had an empty wallet and no job. I must've looked worried, because Dee perked up and laughed it off, like she'd been joking.

"Oh my God, relax," she said. "Please, get out of here so I can leave."

"Thanks, Dee," said Jamie.

"Yeah," I said. "Thanks."

Dee waved us out the door, and in the parking lot Jamie surprised me by asking for a ride home.

"You didn't bike?"

"I got dropped off," she said. She was trying hard not to smile, and my stomach dropped like the ground had disappeared from under me. *So Natalie was the reason for the mascara.* It was clear she wanted to be asked for details, but I didn't want to hear it from her. I'd find out later, from Ronni, from Alexis. Instead I just nodded toward my car, and for the first time since she dumped me, Jamie climbed into my passenger seat.

As soon as I turned the car on, a song from my *Moving On—I Mean It This Time, 2.0* playlist blasted through the speakers. I grabbed my phone to turn it down, and scrolled through my music for alternatives for a second before landing on the obvious choice. I tapped my screen, and Sweets's *Type Two* took over.

"You're allowed to listen to other things," said Jamie.

"This is what I want," I said.

Jamie nodded and looked out the window. I used to joke she was like a dog, craning her neck out in summer to smile into the sun and wind.

"I'm worried about Triple Moon," Jamie said to the window.

"Me too."

"I wish there was something we could do."

"You don't think they'll close, do you?"

Jamie turned to look at me and suddenly I felt naked, like a helpless, clueless baby. Somehow, until I said it aloud, the thought that Triple Moon might not always be there hadn't really occurred to me. Because I had eyes and ears I knew business wasn't exactly booming, but I assumed it was a rough patch that would mend itself in time. They'd start advertising more, maybe debut some new drink, and the norm would return to half-full from mostly empty.

"I think it's a miracle they've been in business as long as they have," Jamie said finally.

I remembered then the links she'd texted to me: news articles about lesbian bars closing across the country, and the think pieces that followed, wondering why. I remembered feeling like it was, in some way, my fault, even if I didn't live in those places and wasn't old enough to go inside if I did. Meanwhile, Triple Moon—a safe place to drink lattes and do my homework and read gay books and laugh and cry and fall in love with girls—was right here, and I had taken it for granted.

We sat in silence, and I listened to Ruby singing through my speaker. *I've held this person's hand,* I thought. *She's practically famous.* Then I had an idea.

"What if we got Sweets to help us with a fund-raiser?"

Jamie didn't say anything, which was how I knew she thought it was a good idea.

"It could be like a benefit concert," I continued. "We charge more, like ten bucks or something, and then instead of the band keeping part of it, all the money goes to the shop."

"It'd have to be twenty at least," said Jamie. "Maybe more."

"People pay thirty dollars for a concert all the time. They pay a lot more than that."

"Usually the band is, like, famous, but yeah."

"Sweets is thirty-dollar famous for sure," I said. My head was buzzing now, my free leg bouncing against my seat.

"Um, my exit?" said Jamie.

"Shit." I looked over my shoulder and sailed into the turn lane I'd almost blown past.

Turning off the exit, I braced myself, expecting to feel something about seeing Jamie's house for the first time in months. Not that it felt like more than a few days had passed. Every turn was automatic, and every house that led to hers was put there to remind me where I was. In twenty years I'd come home from wherever I was living (San Francisco, or Mexico City, or London, maybe Brussels) and I knew this route would feel exactly as familiar as it did now. I snuck a glance at Jamie, mentally tracing the profile I'd memorized the first time I saw her. I still knew every freckle, and maybe I always would. When we were together I'd thrilled at every private look and every inside joke and every piece of Jamie trivia I could recite as my own. I'd been so proud of how well I knew her, like that made her mine to keep. But now all that knowing felt different, like lyrics to a song I didn't even like but inexplicably knew by heart.

When we pulled into the driveway all I felt was impatient. I couldn't wait for Jamie to get out of my car. I couldn't wait to get home and into my bed. I especially couldn't wait for my picnic with Ruby. Now there were *two* things I wanted to ask her, and I had no idea how she'd respond to either one. Suddenly that not knowing didn't scare me so much anymore.

Fourteen

I meant to spend Sunday morning doing all the homework I hadn't done on Saturday because I was too nervous about my date (question mark) with Ruby. But then it was the day *of* the actual date thing, and the very idea of opening a textbook was laughable. Like I was going to sit down and read about kinetic energy when I was seeing Ruby in eight and a half hours. I needed every minute of that time to pace frantically around the house, wondering why I couldn't have suggested a Sunday breakfast instead of a midafternoon snack. On my twelfth trip through the kitchen my mom finally threw down her book.

"Would you stop? You're making *me* nervous!"

"I can't help it! I don't know what else to do!"

My mom took a big bite of doughnut and rubbed at her temple. "Go get my purse," she mumbled.

I dashed into the entryway and yanked my mom's black

leather bag off the hook by the door. I handed it over, and my mom wiped her powdered-sugar fingers on her pajama pants before digging out her wallet. She peered into it, sighing when she found only a few dollar bills. I held my breath as she slipped her emergency second credit card out of its slot. The last (and first) time my mom had given me that card was for my six-month-anniversary date with Jamie. I'd made us a reservation at the fanciest steakhouse my mom's sixty-five-dollar budget offering could buy. With tip I paid sixty-two.

"You're having a picnic, right?"

I nodded excitedly. I'd been planning to cobble it together from food we already had in the house, but instantly I began to dream bigger: Fresh fruit. Cold deli sides. Buttery European cookies.

"Okay," my mom said. "Forty bucks, max."

"That's plenty," I said. "I mean, it's enough. Thank you."

"You're welcome." She picked up her doughnut with one hand and her book with the other. "Now get dressed and get out of here. And take your time."

And I did. I showered and drove to the fancy grocery store out by La Jolla: the one with carpeted aisles and frigid air-conditioning and the boys my age wearing black polos who bagged your food up for you, where old people and rich people and old rich people bought organic produce and gourmet cheese as normal, everyday food. I lingered over every display, and stopped for every free sample offered to me by ladies with perfect manicures, wearing white chef's coats and discreet hairnets: a tiny shrimp cocktail in a paper cup; a smear of truffled goat cheese on a crispy herbed cracker; four sips' worth of cranberry kombucha, on sale this week for $3.99 a bottle from $4.59 a bottle.

I walked all the way through the store once without putting anything in my basket. I had to maximize my forty dollars, and it was easy to get sucked in by flashy-but-impractical items, like the four-pack of crème brûlée pudding that came in actual glass dishware, which I stared at for a full thirty seconds even though it cost eight dollars. On my second trip through the store, now older and wiser, I picked up a box each of raspberries and blueberries, three blocks of cheese, prosciutto and salami, two kinds of crackers, and a bag of potato chips, just in case. Then I did some mental math and put back the blueberries and one box of crackers.

The subtotal came to $38.41, so I threw a bag of M&M's on top for dessert.

Back at home in the kitchen, my mom now upstairs in the shower, I packed everything neatly into a cooler and then stood back to appraise my efforts. I wished I'd thought ahead to buy one of those special wooden picnic baskets lined with gingham fabric. Something like that would have really pulled the whole thing together. But maybe it was better this way. With the cooler I'd look like I was carrying a couple of basic peanut butter and jelly sandwiches, but when I opened it, and she saw instead an elegant, grown-up feast, Ruby would have no choice but to immediately ask *me* to homecoming. Or something like that.

Twenty years later, I sat in my truck in Ruby's driveway, opening and closing and reopening the cooler to check to make sure its contents were still cold. I'd pulled up at three on the dot, and decided I'd give her until 3:06 before I texted her to let her know I was there. It was breezy out, so I'd dressed in a jean jacket over a flannel, and I could feel sweat prickling my lower back. I opened the window a crack and flapped the hems of all my shirts up and down until it dried. And then it was 3:06, so I gave her another minute. I was deciding whether or not to give her another minute after *that* when the front door opened and Ruby emerged. I inhaled sharply. She wore her hair up, with a bandanna tied into a headband, and a very cool oversized fleece jacket that looked legitimately vintage and not fake Urban Outfitters vintage. Bright blue tights covered the skin the tears in her black jeans exposed, and on her feet were floral combat boots.

Again, I thought, *That is not the outfit of a strict heterosexual.*

We waved at each other through the glass, and smiled at each other when Ruby opened the side door.

"Hi," she said, climbing into the passenger seat.

"Hi," I said. "You look great."

We both blushed, and I turned quickly to look over my shoulder so I could begin the long, backward journey down Ruby's driveway.

"Thanks," said Ruby. With her boot she prodded the cooler at her feet. "Is this for us?"

"Of course," I said.

"Can I look?"

"No."

Ruby laughed. "Fine. Then I get to choose the beach."

I panicked a little. This had not been part of the plan. We were supposed to go to *my* beach, the one with the overlook parking lot, so we could sit in the back of my truck and look at the ocean without getting sand in our food. I wanted us to be safe and at least semi-secluded so we could kiss. Et cetera.

"Which one?"

Ruby smiled. "Just take a right at the stop."

Three turns later, I pulled into the parking lot of one of La Jolla's nicest private beaches, famous for allowing—pause for internal screaming—nudity. I'd never been. I wouldn't say I was afraid of it, exactly; having spent so much of my life in a rowdy girls' locker room, I'd gotten comfortable enough being naked and seeing naked people. But that was a sports thing, and you were only naked briefly in order to get into different clothes. This was just . . . voluntary. And Ruby was not my teammate.

"Don't you have to be eighteen to go here?" I asked, still clutching my steering wheel.

Ruby gave me such a withering look that I half expected to shrink to the size of an ant. "It's a clothing-optional beach, not a strip club."

Even the mention of *strip club* made my face hot. A flashing pink neon sign reading SEX lit up my brain. I was worried if I opened my mouth, it would fall out.

"Are you coming?" said Ruby. Her door was open, and she had one foot on the ground and her beach bag in her lap.

"Yes. Sorry."

"It's mostly going to be old-man dicks."

She was trying to reassure me, but it didn't work. I took a deep breath, grabbed the cooler and my bag, and got out of the car anyway. We stripped off our outer layers and tied them around our waists. Underneath her jacket, Ruby was wearing the red cropped T-shirt she'd worn onstage at Triple Moon, and I wondered if that was on purpose.

As we began the hike down to the beach itself, I was grateful for two things: one, that Ruby led the way, which meant she'd have to see the naked people first; and two, the trail was long and winding, and for a while I was able to preserve the hope that we might never actually arrive. There were several scenic stops along the way, and each time we approached one I prayed Ruby would announce that she was too tired to carry on, and why don't we just hang out here. But she never did. The beach and all its nudity got closer and closer, and then we were there.

We paused near the bottom of the trail, ostensibly scanning for the perfect spot.

"You were right," I said. Among the fifteen or so people I could see, only a few were naked, and they all had one thing in common.

"OMDs?"

I laughed. "Yeah."

"Let's go this way."

We trudged laboriously over the sand, Ruby's hair whipping around in the wind. When we found a spot she liked, she dropped her bag and bent over to untie her boots. I tried to shake the jumbo-sized towel I'd brought for us to sit on, but the wind wouldn't let me, so I flung it down and walked around the perimeter, pulling each corner flat. Ruby watched me, looking amused and a little impatient.

"May I sit?"

"Yes. Sorry. Please," I said.

I joined her, and pushed my tennis shoes off with my feet. For the moment, that was as much as I was willing to take off, even if the sun threatened to burn through my jeans. Ruby tucked her shirt up under her swimsuit top so her stomach would tan, and I tried not to openly stare.

"Are you ready?" I asked.

"For what?"

I pointed to the cooler. "Food."

"Oh. Yes. Sure."

This was not *as* much enthusiasm as I'd hoped for, but I popped open the plastic top and gave Ruby the rundown anyway.

"Wow," she said finally. "This is, like, an actual picnic."

"That's what I promised, isn't it?"

"No, yeah. I just figured you'd bring, like, a bag of chips."

I pulled the bag of chips from my tote bag and set it on top of my fancy spread. "Ta-da."

Ruby smiled in a way I wasn't sure how to interpret and opened the chips. I made myself a cheese-and-salami cracker and popped the whole thing in my mouth. Then I made one for Ruby, hesitating before handing it to her.

"Oh my God—you eat meat, right?"

She nodded, and the panic rising in my throat subsided. I handed her the cracker and she bit into it.

"Good? Do you want another one?"

Ruby blinked. "I mean, I'm still—"

"Right. I'll give you a minute."

I became uncomfortably aware of the sound of her chewing, and my watching her chewing, and my knee bouncing against the towel beneath me. I forced myself to look away, directly at the ocean, where there were no nudes. Except for all the animals. Before I could do anything to stop it, that picture of the giant pink whale penis we'd all been obsessed with for a full week during freshman year was in my head.

Ruby reached over and clasped her arm around my wrist, which made me jump.

"Quinn. Relax."

"Sorry," I said. We looked at each other. My leg came to a halt. Her hand was still on my arm. So I leaned forward, and I kissed her.

This wasn't the plan. We'd just gotten to the beach. We'd barely picnicked at all. The sun was still up. There were naked men not very far away.

But I let all that go as soon as she kissed me back. And it was unmistakable: she leaned forward, and my whole body shifted back with the force of her face pressed into mine. Her skin smelled like almonds. Her lips were soft. Her breath was salty like salami, one of my favorite foods. I reached out, so eager to finally touch her hair, but before I got there she pulled back. Quickly. And just like that, my panic was back in full force. Wind whipped against my ears, so cold it hurt.

"I'm sorry," I said reflexively. She looked down at her lap instead of at me. "Did you not . . ." I trailed off. The polite thing to do, I knew, was to give her plausible deniability. But I'd felt what I felt. She'd wanted to kiss me, too.

She did, right?

"No, I did," said Ruby. "I just . . . it's just . . . I'm not sure."

My living-room floor. Jamie refusing to look at me. Jamie get-

ting up to leave. Months of silence and confusion. I felt it all again, now twice as strong. I thought I might cry, so I leaned back, making a pillow of my flannel shirt, as if all I *really* cared about was working on my tan.

"Don't worry about it," I said.

"You don't want to talk about it?" My eyes were closed and I couldn't tell from Ruby's voice whether she was disappointed or relieved. But I knew which was more likely.

"It's okay, really," I said. I opened an eye to squint at her. "Let's just pretend it didn't happen." She was watching me, so I attempted a smile. "Seriously."

She smiled back, and it broke my heart.

Ruby lay next to me, not too close, not too far away. We were quiet for what felt like hours, and maybe it was. I had wanted to ask her about the band, and the benefit concert, and—I almost laughed out loud—homecoming, but there was no way I could do that now. I couldn't believe I'd let myself count on the best possible version of events. I kept opening my mouth to say something, but then—what? I couldn't come up with a single thing. Eventually the sun started to fall, and the wind picked up, and I could hear the naked people packing up their chairs and umbrellas.

"Are you cold? I'm kind of cold," she said.

"Freezing," I said. "We can go."

My meticulous picnic was still mostly intact, and I knew I'd be sadly chipping away at it in packed lunches all week. The trail I'd appreciated on the way down was torturous in reverse. The worst part was that our backs were turned to the changing sky. The sun set when we weren't looking. The darkness I dropped Ruby off in didn't feel romantic, or exciting, like the good kind of trouble. It felt ominous and cold.

"Thanks," she said in her driveway.

"Sure," I said, wondering what for. I was pretty sure she'd just been on the worst non-date of her life. She slung her bag over her shoulder and jumped out of the truck. *Go*, I pleaded in my head. *Please just go.* But she hesitated.

"See you tomorrow?"

Did I have a choice?

"See you tomorrow," I said. And then she left, and it was over. Once I turned off her street I put on Céline Dion, and I let myself do the crying I'd been holding in for hours.

 **Fifteen**

So, fuck homecoming, if you asked me. Frankly, it was an imposter of a dance—a big bureaucratic hoax. Every year, the student government led a spirit week leading up to the Friday pep rally, where we engaged in the collective delusion that this year, our football team might be good enough to finish the season in triumph. That this year, they'd draw crowds far beyond the players' girlfriends and the handful of students who picked the bleachers as a place to be drunk or stoned on Friday nights. In fact, those kids would stop drinking and smoking altogether. The unlikely scrappiness of our newly beloved Mustangs would turn us all into starry-eyed, well-behaved superfans who got into all the right colleges.

As usual, Monday was Pajama Day. But I did not wear pajamas.

Tuesday was Dress Like the Nineties Day. Any resemblance

between my outfit and those worn in the 1990s was entirely coincidental. In Civil Liberties, Jamie and I presented our debate to our very bored classmates, most of whom wore some combination of baggy jeans and plaid shirts, choker necklaces and ponytails in scrunchies. Mr. Haggerty gave us ninety-one out of one hundred. Jamie was mad. I was thrilled.

Wednesday was Meme Day. Thursday was Halloween, for which I dressed, lazily, as Megan Rapinoe, wearing her jersey and a silver chain necklace. Friday, School Spirit Day. I wore my soccer sweatshirt, but not because I felt spirited. I was just tired of dressing myself by then, and it was the clothing item closest to my bed when I rolled out of it.

Maybe I shouldn't have been as miserable as I was. Every day since our ill-fated kiss, Ruby had texted me, numerous times. Not about the kiss itself, or what it meant, but normal things, like what we would have talked about before. At first I was excited to see her name on my screen, relieved that she would not be taking the total shunning route. But then a day passed, and then another, and she remained so insistently *friendly* that it started to make me feel worse than if she'd never texted me at all.

As if that weren't enough to worry about, Ronni and I had the Beach Cup that weekend, the last tournament of the club team season. Held on the UCSD campus in La Jolla every early November, the Beach Cup was a college showcase, attended by hundreds of coaches looking to make their final selections for the following season. On Saturday every team played three or four games, and on Sunday, depending how well you did, you played up to four more. If, like most girls on my team, you'd already accepted a school's offer, the Beach Cup was low-stakes, a chance to show off, gossip about the other teams, and eat parent-provided snacks on the sidelines. You went home bone-tired and sunburned but essentially happy, impressed with all your body could handle. I'd felt that way as a junior. But going into the same tournament as a senior with no set college plan, it felt like stepping onto a rope bridge stretched precariously between two canyons. I couldn't see the other side, and I couldn't see where I'd land if I fell. After the Beach Cup, the school season started up. And if by our first game, a week after the cup, I *still* didn't know which college team I'd be playing for, my soccer career was as good as over. Some no-name D-II school would surface, offering me the chance to be their very best player, and that would be the last you ever heard of Quinn Ryan.

So it was with this outlook on life that I arrived home on Friday, having bailed at the last minute on the team carbo-loading at Kate's house, citing family obligations. (Mercifully, Ronni, understanding I needed to be alone, changed the subject on the team group text so everyone would stop harassing me.)

I staggered in the door, weighed down by my bag, which was filled with a season's worth of water bottles and socks and various trash. I felt my pocket vibrate but ignored it, sure that Kate or Janelle was still giving me shit. I let my bag drop to the floor and threw myself on the couch before retrieving my phone.

I gasped. My team hadn't texted me. Ruby had.

What are you doing tomorrow night

I gasped again. I bolted upright, watching the text bubble reappear, then disappear, reappear again, disappear again. What was I *doing tomorrow night*, she wrote . . . ? As if tomorrow weren't Saturday, the most datelike of all nights? As if—oh my *God*—tomorrow weren't also the night of the homecoming dance? For a brief, deranged moment, I wondered if Ruby Ocampo was about to ask me to the dance. Then I pictured her saying or even thinking those words—*Will you go to the dance with me?*—and burst into laughter. There was no way.

So then what?

The bubble returned and I held my breath.

David's having a party
if you wanted to come

I exhaled. I had to admit: I was ever so slightly disappointed she wasn't asking me to homecoming after all. But this . . . this was better. This was a party for people too cool to care about homecoming, of which I was not one.

David Tovar? I asked, for some reason. As if it could be any other David.

Lol yes

Idk why I clarified, I wrote.

I would have agreed to any David.

Cool. Pick me up at 9?

I screamed a little.

OK, I texted.

I hugged my phone to my chest, eyes closed, already imagining the following night. Then my phone buzzed again, and I grinned, ready to read another conversation-extending sign-off from Ruby. But this time it was just the soccer group text again, a picture of heaps of spaghetti meant to make me question my choices. Which, now, I was.

Fine. I'll be there in 20, I wrote, and ran out the door grinning.

On Saturday, I used my excitement for the party with Ruby as both fuel and distraction. It helped, under the eyes of so many coaches, to have my mind a few hours ahead, with something more than my athletic fate to look forward to. All the coaches I'd ever spoken to were there, including UNC and UCLA, though I didn't look for them in the stands. I'd emailed both beforehand to remind them of my interest, as was standard protocol, but coaches weren't allowed to talk to players at the tournament, or vice versa. This was fine with me, as it further helped me pretend they weren't there. Before the first game began I did all the pressure-lowering techniques I'd learned in therapy, and they actually kind of worked. We won two of our four games and tied one, but I made some of the best plays I'd made all year, and got team-tackled twice.

By the time I got home I was physically exhausted but mentally amped. When I showered I was pleased to find I'd tanned fairly evenly, which made my teeth and eyes look brighter. I dried my hair before slathering it in wax, then began trying on every combination of T-shirt + pants I owned before landing on a black T-shirt, black jeans, and black Vans, plus my blue jean jacket, for variety. Then I had to fix my hair again, which took more wax, and then more water, and then spray, until it reached a stiff sort of sheen.

When I left, my mom eyed me suspiciously.

"Did you wash your hair?"

"Yes!" I said, but I ducked before the entryway mirror to double-check.

"Oh, so that's, like, the look."

"Mom. Please."

"No, I get it now. You look dope."

"*Mom.*" I opened the front door. "I'm going now. Bye."

She waited at the door a moment before calling out another of her favorite jokes: "Don't get pregnant!"

I tried to suppress my smile. I didn't want to encourage her.

On the way over to Ruby's I sang along to a playlist called *Modest Expectations,* formerly *Everyone Is Counting on You.* (Ronni's revision.) It was a playlist I typically listened to within the privacy of headphones on the bench before soccer games, but I needed its (modestly) hyping effect now more than ever. World Cup anthems blasted through the speakers until I turned onto Ruby's street and abruptly turned them off, figuring she'd be less likely to judge me for a silent car than one playing Shakira's "Waka Waka." Good thing, too, because this time, Ruby was waiting at the bottom of her driveway. She was tapping furiously at her phone, but she smiled when she looked up and saw me.

If what happened at the beach had happened any differently, I might have been positive Ruby was dressed up for me as much as she was for the party itself. She wore a cool oversized jean jacket over a black T-shirt and a stretchy, short black skirt I blushed to look at. On her feet, Vans high-tops. Her hair was pulled into a high, royal blue–tipped bun. When she opened the door and climbed into my truck the first thing I said was, "You changed your hair. I like it."

She lightly squeezed her bun as if to remind herself of its color. "Thank you," she said. "It's darker than I wanted."

"It'll fade."

"Yeah."

Ruby settled into her seat, and the safe-seeming silence

became immediately stressful. I drove to the end of the street, waiting for her to direct me. But she was absorbed by her phone and didn't notice that we'd been stopped at the stop sign for a full ten seconds. I stole a glance at her screen but couldn't read the name of the person she was texting. I had a pretty good guess, though. I cleared my throat, and Ruby flipped the phone facedown in her lap.

"Sorry."

"No, it's okay," I said. "I just, um. Don't know where I'm going."

"Oh," she said. "Right. Turn left."

As it turned out, the Tovar house was only about a mile uphill from Ruby's, and even more imposingly palatial; it looked like the kind of house an evil twin from a soap opera would make threatening phone calls from before taking to the balcony with a bottle of Scotch. When Ruby saw me see the house she explained, "His dad's a plastic surgeon to, like, famous people."

The street was lined with BMWs and Lexuses (Lexii?) and Mercedes-Benz SUVs, a number of which I recognized from the school parking lot. I did a quick, impressive parallel-parking job (Ruby said so herself) a few houses down, and we made our way up the wide, pitch-black street. There were never any streetlamps or sidewalks in the rich neighborhoods, I'd noticed; everyone wanted to pretend they were neighbor-less and alone at the edge of the ocean. In the dark, Ruby's hand brushed past mine, or maybe it was mine that brushed past hers, and I felt the short route of her fingertips across my skin like fire. To keep it from happening again—unless Ruby really, really wanted it to—I stuck my hands in the pockets of my jacket for the remainder of the walk up the driveway.

Ruby did not ring the doorbell, or knock; she pushed the door open with the familiarity of someone who'd let herself in a hundred times. She'd told me Sweets practiced in an un-used bedroom David's father had lined with soundproof foam. His folks were out of town at the moment, in Las Vegas for a plastic-surgery conference, Ruby explained, and a wave of nerves washed over me, imagining the debauched scene in-side before I actually encountered it. All the parties I'd been to had been thrown by soccer girls or water polo guys, and they all blended together in my head, the same forty people drink-ing out of the same red Solo cups and dancing to the same five songs. As a sophomore and a junior there was nothing I'd looked forward to more, and as a senior I took pride in being one of the seniors laughing at the overeager, quickly intoxi-cated sophomores and juniors. But now, walking into what I assumed would be a very different sort of party, I felt newly and frighteningly aware of the limitations of my experience. In my own familiar setting I was reasonably cool, and well-liked, a jock among jocks. In this one, I could only hope that arriving with Ruby granted me acceptance by proxy.

Inside the dimmed foyer, Ruby pointed me to a sea of shoes

spreading across the white tiled floor, and I reluctantly bent over to untie my laces as she sat on the steps to do the same. I said a silent prayer of thanks that I'd worn normal white athletic socks and not novelty ones, and slid my boots underneath an end table covered in silver-framed pictures of David's family. David frowned handsomely in every last one.

"I was not expecting a shoes-off vibe," I yelled over the music.

Ruby grinned. "It's his mom's one rule."

Together we slid down the hallway into the kitchen, where we took in the scene. A spacious granite island countertop was covered in liquor bottles and empty cardboard six-packs and red Solo cups, misplaced or abandoned for new ones. David stood behind it, pouring drinks for Alex Grant and Emily Heidegger, who were laughing so hard their cups shook. Vodka trailed down Alex's hand and wrist, and Emily licked it off. "EW!" Alex screamed before licking the rest off herself. David noticed Ruby and raised the vodka bottle in triumphant greeting. "RUUUUUBE!" he yelled.

She looked at me. "Let's get a drink, yeah?"

I nodded urgently.

David scrambled around the island to hug Ruby. He also gave me a wave over her shoulder, which was more than I expected.

"How's it going," he said. "What's up," I replied. Two questions uninterested in answers.

Ruby extracted herself from David's drunken death grip and slid two cups off the stack for us, handing me one.

"Always gotta be fashionably late," David teased, and I realized nine wasn't when the party started for anyone but Ruby. Which made the drunkenness levels around me more logical. Alex and Emily, for instance, were shiny and squinty-eyed, no longer competing with each other for David's focus but huddled together, united against their new common enemy: Ruby, who was oblivious.

"What do I want?" she asked herself, touching every bottle.

"May I?" I reached for her cup and she handed it to me. If I'd retained one piece of useful information from the soccer parties I'd been to as an underclassman, it was how to assemble a decent cocktail from the supplies in my rich classmates' gleaming refrigerators. I found lime juice and lemon juice and honey in various cabinets, and then remembered David was standing right there, and asked him if I could use them.

"Sure, but I want one."

"Me too," said Alex and Emily.

As I threw together our drinks, two more drunk girls wandered over, and then Ben and a few other guys, and soon I was bartending for half the party. People were acting insane, like my drink was the most delicious thing they'd ever tasted, when really it was pretty easy to improve upon a flat, watery beer or a mix of cheap flavored rum and Diet Coke. I let them be impressed. Though Ruby found her way to the other end of the island and was talking to David and Ben, she kept looking over to laugh at my hustle. When the crowd finally cleared, she came back over and handed me her empty cup.

"Not to make you make me another one, but . . ."

I grinned and took a big gulp of my drink, which I had to admit was pretty good. I felt the tequila warmth spread all the way down to my toes. I made Ruby a new one and topped off mine, and before I could get roped into making two more for the newest arrivals, Ruby pulled me away by the sleeve. "You've done enough," she said to me. "Sorry, she's off duty," she told the annoyed-looking girls at the counter. They shrugged and filled their cups with whatever.

I followed Ruby out of the kitchen and past a den, where eight or ten boys sat immobilized by the contents of the giant green bong on the coffee table, into a room whose original purpose was unclear (houses like these always had extra) but that was currently serving as a dance floor-slash-mosh pit.

"What *is* this?" I yelled in Ruby's ear. I couldn't help myself. The music blasting through the thousand-dollar speakers was, like, EDM meets . . . something angry and bad.

Ruby shrugged and yelled something back that sounded like "Peter Rabbit," or maybe "Peter Abbot" was more likely, but it didn't matter, because I had no plans to look them up later.

"I miss Ariana Grande!" I yelled.

"What?"

I shook my head, and Ruby laughed. In universal loud-party sign language, she motioned for me to finish my drink with her before wading into the crush of sweaty bodies. I tipped my cup to hers in cheers, and then we drained them. We grimaced and grinned at each other, and Ruby reached her hand across the short distance between us and wiped the corner of my lip with her thumb. My whole body felt golden and sparkled where she touched me. *I'm possibly a little drunk,* I thought. Immediately I forgot everything I'd promised myself about making risky first moves and took Ruby's hand to lead her into the crowd.

I didn't know how long we danced. Every song blended into the next, or maybe it was just one very long one. We jumped and swayed and nodded. Ruby pulled her hair out of her bun so she could whip it around, and I had to step back to avoid being hit. Then we got sweaty and she put it back up. Three different people came over to hug Ruby and dance near her. A few times the crowd pushed us apart, and I found myself dancing with no one. But I didn't care. I felt light and alive and in love with everything. And eventually, Ruby and I danced our way back to each other.

At some point the glow started to fade, and I realized my throat was dry and I needed to pee like never before. I transmitted this information to Ruby as best I could, and tried not to be too disappointed when she didn't follow me. After I went to the bathroom, I found my cup on the sideboard and carried it into the kitchen, where I filled it with water from the Tovars' fancy built-in filter. Forget my punch—that water was the best thing I'd ever tasted in my life. I gulped it down standing by the sink and refilled it. Since I'd been in there last, the scene in the kitchen had deteriorated considerably. Empty bottles had spread over every surface like a virus. A small pile of radioactive-looking Cheez Balls sat at the edge of the counter, overlooking a few fallen compatriots on the floor. And then there were the people: slumped, splayed, splotchy. Yelling for no reason. I wasn't drunk enough to not find them annoying, so I poured some of the nearest warm vodka and warm Diet Coke in a cup and grimaced through it with my eyes on the doorway to the dance room. *Any second now,* I thought.

Sixteen

Ten hours later, Ruby appeared, rosy and glowing. I smiled until I saw her expression, which was certifiably Pissed Off. A second later, the reason why staggered through the doorway after her: Mikey. I hadn't seen him in there, but then again, I hadn't been looking for anyone else.

Ruby saw me, and our eyes locked. My adrenaline kicked into high gear. I flew across the kitchen to Ruby's side, inserting myself between her and Mikey.

"Are you okay?" I asked. Ruby nodded, but her eyes were on Mikey, who didn't seem to notice I was there. He was the kind of drunk you could see, and smell. He propped himself up against a cabinet, glowering.

"We're having a private conversation," he said, and finally he looked at me. I hated him so intensely in that moment I wanted to hit him. I imagined him trying to pull Ruby closer by the wrist, and her resisting, then me knocking him flat with a single, well-placed punch. I imagined Ruby thanking me, throwing her arms around my shoulders. *My hero*, she'd say. It wasn't that I wanted him to hurt her, but I thought that maybe if I saved her before he could make her cry she'd realize how much she wanted me.

But he didn't grab her, and Ruby didn't say anything, so instead of the savior, I was only a creep, still standing between two people who didn't want me there.

"Sorry," I muttered. I walked out of the kitchen so it looked like I had somewhere else to be anyway, when of course I didn't. In the house's dark and empty entryway I sat on the steps presiding over the sea of shoes and held a hand to my mouth so no one would hear me cry. I felt so stupid for so much: my unrealistic imagination, the gap between the way I wanted to be seen and the way these people actually saw me. For drinking too much, past the point at which I knew I became angrier than I wanted to be. Two drinks was safe. Any more and I ran the risk of reminding myself of my dad. *Ugh, my dad.* He still hadn't told me when, or if, he was moving back, and I hadn't asked for more information in weeks, not wanting to remind him to ask me about college again. I hoped that by Monday, when the tournament was over and the club season with it, I'd have something good to tell him. But I didn't want to think about that now.

I heard a couple of people coming around the corner,

maybe to get their shoes and leave, so I leapt up and took the stairs two at a time. The second floor was dark, and most of the doors were closed. I turned my phone's flashlight on and then plugged my ears as I ran by every bedroom, searching for an unoccupied bathroom. I found one at the end of the hall. When I flicked on the light I gasped; it was bigger than my bedroom, and maybe my mom's as well: tan granite and dark tile everywhere, and a glass-enclosed shower so cavernous it creeped me out a little. I closed the door behind me and stepped closer to the giant gilded mirror to examine the damage. I was puffy, but not terribly so, and the little bit of eyeliner I'd put on had mostly remained in place. It took me a minute to figure out how to work the sink, but when I did I ran my hands under cold water and pressed them to my face. I looked at the curved metal faucet and had an idea I knew, as I had it, was a drunk one. I leaned forward to press my puffy eyes against it, figuring this was basically the same technique I'd seen my mother use with spoons she kept in the freezer. Anyway, it felt good, and grounding somehow, and I stayed hunched over like that for longer than I planned to, until someone knocked on the door, and in my hurry to get my face off the faucet I somehow poked myself in the eye with it.

"Ow!" I yelled.

"Quinn?"

"Ruby?"

With one hand cupped over my presumably empty eye

socket I opened the door slowly until I confirmed that it really was Ruby on the other side.

"What happened?"

"Nothing," I said, knowing this was a ridiculous answer as long as my hand was covering my eye.

"Let me see."

"No."

"Come on."

"It might be really gory. I hit it really hard."

Ruby tried not to laugh. "Okay, well, I'll steel myself." She lifted her hand to mine and pulled it gently away. I wanted to be mad at her, for having the nerve to come here and touch me like that just minutes after her freaking lovers' rendez-vous in the kitchen, but I also didn't want her to ever stop touching me. When she saw my eye she gasped, which made me gasp, and I whirled to face the mirror to find my injured eye . . . mostly identical to my uninjured one, save for slightly smudged eyeliner.

"You scared me!"

Ruby shook with silent laughter.

"It really hurt. It really felt like I broke something."

"What were you *doing*?"

"Nothing weird. It doesn't matter."

"You're drunker than I thought."

"Yeah, well." *I had to cope somehow,* I thought.

"What's that supposed to mean?"

I felt the rest of my face redden to match my eye wound. I didn't really mean to get into this, but I could already sense my feelings threatening to spill from my mouth. I knew they weren't all fair, but it felt like if I did not say them, I would die.

"You didn't come with me. I didn't know what else to do."

Ruby smirked, but not meanly. "There are, like, a *lot* of other people here to talk to."

"Yeah, but nobody else I want to talk to." She looked at her feet, watching them take a tiny step closer to me. I stayed where I was. I'd been this person so many times before, even before I understood what it meant: waiting for a girl to choose me the way I'd chosen her. My entire middle school experience was defined by girls I was crazy about abandoning me the moment they got boyfriends. None of them understood why it hurt me so much. I knew why, but couldn't put it into words. Boyfriends, even ex-boyfriends, remained a somewhat special presence in my life. I envied them, and I was afraid of them, and when I'd had a little to drink, I hated them. "You have . . . people here."

"Like Mikey, you mean."

"Among others." I shrugged, as if that weren't exactly what I'd meant.

"You're an idiot," she said.

"What?" I said. But then she kissed me. *Really* kissed me. Pushed me into the wall behind me kissed me. Her hand on the back of my neck and both of mine on her shoulders, her back, her hips and waist, the top of her butt. I felt her blindly wave her unoccupied arm at the door until it was closed, and the lock clicked. There was no going back after a kiss like that.

I woke up in Ruby's bedroom not believing where I was. I saw her in bed, above me, from where I slept in the nicest sleeping bag I had ever encountered, and still it seemed fake. I felt around for my phone to look for evidence that I wasn't losing my mind. It was 6:32. I had texted my mom at 12:17, during a make-out break, to let her know I'd drunk too much to drive home and would be sleeping at a friend's house. She'd sent me a thumbs-up emoji and a drop of water, meaning: *drink some*. If she knew *friend* referred to Ruby, she didn't say so, and I loved her for it.

Sometime after that we half ran, half walked from David's house to Ruby's, holding hands up and down the tar-paved hills in the dark.

Ruby's parents were long asleep by then, and she made us tiptoe in the side door, across the entire first floor, and up the stairs that curved around their grand octagonal foyer. Twice on the stairs the wood creaked loudly beneath my unpracticed feet, and each time, Ruby reached out to grab my arm and hold me firm in place, freezing us both until she was sure her parents hadn't woken. Instead of getting off at the second floor as expected, Ruby pulled me toward another set of stairs, which

I climbed with one hand in hers and the other clinging to the banister. I was afraid of heights, particularly those witnessed from staircases, but I made myself look over the edge at the foyer growing farther below us. I tried to think if I'd ever been in a house with three stories before but could only come up with some historic miner's mansion my fifth-grade class had toured on a field trip we took during our Gold Rush unit. And even that might have been more like two and a half.

Ruby's bedroom took up nearly the entire floor, and I briefly worried she'd have me sleep on the couch at the opposite end of the room from her bed. (A *couch*. In her *bedroom*.) But then she closed the door and pulled me toward her bed, and I stopped thinking altogether.

We didn't have sex, though it was obvious we were both wondering if we would. During a break in the kissing she looked up at me and I felt like she might be waiting for me to ask her if we could, but I couldn't come up with the words, and something about being put in that position made me stubborn. Replaying it in the early-morning sunlight, it felt silly to think of it that way, but at the time, I didn't want to be something Ruby just went along with.

Eventually she'd pulled a sleeping bag from her enormous closet, and I was surprised by my own relief. Not that I'd really thought I'd sleep with her in her bed, because if she had the kind of parents you tiptoe around, they probably weren't the kind of parents who'd be cool with an obvious lesbian sharing their daughter's bed. But when we were still lying there together, mouths numb from liquor and kissing, I'd felt lonely and claustrophobic and homesick and embarrassed by all of these feelings and more. I'd never been much for sleepovers as a kid—something about another house's smells and sounds felt foreboding in the dark, and though I always woke up first, I was afraid to leave my friend's bedroom without them, convinced I'd encounter her pajamaed dad in the hallway, and he'd awkwardly ask if I slept okay, and I would have to lie. (This had happened to me once, at Melissa McDougal's house in second grade, and that was enough.) But in my sleeping cocoon, after we'd said good night and Ruby's breathing slowed, I felt better. I clutched my phone in lieu of the ragged teddy bear I pretended was only decorative, reading through text threads with Ronni and my mom and Jamie to remind myself I was still me, and in the morning I would go home.

Now it was 6:41, and I had to be at the tournament, ready to play. I'd heard footsteps descending the stairs when I first woke up, and now ambient TV and kitchen sounds drifted up from the first floor. I slithered out of my sleeping bag, tiptoeing out of the room and into Ruby's bathroom around the corner, which revealed itself to be the second most glamorous bathroom I'd ever seen in my life, both within the last twelve hours. The towels were plush and a creamy, impractical off-white. There were weird spiky sprigs of dried plants arranged in rose-gold vases on the glass shelves, which also held a number of lotions and creams and other mysterious liquids, all neatly arranged. There wasn't even one water spot on the mirror. I was afraid to touch anything, but I was more afraid of showing up to my game unshowered, smelling like liquor and hormones. I retrieved a spare towel as delicately as if it were booby-trapped, and stripped out of last night's outfit. I held my hand under the showerhead (perfect water pressure) until the temperature was right, and then I stepped in. I luxuriated in flicking open each of Ruby's several shampoos and conditioners and body soaps and sniffing their contents. Unable to choose, I made blends of all three.

By the time I got out, my butt and back were bright pink, and the mirror fully fogged. Reluctantly, I got dressed in the clothes I'd thrown on the floor. I found toothpaste and squeezed some onto my finger, my makeshift toothbrush, and snuck back into Ruby's room. Her back was facing me, and I assumed she was still asleep, but when I got closer she murmured, "You smell good," which scared the shit out of me.

She turned over in bed, peering at me through smeared black eyeliner. "You took a shower already?"

"Yeah. Sorry. I wake up early."

She lifted her phone from her nightstand and laughed. "Wow. No kidding."

"Sorry."

"No, it's fine," she said. I was still standing three feet from her bed, unsure what to do with myself. I couldn't get back into my bag, but Ruby made no signs of getting up either. "I'll get up," she said, but she didn't move.

"No, no," I said. "I've gotta get to my tournament soon anyway."

"Oh right," she said.

I couldn't stand it anymore. I sat at the foot of her bed. In response she stretched out her leg so it grazed my thigh through the blankets. We smiled at each other, and laughed.

"So what now?" she said.

"What do you mean?" I said. I knew what she meant.

"Are we like . . ." Ruby gestured at the space between us.

"Engaged?" I suggested.

She laughed, a single, loud *ha!* that reminded me of Jamie at the worst possible time.

"I'm kidding," I added.

"I know."

"We can be whatever you want us to be."

"But what do you want?"

I looked at her, lying in the bed we'd made out in hours earlier, days after I'd kissed her first, weeks after this very scene would have seemed laughably unlikely, months after I got my heart broken, and felt there was only one possible, reasonable answer.

"I want you," I said.

Finally, Ruby sat up and scooted down the bed to my side. The gears in my heart whirred to life. She leaned in close to me, waiting to be kissed. She had morning breath, which was comforting, in a way. It meant I wasn't dreaming. This was really happening. I kissed her, still waiting to believe it.

Seventeen

I couldn't remember the last time I'd been so excited to walk into school on a Monday morning. I strode into the building feeling like the post-makeover scene in every teen movie, hoping everyone else was seeing me pass in glorious slow motion. I was still wearing my normal clothes and I still had the same haircut, but surely I looked different. I wasn't just Quinn anymore. I was Quinn, Ruby's girlfriend. Ish. I reminded myself at every opportunity, willing it to feel real. When I saw a pair of freshman soccer players in the hall I imagined them thinking, *That's Quinn. She's dating Ruby Ocampo.* I grabbed my books from my locker and thought, *I wonder what my girlfriend, Ruby Ocampo, ate for breakfast.* Then I remembered she'd told me she didn't eat breakfast. *Pancakes just for me, thanks—my girlfriend doesn't really like breakfast food.*

I'd more or less confirmed our status via text message the night before, in what was hopefully a very restrained, almost ambivalent manner. Ruby had finally texted me that afternoon: the slant-mouth emoji with a bandage on its head, which briefly made me panic she was about to write the whole thing off as a drunken mistake. I didn't think she'd been very drunk the night before, and definitely not that morning. But before I could decide how best to respond, she sent the kissy-face emoji, and I knew she wasn't going to take it all back. Later, when I asked her if all this meant we were together, she replied **Lol so formal.** But then she added, **Yes, I guess it does.** Smiley face.

So that was that. We were official. I took a screenshot, just in case I wanted to print it for a scrapbook someday. I wanted to give her something of mine, because just saying the words didn't feel like enough. *There should be a high school couple registry*, I thought. I wanted my name listed next to Ruby's on some sort of permanent record. Maybe even a plaque.

Instead I decided to wear my great-grandfather's bracelet to school in order to give it to her. Not to keep forever, unless we were together forever, but to wear for now. It felt important, and a small, secret part of me knew it was because I didn't think people would believe we were together otherwise. I knew if Jamie found out she would scold me, say I was being patriarchal and probably somehow capitalist, too. She would say I was trying to mark my territory, but it wasn't like that. Or if it was a little like that, it was more that I wanted to be marked as Ruby's.

Now, more than ever, it felt cosmically unfair that Ruby had B lunch period when I had A. But I practically skipped into the cafeteria anyway, plotting how to share my news without screaming it before I sat down. Ronni and Jamie were already at the table, which meant Alexis was probably still in line for her usual salad and french fries.

"Hey," I said, easing my backpack off my shoulders. *Good start.*

Jamie's mouth was full, so she gave me a wave, and Ronni clapped me on the back.

"What's up, Q?"

"Not much," I lied, stalling. I didn't want to say anything substantial in front of Jamie before Westville's *TMZ* joined us. "How've you been since . . . twenty hours ago?"

"Good," said Ronni. "I ran a six-twenty-five this morning."

"Are you kidding me?" I asked.

She smiled smugly, then glanced at Jamie. "Jamie was actually just telling me about *her* weekend." Something about the way Ronni said it made my face go hot with worry.

"I went to the dance," Jamie explained.

My stomach dropped into my feet. Immediately, I had ten million questions, but I was too shell-shocked to ask any of them. *Who?* (Natalie?) *What? When? Where? WHY?* As of last week, as far as I knew, Jamie had had zero plans to attend the dance. I knew this because I'd listened very carefully anytime Alexis and Jamie talked about Alexis's homecoming drama on the other side of the lunch table, and Jamie had made no indication she would also be there. *How did she even get a ticket so last-minute?* I wondered, ridiculously, as if our crappy school-gym dance tickets typically sold out like Coachella.

"What's happening?" said Alexis, who, apparently sensing potential drama, had rushed over to the table with tray in hand. I realized I still hadn't said anything.

"Jamie just told us she went to homecoming!" I exclaimed brightly.

"Oh. Yeah. She was sorta my date." Alexis grinned, leaning into Jamie as she sat down. I felt a flare of jealousy, even as the relief that Jamie hadn't gone with Natalie (at least not formally) rushed through me.

"How?" I said. "I mean, what about . . . Jacob? Or those other guys?"

"Please," said Alexis. "Bringing a boy to the dance is so nineties." She threw her arm around Jamie, and they looked deep into each other's eyes. Then they cracked up, evidently at some incredible homecoming-related inside joke I hadn't been there for, and would never be part of. I had a horrible feeling I would be hearing about this dance for the rest of the year, if not the rest of my life. My own Saturday night felt impossibly far behind me, the details increasingly fuzzy and dull.

"I wasn't going to go, but Alexis played the feminist card, and I couldn't refuse," explained Jamie. I wondered if this was for my benefit, but then, why would she think I'd care? (I was of course wondering if Natalie had gone too, maybe with band friends, and who she'd danced with, and if that included Jamie. But that was just curiosity.)

"It's actually really progressive for a lesbian and a straight girl to go together," Alexis agreed.

Jamie cocked her head. "Well . . ."

Alexis gasped excitedly. "Wait. Do you think anyone thinks I'm gay now?"

"No," the rest of us said. Alexis's shoulders slumped a little.

"What did you wear?" Ronni asked Jamie. We'd all seen about two thousand pictures of Alexis in her dress weeks earlier, when she'd asked us to vote on her six different options. "Where are the pictures?"

"Don't tell her—I'm still editing them," said Alexis, holding her hand out to stop Jamie before she could ruin the surprise. "Anyway, you get way more impact posting on a weekday."

"Right, of course," said Ronni. I could hear the slightest sarcasm in her tone, and I knew it was meant for me, but I couldn't bring myself to look at her. If she saw my eyes, she'd know I wasn't okay. And I worried that if she knew I wasn't okay, she'd be disappointed in me, for not being tougher, for taking everything so personally.

"A lot of people were there with friends, actually," said Alexis. "You guys should have come."

Ronni shrugged, and I knew this was my chance, the clearest opening I was going to get. *Like Natalie Reid?* I wanted to say. But I couldn't let Jamie have that. I would have to find out later. Instead I had to take control. I had that weird, out-of-body feeling I sometimes got when I was about to say something I was scared to say, like the only way to get to the other side of it was to make my mouth say the words, even though the rest of me was somewhere else.

"I went to a party with Ruby," said my mouth.

Alexis smacked her hands against the table, making us all jump.

"Alexis, please," said Ronni. I'd told her everything on Sunday at the tournament, of course, so this was old news to her. I took a risk and glanced at Jamie. She was staring right at me, and I looked away.

"What happened? Whose party? David's? Was it amazing? I've never been. I *was* invited last year one time, but then I got food poisoning, remember? I honestly wanted to die. I almost went anyway but then I threw up in my garage," said Alexis.

I remembered that day perfectly, because Jamie and I had been together when Alexis had called, crying, post-vomit. Jamie had switched it over to FaceTime so we could both talk her down, and at the sight of her pale, sweaty, mascara-streaked face, we'd accidentally burst out laughing and couldn't stop. Alexis hung up on us and, eight seconds later, called us back, laughing too.

"I remember," I said. "I wish you could have been there."

Alexis smiled gratefully. "Okay, seriously. Tell us everything."

So I did, vaguely. I made my mouth say the words. Ruby texting me, me picking her up, making everyone drinks, us dancing. "It was fun," I heard myself say, like it was any old Saturday night. Somewhere far above me, I was trying to read Jamie's mind—hard enough when I was looking at her, and impossible when I wasn't.

"Did anything happen?" said Alexis.

I nodded, grinning involuntarily. "I mean, yeah. We kissed."

"Kissed, or like made out?"

I grinned harder, which gave Alexis her answer.

"Are you together?" she squealed. I nodded, and she squealed harder. I risked another glance at Jamie, who was very much focused on her cafeteria burger, so flat it was almost two-dimensional. Then she spoke.

"That figures," she said.

Instantly, I deflated. Jamie could do that to you. It didn't matter how many words she used; I'd seen her do it in one. There was a tone she had, when she found something you said so completely boring, or stupid, or predictable, that made you feel embarrassed for having ever had the nerve to be born.

I had rarely been on the receiving end, but I'd seen it done, powerfully: to some senior water polo player when we were juniors; to some random homophobe at the movie theater; to her mother, once. It was a power she used mostly for good, or at least I almost always thought it was deserved. But to me, for this? She had no right.

"What is that supposed to mean?"

She looked up, all faux surprised I cared. "Nothing. Just, I think we all saw that coming."

"It's been clear she likes you," Ronni said, looking nervously between Jamie and me. But I knew that wasn't what Jamie meant. Jamie meant that Ruby thought I'd be a fun experiment, and I was the sucker willing to go along with it.

"People are going to lose their shit," Alexis said. "Not that *I'm* going to tell them."

"It's okay," I said. "I mean, yeah, maybe don't announce it over the intercom, but like. It's not a secret."

Alexis beamed, and I could practically see the flowchart of people she planned to tell unfolding across her forehead. I'd been excited for people to know I was with Ruby, and I still was, but Jamie's comment had shaken me a little too. What if I was just revenge? What if she really was straight, and the kiss was a curiosity she now had an answer to? I knew, like Jamie knew, that we shouldn't assume anyone was straight until proven otherwise. But it was hard not to. Statistically, most people were. And though neither of us wanted to admit it, there was something in us both that was capable, in weaker moments, of black-and-white thinking, and shutting people out.

Being a good queer was exhausting sometimes. Jamie and I used to joke about all the things we could think about instead, if we were straight: tree houses, purses, baby showers, NASCAR.

There was a part of me that was still afraid. That still felt that it'd be somehow worse for Ruby to dump me for Mikey than it would be for her to dump me for another girl. But I thought of the way she'd kissed me in the bathroom at David's house, and again, later, in her bed. These were not things a straight girl did. Straight girls held your hand and hugged you too long and leaned their head on your shoulder. They took you right up to the edge of plausible deniability, and then they left you there.

This was different. I was almost positive.

Word spread in the style of wildfire: slow, then all-consuming. By Civil Liberties, the first time I even saw Ruby all day, it was obvious everyone knew. Which is not to say that everyone cared. But it seemed as if homecoming itself had provided disappointingly few good stories, and people were desperate for drama. Personally, I was more worried about Friday's school-season opener game against Granite Hills, not only because they were very good, but because, traditionally, season-opener day was also College Day, when all the seniors on the team were supposed to wear their new school's shirts to school. It wasn't a school-sanctioned tradition, and in fact Coach Swanson seemed to dislike it, probably because there were always girls who didn't have offers yet, girls who'd end up at some D-III school with a cornfield for a campus, girls who would quietly drop out of college soccer altogether. I was not supposed to be one of those iffy girls.

But the chances that I would be able to get into UNC by then—and make use of the UNC shirt collecting dust at the bottom of my drawer—were looking increasingly slim. Over email, both they and UCLA had told me they'd let me know within a week of the Beach Cup, and that week was running out. I had thought about asking Ronni to overrule our team's College Day precedent, make it in March or something, but everyone wanted to do what the seniors before us had done, and the seniors before *them* had done. And while it would be embarrassing for me to show up college shirt-less on Friday, it would be worse if Ronni moved it and everyone found out why. Which they would.

But there were four full days to get through before then, and I intended to focus on the good things, like my beautiful, perfect girlfriend, sitting across the classroom from me, beautifully and perfectly.

After class she waited for me outside the door, oblivious to the girls looking back and forth between us. I watched them over Ruby's shoulder until they stopped.

"Hi," said Ruby.

"Hi," I said. I stepped in closer so our faces almost touched. I'd never kissed a girl at school before. Jamie never let me, because school-grounds PDA was against the rules, per the student handbook, and Jamie took the student handbook very seriously, despite having successfully lobbied the administration to remove gendered language from the dress code during our sophomore year so that *no one* could wear baseball hats or skirts shorter than their fingertips fully extended. She was a very complicated woman.

I decided not to go for a kiss just yet, and instead took Ruby's hand. Then she laughed, and I dropped it like a hot plate.

"No, sorry," she said. She grabbed my hand from my side and swung it back and forth a little as we walked. "You just surprised me," she added. "It's cute." But the way she said *cute* was the way you'd say *cute* if your friend brought a metal Disney-themed lunch box to school instead of a plain paper bag, so when we reached the end of the hall I released her hand, pretending I had to adjust my backpack. I felt my great-grandfather's bracelet fall heavy against my wrist, and realized there was no way I could ask Ruby to wear it. I was embarrassed I'd ever considered it. I brushed the thought aside and pushed forward.

"Want to come over later?" I asked. "After practice?"

"I can't tonight," she said. "I've also got practice."

"Ah, okay," I said. Suddenly I felt like crying, and made a mental note to check when I was supposed to get my period. Band practice meant Ruby would be with Mikey, and even though I knew they were over, I knew how confusing it could feel to be around an ex, doing something you used to do when you were together.

"What about Thursday?" said Ruby.

Thursday felt like a million years away, but I was still relieved she said it.

"Thursday is great," I said.

"Okay, cool. Text me," she said. And then she kissed me. It was brief, barely long enough for me to smell her shampoo, but I still felt light-headed when she pulled back. I looked around to see if anyone had seen us, if any faculty member was rushing toward us to give us detention, but nobody seemed to have noticed. I was more disappointed than relieved. (If you commit illegal PDA on school property and nobody sees it, did it even happen? What's the point of so flagrantly breaking a rule if you don't get caught?)

Ruby and I said our see-you-laters, and as soon as she was out of sight I ran to the locker room, where I knew my teammates would gas me up as soon as they saw me. And I was right.

"Q, you STUD!" yelled Kate. She ran over and whipped me in the butt with her jersey.

"I don't know how you did it," said Janelle. "But I'm impressed."

"What do you mean, you don't know how?" I grinned, pointing to my face. "Have you seen me?"

Janelle rolled her eyes, and the other girls laughed and hollered over each other. It felt good to pretend I was really that sure of myself. In here, with my team, was the closest I came to feeling invincible.

I maneuvered my way over to my locker and found Ronni seated on the bench behind me, tying up her cleats.

"So did you tell them, or is this all Alexis's work?"

"Oh, Kate was texting me for confirmation by fifth period. This is all Alexis and associates."

"God love her," I sighed. My earlier worries about everyone finding out only for everything to go south were slightly ameliorated by our hallway kiss, and I only wished I had a picture for posterity, and proof. Maybe there was a security camera around there. I could check tomorrow after—*No*, I thought. *Calm down. Don't be crazy.*

"I think Jamie was upset," Ronni said, so quietly I only heard it on delay. I didn't know she could even speak at that volume. I shut my locker door and sat down next to her.

"Really?" I asked.

She nodded. "I walked to class with her after." *She feels sorry for Jamie*, I realized. Which was outrageous.

"What did she say?" In my head, totally without my permission, I heard Jamie's voice say: *I still love her. I miss her. I never should have broken up with her.* I ran my hand over my hair, like I might wipe my brain clean. Jamie would never talk like that, and I knew it.

"Nothing, really. It was just how she seemed."

I bent over to pull on my cleats so Ronni couldn't see me wilt. "I'm sure she doesn't care," I said. "She has Natalie."

Ronni shrugged. "I dunno."

"Doesn't she? Were they at homecoming together? Did Alexis say?" My heart raced suddenly. I didn't want to know. I had to know. I'd scoured Instagram for evidence after lunch and found nothing.

"She was there, but I don't know if they were there 'together,'" she said. "Alexis said it's complicated."

My eyes closed reflexively, like I could keep what Ronni had just said out. *Complicated* was not good. Complicated means there was something to complicate.

"Why'd you bring this up, anyway?" I said. "Jamie and I are friends. Like she wanted. She should be happy for me. And so should you."

"You know I'm happy for you."

"I thought I did."

Ronni stood up, annoyed with me now. "Look, I just thought you'd want to know. I know you still care."

"Not like that, I don't."

Ronni looked at me steadily, seeing right through me.

"Okay," she said. The *if you say so* was implied.

I was mad all the way through practice, and all the way home. This was not the triumphant Monday I'd envisioned. My friends didn't care that I had a new girlfriend. Apparently, the only girlfriend I was allowed to have was Jamie. Never mind that I hadn't been the one to end that—Ronni was going to make sure I felt guilty about it, as if Jamie's feelings were still my responsibility. Jamie, who went to freaking homecoming without me. (*Jamie! Homecoming.* I still couldn't believe it.) It wasn't like she was sitting at home all weekend, every weekend, crying her face off over me. She'd moved on, to another girl, to a life without me. Why wasn't I allowed to do the same?

When I got home, after I showered, while I was eating last night's reheated salmon and vegetables and once again searching all social media for photos of Jamie and Natalie together at homecoming, Jamie texted me, and I nearly choked to death on asparagus. Imagine that obituary.

Hey, she said.

I closed out of Instagram, worried she might somehow be able to see what I was doing, and waited. Forty-two full seconds went by.

We should probably get together to talk about Triple Moon stuff this week

Shit. Another thing I hadn't thought about as much as I meant to.

OK, I replied. **When?**

Tomorrow night?

Your house?

My stomach flipped. I'd assumed we'd go to Triple Moon to work on saving Triple Moon, which, in retrospect, seemed stupid. Neither of us wanted Dee or Gaby to know what we were up to until we had a legitimate plan to present to them. Jamie hadn't been over to my house in a long time, and I didn't know how I felt about seeing her there again. But I also knew how much Jamie hated having anyone over to her house, and how many questions her mom would have for her if I were to show up there again. My mom, at least, would attempt restraint. Hopefully.

Yeah, that works, I wrote. **I'll be home by 7.**

Cool, she replied. **See you then.**

She was still typing, and I caught myself holding my breath. Partly to keep myself from watching that bubble and partly because I missed her, I texted Ruby, just to say hi. Then I remembered she was at practice and felt bad for bothering her until I went to bed. I was already asleep when she replied, **hello and good night. xx.**

 *Eighteen*

The next day I got home from practice later than I hoped. As a team we'd collectively played like shit, and Coach Swanson's lecture ran us five minutes over. Then the drive home took thirty-five minutes instead of twenty, thanks to an unexplained road closure, and by the time I got home I had exactly twelve minutes to shower and make myself and my room presentable for Jamie. I showered in three, made my bed, and stared at my room from the doorway, searching for anything embarrassing I was too familiar with to see. Finally I called my mom into my room just to get a second, more judgmental set of eyes on it.

"You might wanna make your bed," she said.

"Are you kidding? I *did*!"

She gave me a rather patronizing look and crossed the

room to pull my quilt tight over the corners and fluff the pillows. Fine. It looked better.

"Anything else?"

"Nothing we can fix in five minutes."

I elbowed her in the arm, and she twisted her leg to kick me in the butt, a signature Mom move I'd outlawed in public places when I was ten.

"So she's just coming over to work on a project?" she asked.

"Yes, Mom. Nothing's happening."

"And you're okay with that?" She peered at me over the top of her reading glasses, which she kept on a beaded chain that could only be described as "funky" and which she was at least fifteen years too young for. *Maybe I'll get her a new one for Christmas*, I thought. Did they even make cool glasses chains, or was that like hoping for fashionable headgear?

"Quinn?"

"Yeah," I said, a little too emphatically. "Sorry. It's all good."

I cringed inwardly. I had never said *it's all good* before, and my mom knew it. But she let it go and retreated to her office. A minute later, at seven on the dot, the doorbell rang downstairs. Jamie took being on time very seriously.

I descended the stairs and opened the door to find Jamie with a three-paneled poster board in one hand and a bag of markers in the other.

"Oh God," I said. "Tell me we're not doing a presentation."

"No." She shook her head, stepping past me into my house. "Well, maybe. This is for us to brainstorm, but if it looks really good when we're done I'm going to want to show them."

"Dee will laugh us out of the cafe."

"Gaby won't," said Jamie. She sat cross-legged on the couch and began arranging her supplies on the coffee table, and it could have been any of the last three years, watching her work on any number of projects for which she decided a three-paneled poster board was necessary. And, if I'm being honest, I always did. On projects we did together, Jamie never let me do any visuals. She once said my handwriting looked like that of a child on cough medicine writing a letter to Santa. I wasn't even mad, but I gave her the silent treatment for as long as I could anyway, not wanting to give her the satisfaction of being right *and* funny. I lasted maybe a minute before bursting into laughter. I smiled even now.

"What?"

"Nothing," I said. "You're right."

Jamie blinked at me. "What?"

(It was possible I'd never said those words, in that order, to her before.)

"You want some water? A snack?"

"Do you have a ruler?"

"Umm. I think so. I'll look."

I went into the kitchen and opened one junk drawer after

another. (We'd started with just one—my mom liked to joke that the rubber bands and paper clips and instruction manuals and tape rolls were breeding.) Near the back of the third, under a waxy sheet with a single gold-miner stamp remaining in the corner, I found my ruler, orange plastic and rough-edged from ten years of use. I brought it and a bag of chips and two glasses of water back into the living room, where Jamie had written *SAVE TRIPLE MOON COFFEE SHOP* at the top of her poster board in pristine purple block letters.

"Purple for gay?"

"Yeah," said Jamie. "I was gonna do rainbow, but that seemed over the top." She took the water I offered her and downed half the glass in one go.

"Should you do a black outline?" I suggested.

"No."

I rested my chin in my hand, using my palm to suppress my smile. Jamie drove me crazy, and right now, for some reason, I missed it. She held a black marker in her hand, hovering over the board, and we both stared at it for a minute, waiting for the rest of the plan to fill itself in.

"I still think we should do a benefit concert," I said.

"What if we got someone famous to be the face of the campaign?" said Jamie.

"Who? Like Ellen?"

"No, not like *really* famous, but like California famous. Like Linda Weller."

"Who?"

Jamie sighed pityingly. "Our state controller?"

"I'm sorry," I said, "but I didn't know that was a thing until right now. Which makes me think she is maybe not that famous."

"Influential, then. She handles budget stuff. So she's possibly even more powerful than a high school band."

I ignored the dig. "Is she queer?"

"Does she have to be?"

"It would be nice."

"Well, sure. She could be. I don't know. She has a husband. But she refers to herself as an ally." Jamie was flustered, frustrated I wasn't immediately convinced by her brilliant idea.

"So, probably not."

"If you know of any queer, local, powerful politicians and/or celebrities who would care about the preservation of a small lesbian coffee shop, I'm all ears," Jamie huffed. She watched me think about it, looking annoyingly smug.

"Fine. I don't know anyone."

"Thank you. I'm writing down Linda Weller." Jamie triumphantly uncapped a blue marker and began drawing a large *L* in a prominent, central position on the board.

"Leave some room for other ideas, too," I said. "Like Sweets."

Jamie sighed. "Fine." After about an hour she finally finished Linda Weller's *R* and selected a new, light pink marker and wrote *Sweets* in small, barely visible letters on the right-hand panel of the board. "There."

"Are you kidding?"

"What?" Jamie sucked in her cheeks, trying not to laugh. Which made me laugh.

"You're such an ass!"

"I know. I'm sorry. I'll write over it in blue." She uncapped a new marker and traced thinly over her work. "How's that?" She was giggling uncontrollably now, leaning back into the couch; we both were.

"Barely better," I wheezed.

I pulled a leg up onto the couch, and my knee grazed Jamie's. I expected her to recoil, or move back, or otherwise remind me that we weren't allowed to even accidentally touch anymore. But she didn't. Neither of us moved, and I wondered if she could feel the inch of air between our knees crackling too. It wasn't even sexual tension, or romantic, as much as it was that I missed the ease of being near her without thinking about it.

"So how's it going, with her?" Jamie said.

At first I thought Jamie meant Linda Weller. That's how impossible it seemed that she would ask me, directly, about Ruby. I was so shocked I didn't know what to say besides, "Good. Yeah."

I knew I should feel grateful Jamie asked, that she was actually trying to be my best friend and not just my ex, but instead I felt raw, exposed. I didn't want to know how Jamie would respond to any real detail. I didn't want her to put doubt in my head. I didn't want her to be too happy for me either. It was for me to decide if I was better off now, with Ruby, than I was last year, with her. I felt silly, all of a sudden, like Jamie had seen all of this coming, and I was just following her script. But she didn't know everything. What I had with Ruby was mine, and Ruby's, and I wanted to keep it that way.

Jamie watched me, nodding slowly. "That's good," she said.

I braced myself for a follow-up question, but it never came. So I changed the topic to the first thing I could think of. "How's Natalie?"

Jamie's eyes widened so slightly nobody else would have noticed. *Success.*

"She's good," she said. A pinch, somewhere behind my rib cage. Maybe a heart attack would kill me right now. Then UNC would be sorry.

"Great story," I said.

Jamie chewed her bottom lip and fiddled with the worn, frayed friendship bracelet I'd made her when we were freshmen. The one she made me, far more intricate, had fallen off long ago, probably on some other school's soccer field, but somehow my simple three-yarn braid had held on. Dark blue, light blue, bronze: Ravenclaw colors. She looked like she was going to say something else.

It was so quiet I could hear the neighbor's dog's collar tinkling as he puttered around their yard. Even my breathing seemed cacophonous. Then Jamie cleared her throat, and I froze, watching her lean forward to grab a new marker from the pile. Still, nothing.

Just ask her again, I thought, but did I really want to know more? I didn't want to seem too eager, and I didn't want to invite follow-up questions about Ruby, either. I couldn't be mad at her for giving me exactly as much detail as I gave her. It wasn't fair. As if that ever mattered.

Finally she spoke.

"Do you think your mom would contact her for us?"

"What?"

"Linda Weller. I think we're much likelier to get a response if a reporter contacts her."

"Oh," I said. For a split second, I'd wondered why Jamie wanted my mom to call Natalie Reid. "I mean, we could ask, but she's a crime reporter. For a local paper. It's not like she's . . . Rachel Maddow!" After a brief panic in which I'd struggled to remember the name of any political journalist, I was quite pleased with myself for that.

Jamie cocked her head. "Well, no, but it's an elected office, and your mom is a constituent, which means a lot in itself. Or should mean a lot."

"Okay, so what do you suggest we do?"

"Write a letter, and have your mom send it on *Union-Tribune* letterhead."

"A letter? Why don't we just send a telegram?"

Jamie cocked her head, exasperated. Sometimes, like now, I said something just to provoke that particular head movement. It made me laugh.

"You're playing dumb, but I know you know why sending an actual letter is nice."

"Okay, okay," I conceded. "So what do we say?"

"I'll write down some themes," Jamie said excitedly. She slid off the couch to be closer to the poster board and uncapped a bright red marker. Then she turned to me expectantly.

"Gay rights!" I yelled.

Jamie laughed and wrote it down. She looked at me again.

"Ummmm."

"Small business owners?" Jamie offered.

"Ooh yeah," I said. "That's great."

We went on from there, Jamie suggesting things and me agreeing with them. My mom came downstairs after a while to get a second or seventh can of Diet Coke, and we told her about our plan. Like I had, she reminded Jamie that she was a crime reporter, and the *Union-Tribune* a small paper. But she agreed to send our letter when we'd written it. By then it was a quarter past ten, and I was starting to fade, and Jamie's week-day curfew, the last I'd heard, was ten-thirty.

"Aren't you going to be late?" I asked. The poster board was full, with various themes and bullet points surrounding Linda Weller's name in red and orange and green. In the end, the board was rainbow-colored anyway. The Sweets plan, which Jamie kept calling plan B, remained isolated and undeveloped off to the side. I'd wanted us to take it seriously, but Jamie was so excited about her idea, and I couldn't quite bring myself to ask what we'd do if it didn't work. It was strange: we'd worked on a project together just weeks earlier, but it felt like much longer ago. Something felt different now, and it wasn't just that this was a project we really cared about and the other one was homework. Something between us had started to mend. If our breakup had burned our relationship to the ground, it felt like we'd just finished work on our new first floor. It was familiar, and still us, but it was smaller, and more thoughtfully built. I felt more aware of what we were and could be to each other, when for so long I'd taken for granted that we'd always be each other's everything. It wasn't that I wasn't sad (and in fact I was pretty sure I'd cry as soon as Jamie left), but I felt lighter, too.

"Yeah, I guess you're right," said Jamie. "I should go."

I helped her clean up and took our glasses into the kitchen. She pulled on her jean jacket, and I carried the poster board out to her mom's car, which she'd borrowed for the night. I slid it gingerly into the back seat under Jamie's close observation, then stood with her next to the door.

"Okay," I said.

"I'll put together a draft and send it to you tomorrow," she said.

"Okay."

Tentatively, she raised her arms, and I did the same. We laughed, and stepped together, her arms around my shoulders and mine around the safe middle of her back. Soon I'd throw my arms around her without worrying where exactly they landed. Soon, but not yet.

It figured I would get the email on a Thursday. Historically, I *hated* Thursdays.

When I didn't have a girlfriend (which, so far, was approximately 99.5 percent of the time), there was nothing particularly special about Thursdays. Even their proximity to Fridays, and therefore the weekend, was tempered by the usual need to start *and* finish the homework and studying I'd meant to start earlier in the week, plus the nerves that settled over me the night before a big game. And lately, every game felt like a big game.

I should have been grateful, I guess, that she emailed me after practice, when the other girls were already getting in their cars and driving out of earshot. I wondered if she knew, and was trying to minimize my humiliation, or if it was just coincidence, and I was the last, least important thing on her checklist that day. An unwanted task between her and freedom.

The email read, in full:

Dear QUINN,

We are writing to let you know that all letters of intent for next season's women's soccer team have been signed, and the UNC recruitment process is now complete. Thank you for your previous interest in our program, and best of luck in your college career.

Best,

Carla Martinez

Coach, University of North Carolina

Women's Soccer

It wasn't even personal. My name was auto-filled by form, just one of who knows how many sad, hopeful seniors hoping to be the exception to the recruitment calendar we'd all had memorized since freshman year. We'd memorized the exceptions, too—the friend's sister's friend who got a full ride from Florida on Christmas Eve because a previous recruit decided a lesser offer from Georgetown was worth more if it meant she could stay on the East Coast with her boyfriend, or whatever. It was never a direct connection. I never knew these girls myself. The girls who were seniors when I was a junior all took their first offers and were set on their teams by October. If you had an offer, you could sign your letter of intent to play for that school anytime between mid-November and April of your senior year—the sooner the better, if only for College Day.

The UNC T-shirt my dad had bought for me as a freshman was clean and folded and waiting in my dresser. At the beginning of the year it had been at the top of the pile, but as the months went by it dropped lower and lower, buried beneath the shirts I actually wore. I told myself I still had hope so long as I could see that stripe of Carolina blue when I opened the drawer.

What was I going to tell my dad? I'd been deliberately not in contact, not ready to know yet if he was taking the San Diego job. Neither had he made any effort to update me. Maybe he was going to take the job, and was afraid to tell me he wouldn't be in North Carolina when I got there. The thought of having to be the disappointer rather than the disappointed was too much for me, and so I said nothing.

My mom, I thought, somewhat bitterly, would be thrilled if it meant I stayed in California. She would, of course, perform the sympathy required by a rejection like this one, but I knew she wanted to be able to drive to see me, and have me be able to drive home every long weekend we got. I wanted to be geographically excused from that responsibility, and guilt.

I didn't want the crutch—if I *could* go home easily, I feared I always would. It wasn't that I didn't think I'd miss her, but that I wanted to be somewhere new long enough to actually miss her.

Technically I could have accepted any number of recruitment offers from D-II schools on the East Coast, or even the Midwest, but then I'd have to tell my team that I was going to play on a division-two team, and they'd feel sorry for me. Even the ones going to D-II or D-III schools themselves. Some of them weren't as good as I was, or didn't care as much as I did, and planned to do other things with college life anyway, like join sororities and date frat boys. But soccer was all I had, and I had a sinking feeling that everyone who knew me knew it.

Soccer *and* Ruby, I reminded myself. She was going to Stanford. A five-hour, forty-three-minute drive from UCLA, without traffic. (Ha.) And I could visit Ronni there too.

If I got off the wait list.

Here was the one good thing about Thursdays, when I had a girlfriend: it was closing day for the *Union-Tribune,* which meant my mom stayed late at the office, scrambling with the other reporters to get the weekend edition ready for print. So at least when Ruby came over, I knew we'd have until ten at least before I had to worry about my mom waltzing in. I wasn't sure tonight was the night we'd have sex, but I wanted to, and I was pretty sure Ruby wanted to, too, and now with the news from UNC I was even more eager to focus on something that felt good. Even if it was just my body pressed into hers. Even if she just held me.

We said six-thirty, but my doorbell rang a few minutes after seven, which meant I ate half a bag of chips sitting at the kitchen table, creepily peering through the blinds for Ruby's car, which I'd learned she wasn't allowed to drive to school ever since she rear-ended someone in the parking lot junior year, causing fifteen hundred dollars' worth of damage to the bumper. This regulation didn't make a lot of sense to me, or to Ruby, who pointed out to her father that she was probably much likelier to get in a car accident outside the school parking lot, where people drove faster than ten miles an hour, but Mr. Ocampo had told her that at least those people weren't all "sixteen and hormonal." She had hoped to win her dad over by this point in the year, but so far he'd held steady, leaving her to rely on rides from bandmates or "friends" like me. Not that Ruby had a very difficult time finding someone willing to drive her wherever she wanted.

When Ruby pulled into the driveway I leapt to action, dusting chip crumbs off my pants and sucking salt off my fingers as I rolled up the bag and threw it into the cupboard. I dashed up the stairs, so that when she rang the doorbell, I'd take at least as long to answer the door as it took me to descend them. I checked my teeth and my hair in my bathroom mirror and then waited. And waited. Just as I was starting to worry, because it didn't seem possible anyone could take that long to get from the car to the front door, the doorbell rang. I casually walked down, made myself count to three, and opened the door.

"Hi," said Ruby.

"Hi," I breathed. "Sorry. I was just doing push-ups upstairs."

Ruby smirked. "Cool."

"Come in," I said, and when she stepped through the door I leaned in for a kiss. I felt like a fifties housewife, home all day, and here, at last, was my husband, the rock star. I took her jean jacket and draped it over the banister. "How was your day, sweetheart?"

There was the smirk again.

"I'm kidding. In my head it was like you were coming home after work, and I've been here waiting," I explained.

"Yeah, sorry I'm late," said Ruby.

"Oh—that's not what I meant! You're fine." I was flailing. I could feel it on my face, which meant she could see it. Why did I have to make everything so awkward? Why had I just told Ruby I was fantasizing about us living together?

Ruby looked around. "Do I get to see upstairs this time?"

"Oh, uh." I blushed. "Yeah, if you want."

She looked at me expectantly.

". . . Now?" I asked. She laughed and took my hand, and I

led her upstairs, naming each room as I went as if it weren't obvious what each one was for.

"That's my mom's room and bathroom. It's a mess. That's her office, which is also a mess. This is my bathroom, and this is . . . my room," I finished. I flicked on the light, and watched her scan the dresser, the desk, and finally the bed. Her face broke into a grin when she noticed the poster affixed to the ceiling above it, its corners reinforced with layer upon layer of graying tape.

"Is that Justin Bieber?"

"It sure is," I said. "I was so in love with him."

Ruby raised an eyebrow. "You were."

"That, or I wanted to be him," I said. "Both things, I think."

Ruby crossed the room to my bed and sat down, looking up. My stomach flipped. "You guys have kind of the same hair," she said, looking back and forth between us.

"Not a coincidence," I said, and she laughed.

I joined her on the bed, both of us facing the rest of my room, studying my things.

"So many trophies," said Ruby.

I beamed.

"There's a really good energy here," she continued.

"In my room?"

"The whole house," she said. "I like it."

We looked at each other then, our faces just inches apart. Whatever she saw, I wanted to see it, to be it. She didn't yet know I wasn't as impressive as all my trophies made me seem. She didn't yet know how lonely this house could feel with my mom and me both in it. I wanted to be her version of me. I wanted to shrink myself down and curl up in her body. I wanted her mouth on mine. I wanted—everything.

"Kiss me already," she said, so I did.

Sometime later—twenty minutes or two hours or three days, I would have believed anything—we lay upside down in bed, our feet resting on my pillow, our hands clasped and flopping back and forth in some made-up game only we knew how to play. We looked up at Justin and laughed.

"Look at that smile," said Ruby. "Perv."

"He's seen a lot," I said. Ruby raised an eyebrow teasingly. "Okay, not that much."

She laughed. "It's okay if he has. I don't mind."

It wasn't that I wanted her to be jealous, exactly, but her apparent ambivalence deflated me just slightly. Obviously she knew about Jamie. But did she think I'd hooked up with other girls here too? She was only the second. I wondered what I was to her. Then I immediately felt bad for wondering. It didn't matter, of course. Intellectually, I knew that. It was just that my brain was unavailable to me at the moment.

"What about . . . your room?" I said. I pictured waking up there, in my sleeping bag, astonished to be where I was.

"You've seen it." She grinned. "My mom is always just . . . *around*, like unnecessarily changing a light bulb in the hallway outside my room or something. Anytime Mikey came over to hang out she made me leave the door open," she said. "Other people's houses are better." I sent a silent thank-you to my mother, and to divorce, for making my modest love life possible.

"Well, you are welcome anytime," I said. "I only wish this bed was bigger." I was pressed against the wall so Ruby wouldn't fall off the edge of my twin, and my free arm was underneath me and starting to go numb.

"Here, follow me," said Ruby, and rolled onto the floor. I laughed and I followed, letting myself fall right on top of her. That led to some more making out, and I had the thought that if it weren't for food, or having to go to the bathroom, I could have lived there, on the floor, with Ruby forever. When we came up for air Ruby scanned the vast collection of crap stored under my bed, made plainly visible by the blankets we'd pushed aside.

"I wanna see little Quinn pictures," she said.

I laughed and reached over her, pointing to the plastic Disneyland album where I kept some, and she slid across the floor so she could reach it. I listened to her rooting around, pushing things out of the way—old cleats, a board game. Incredibly, it never occurred to me she might grab something I didn't want her to see. The shoebox literally and idiotically labeled BABY PICTURES did not cross my mind. My brain was still sex-fried and hazy and totally useless. I just lay there, waiting, flat on my back, comfortably sleepy and pleased with myself.

"What's this?" said Ruby, and my heart stopped cold. It was her voice: not teasing, not cooing, but confused. Smiling, but not laughing. I remembered. I sat up.

My album of photos, safe and cute, remained under the bed. Next to Ruby's legs, the shoebox. In her hand, a worn sheet of loose-leaf. I didn't have to see the front to know which one.

"'Straight Girls We Wish Weren't,'" Ruby read. "'Number one: Ruby Ocampo.'"

Slowly, I lifted my eyes to meet hers, and I was surprised and relieved to see that she was smirking, amused.

"I'm sorry," I said. "Jamie and I—we made that list ages ago. It has nothing to do with us. I wasn't trying to, like, achieve something with you. I swear."

"I believe you," she said. She scanned the rest of the list. "Indya Schoenberg? Interesting."

"Like I said. A long time ago." Ruby raised an eyebrow. "Not that I wouldn't still put you in first place," I added hastily. "I mean, I wouldn't make this list now, obviously. I don't know what I'm saying. I'm trying to compliment you, but it's not coming out right."

"Try again," said Ruby. She set down the list and leaned back against my bed frame, arms crossed. My cheeks reddened.

"You're beautiful," I said. "Even more now than . . . back then." I gestured at the list. I wished I knew magic, so I could blink and the paper would—*poof*—explode into dust. I tried it anyway. Nothing happened.

"Thank you," she said. Her arms remained crossed, I noticed.

"Are you mad?"

Ruby shook her head slowly. "No, I'm not mad." She looked at me steadily. "I just think it's funny how you guys decided I was straight."

So she's a little *mad,* I thought. Girls didn't say *I just think it's funny how* unless they were at least a little mad.

"Weren't you?" I said. "At the time?"

"I was, what. Fourteen?"

"We made it in the spring, freshman year, so probably more like fifteen," I explained, knowing full well I was losing whatever the argument here was. "You were dating that guy, Mitch." I didn't know his last name; he'd been a junior then, a shaggy, skinny stoner. Very cool, of course.

"So?" she said.

"So I guess we assumed you liked boys?" I said. I was embarrassing myself, which made me defensive. "We didn't spend a lot of time analyzing every possibility. It was just a stupid list."

"You know, there are these people who like boys *and* girls," said Ruby, like she was a teacher and I was a small, dumb child. Which was how I felt.

"I know," I said. I watched her uncross her arms and pick up the list again. *Ugh.* What was I thinking, sending her under my bed? Why had she picked this paper up, anyway? I had clearly pointed out the box of photos, now sitting forgotten by Ruby's left knee. This was supposed to be a cute moment, looking at pictures of me as a toddler tomboy, nestled into each other's necks. Instead I felt like I was on trial for something ancient and private, something meant only for Jamie and me. Surely Ruby had written things in old diaries she wouldn't want me (or anyone) to see now. That was the whole point.

"I'm not straight," said Ruby.

"I get that now," I said.

"I've known I liked girls since I was ten," she said.

I waited a moment, trying desperately to swallow a reflexive, competitive *Well, I was five.* "Who was it?"

"Maddie," she said matter-of-factly. "Of the Disney Channel classic *Liv and Maddie.*"

I laughed. "The tomboy twin. Naturally. I liked Liv."

Ruby smiled, and I felt it was safe then to scoot closer to her. I rested my hands on her bare knees. She looked down, and put her hands on top of mine.

"I'm sorry," I said. "When Jamie and I came out, we were

the only people like us we knew. Before her, I had nobody. And for so long, it felt like all *anybody* would talk about was boys. So I pretended I liked them too, all the way through middle school. I didn't think I'd ever have another option until I met her. And then, right away, I knew she was different like I was different. So we became a team: us versus everybody else."

I paused until Ruby finally looked up at me.

"It wasn't like we consciously believed we were the only girls alive who liked girls. But we *were* the only ones who were public about it, for a really long time. Even when we started the gay club." Thinking about the club made me want to cry for some reason, and I retrieved my hands from Ruby's lap, pretending to examine my nails. "Did you ever think about coming to one of our meetings?"

Ruby frowned. "This is the first time I've ever heard of a queer club at our school."

"Are you serious?" I was flabbergasted.

"Dead," she said. "Did not know that was a thing. Is it still going . . . ?"

"No," I said. "Because nobody really came. But we had flyers *everywhere*."

Ruby smiled sheepishly. "I would remember if I saw your name on something like that."

I flushed, feeling shy and shocked and defensive and strangely giddy all at once. I reached into the shoebox and pulled out a creased, bright pink Westlake GSA flyer, and handed it to Ruby.

She studied it for a moment, smiling a little. "How long did you have it for?"

"It felt like forever, but I guess it was closer to . . . two months? Ish?" I blushed. Could that be right? We had *so* many meetings, I thought. We waited for our community to find us until we couldn't wait any longer.

"I never knew," Ruby said again.

"Would you have come if you did?"

"Maybe," she said. "I might have been too scared of you guys."

"Me?!" I said incredulously.

"Yeah," said Ruby. "Well, more Jamie, but yeah."

"She is scary," I agreed.

Ruby studied my face. "She means a lot to you."

I could feel myself redden. "Yeah," I said. "So do you, though."

Ruby leaned over and kissed me softly on my jaw, sending goose bumps up my arms.

"Okay!" I said, standing up to grab a pen from my desk. Ruby watched me curiously. I sat down again, and held out my hand.

"No, don't," she said. "It's an antique."

I picked up the list myself. "It's a living document," I said. "Like the Constitution."

"Okay, Mr. Haggerty." Ruby grinned. She watched as I drew a line through the word *Straight* and then another through *We Wish Weren't.*

"There," I said.

Ruby laughed. "'Girls.' Great title."

"It's honestly more accurate this way," I said. "That's all we were thinking about."

Ruby leaned forward and kissed me on the corner of my mouth. "Thanks," she said.

"Of course," I said. "Just out of curiosity, how *do* you want me to, like, describe you?"

"Incredibly talented, brilliant, beautiful," she said, deadpan. I rolled my eyes, and she laughed. "I'm bi," she said firmly. "It's not a secret, at all. It's just that nobody ever asks."

I nodded. "Cool. 'This is Ruby, my girlfriend. She's bi,'" I said, mock-introducing her.

Ruby winced, just slightly, and my heart dropped into my gut.

"About that," she said.

"Oh no," I said, accidentally.

"No, it's okay," she said. "We hadn't talked about it yet, but I would prefer if you don't call me your girlfriend."

Oh my god, I thought. *I am being dumped for the second time in a calendar year.*

"I'm not ending things," she said, reading my mind. "I just don't like that word as applied to myself."

"Okaaay," I said.

"It's not about you," she continued. "I didn't let Mikey call me that either."

It was hard to tell how consoled I should feel. I said nothing.

"Other people said it, maybe, but he never did, and neither did I," she went on.

"But why?" I sputtered. I sounded like a baby. *Baby moron.*

Ruby puffed up her chest and held up a politician's fist for emphasis. "I'm a strong, independent woman living in the twenty-first century," she said in a deep voice that made me laugh. She smiled, and resumed her normal slouch. "Maybe when I'm in college I'll get it, but right now, at this age, it doesn't make sense to me to belong to somebody else like that."

"I get that," I said, though I didn't, totally. I *loved* to be called someone's girlfriend, and to call someone else mine. I could only imagine how I'd one day feel to say *wife.* I could make myself faint just thinking about it.

Ruby took my hand, and I looked at it, my palm pale and open in hers. "Can't we just like each other, and spend time together? You like hanging out with me, right?"

I nodded, wondering to what extent *hanging out* was the point. What she wanted sounded so simple, and impossible at the same time. But I would try. I was trying. I smiled, to prove it to her.

"I *really* like hanging out with you," I said. I leaned forward and kissed her, slowly, running my thumb across her cheek. I didn't admit it to myself then, but I was going for the kind of kiss that makes a person renounce her values and decide she loves you, and only you, after all.

When I pulled back I realized I still hadn't told her about UNC, but something about the way she smiled at me made me decide it could wait. I watched as Ruby picked up the piece of paper with her name on it, and replaced it gently inside the shoebox. If she knew what the box memorialized, and to whom it was dedicated, she treated it with respectful indifference, like the gravestone of someone who'd died long before she was born.

 # Nineteen

I woke up on College Day feeling sick to my stomach with dread. For a solid twenty minutes I contemplated various theatrics that might allow me to plausibly stay home: a fever (no—the thermometer would easily disprove it), a cough (as easy to fake as it was obvious), diarrhea (presumably wouldn't be asked to provide proof). My mom suffered fairly regular migraines, and while I had yet to inherit them, I could pretend today was the day they began. I could have the day to wallow in peace. But if I missed the game, the first of the school season, my team would be so disappointed in me, and they'd spend all night talking about it, and Ronni could only do so much to protect my shameful secret. Ultimately I decided suffering through the day was worth a paranoia-free weekend. If they were going to find out about UNC eventually (and they would), it would be better, in the long run, if they heard it from me.

So I got up, and I showered, and I got dressed in my favorite Westville Soccer T-shirt. It was from sophomore year, faded and soft, the letters of my last name partly eaten away by so many washings. That year, it had been only Ronni and me on varsity. That year, I'd had no doubt where I'd end up. Had I gotten worse since, or had I just been that wrong back then? I didn't want to know.

The night before, after Ruby went home, I'd texted Ronni to ask if I could drive her to school the next morning for moral support. When she opened the door to my truck, I handed her the box of doughnuts I'd picked up for her and the other girls—part congratulations, part distraction—and she slid into the passenger seat, selecting the powdered-sugar doughnut with lemon filling I'd picked out for her. She took a bite before gently asking which shirt I'd decided to wear.

I unzipped my bomber jacket and pulled it open at the chest. Like a superhero whose superpower was being bad at soccer.

Ronni nodded. "Good choice." She held out the box, and I grabbed a cinnamon sugar, my second so far. It was going to be a very long day, and I was grateful to Ronni for knowing I only wanted to say what I had to say to get through it.

The seniors on our team congregated in the hallway before first period, outside the captain's locker, as was tradition. The other eight were already there when Ronni and I arrived, and they shrieked and clapped when they saw me carrying my big pink box of doughnuts. Halle and Kate lunged for it, claiming their favorites before anyone else could, and I handed it over, releasing myself from the spotlight. I breathed in and out slowly, trying to slow down time, to prolong those last few moments of ignorance. Then Halle, mouth dotted with sprinkles, used her free hand to lift up her sweatshirt, showing us her crisp, white Saint Mary's shirt. Everyone cheered, and then it started, and there was nothing to be done but wait.

When it was my turn, I cleared my throat, puffed myself up to make an announcement.

"I'm excited for you all, and no offense, but I'm actually playing for the best team there is," I said. Ronni watched me with a funny look that I ignored. I unzipped my jacket slowly, and then all at once. "WESTVILLE FOREVER, BABY!" I hollered.

Janelle and Alex cheered, and a few of the other girls clapped confusedly.

"I haven't decided yet," I explained.

"You haven't heard from—" Halle started. She was interrupted by Ronni, letting her backpack fall to the floor with a thud.

"Last but not least, people!" she yelled, and whipped off her sweatshirt to reveal her Stanford T-shirt. Everyone cheered, and I gave her a small, grateful nod.

Then the first bell rang, and the few remaining doughnuts

were quickly seized. "Thanks, Q!" my teammates said, running off to class, and soon I was left with just Ronni, holding the empty, sticky pink box. I wiped at a smear of raspberry filling with my thumb and stuck it in my mouth.

"Okay," said Ronni. "The worst part is over."

I nodded, though I wasn't sure I believed her.

It started raining sometime during second period, and I spent the day shuffling between classrooms only to stare out different windows, praying, reciting the words *Please lightning, please lightning, please lightning* over and over inside my head. In order for a soccer game to be rained out, you needed lightning, or you needed such a torrential downpour that to play in it would significantly damage the field. (If you played on turf, you were out of luck.) The rain I watched was soft and pathetic, and even when it hadn't stopped by fifth period, I knew it wouldn't be enough.

So this is how the fall season ends, I thought. Damp. Gray. Collegeless.

In Civil Liberties the windows were behind me, so whenever I could I looked at Ruby instead. She teased me, batting her eyelashes and mouthing things I couldn't read. Once, she even licked her lips, and I choked on nothing. She cracked up, silently, as I tried to cover for myself by taking a swig from the water bottle in my bag. After class, she met me in the hall, looking very pleased with herself. Jamie brushed past me, turning to wave.

"See you at the game?" I asked. She and Alexis had promised they'd come, though that was before it had started raining. Jamie nodded, and patted her backpack. "I have a poncho," she explained, continuing on her way.

I grinned. Personally, I'd had no idea it might rain, but Jamie was on top of the ten-day forecast at all times. She had three different weather apps on her phone.

"I'm sorry I can't make it," said Ruby.

I turned back to face her, and she looked so cute and remorseful I couldn't help but kiss her on the nose, then the forehead, then the mouth.

"It's okay," I said. "It's gonna be miserable out there."

"Yeah, but your friends are going."

"Yes, but my friends don't have important family stuff to do, which is a really good reason not to sit in the rain." Ruby's aunt (her mom's closest sister) and her cousin, the aunt's fifteen-year-old daughter, were in town, fresh off a separation from her uncle, who'd apparently been—rather uncreatively, I thought—sleeping with his administrative assistant. As Ruby had described it, they were having a forced "girls' weekend," involving lots of spa time, delivery food, candy for the girls and wine for the adults. "A total nightmare," she'd called it.

"I honestly can't tell you which sounds worse," said Ruby. I made a mock-offended face, and she laughed.

"Can I call you after?" I asked.

"Text me," said Ruby. "I might be forced to watch *Legally Blonde* or something."

I stuck out my tongue, performing disgust (despite my actual feelings about *Legally Blonde*, which were that it was a perfect movie). I reminded myself of the conditioning experiment we'd learned about in psychology: the rat who discovers that when he pushes the lever, he gets food. I was like that rat, pushing the lever over and over and over again, but instead of food, all I wanted was for Ruby to smile. But every time I thought I'd figured out what worked, it stopped working. Ruby only sighed and checked her phone.

"I better go," she said.

"Me too." The parking lot and the locker room lay in opposite directions, so Ruby gave me a quick kiss and a wave. I stood there, counting to ten. At four, she turned around. My eyes flew to the ceiling, and I whistled, pretending I got caught. When I let my eyes drop, I saw she was smiling. *Success.*

By the time we got out to the field, the rain had slowed to a mist, too fine to see but not to feel. The mostly triumphant mood of that morning had dimmed, but rather than being comforted by my teammates' shared misery, I found it patronizing. They were going to Stanford and Florida State and Saint Mary's, or they were going to D-II schools and were thrilled about it. It didn't have to matter to them if this one game was miserable, because they knew this wasn't the end. I, meanwhile, had panic-sent another email to UCLA, asking if they were still finalizing the lineup, and I hadn't heard back yet.

"I need us to win," I muttered to Ronni, seated next to me on the bleacher.

"That's generally the goal," said Ronni.

"No," I said. "I *need* to win."

We were playing Torrey Pines, and this year they were good for the first time since I'd known them. They got ahead early with a 1-0 lead, and when the ball sailed past Halle's hand I threw up my hands and groaned like everyone else on my team. But secretly, my chest burned with excitement. I loved come-from-behind victories, and I especially loved leading them. There were girls on my team who got down on themselves at the first sign of trouble, playing badly and getting upset and playing even worse as a result. But I thrived under duress. I loved imagining the spectators underestimating me, assuming the game was over, and then watching, stunned, as I proved them all wrong.

So that's what I did. With seconds left in the first quarter, I landed a header in the bottom left corner of the goal, thanks to a perfect pass from Ronni. We clasped hands and hugged like we'd just won the game, which probably annoyed the Torrey Pines girls, but I didn't care. Ronni was so visibly proud of me. And then I scored again, barely a minute into the second quarter, and the whole team rushed me as I threw out my arms in the Pinoe power pose. I knew that they knew from this morning's anticlimactic T-shirt reveal that I needed this, and instead of letting myself feel pitied, I decided to feel grateful. I didn't know if I'd ever matter to another team the way I mattered to this one, and I wanted to live inside every second of it.

The final score was 3-2, Torrey Pines tying us shortly before a truly spectacular shot by Ronni, suspended almost horizontally in midair. Our crowd, though smaller than usual due to the weather, erupted, and our teammates boosted Ronni and me onto their shoulders like kings. Coach grabbed us each by a shoulder in her trademark death-grip congratulations, oblivious to our wincing. "Great game," she said. "That's what I like to see. Great, great work." Ronni and I beamed. When Coach was overcome with pride there were only about six words she could come up with, and she leaned on them heavily.

I grabbed my water bottle and took a big gulp as I scanned the crowd for Jamie and Alexis. I found them near the top of the bleachers, still talking intently, but then my eyes were drawn elsewhere. A woman I recognized but couldn't place was briskly working her way down the bleachers, and when she saw me looking, she waved.

"Quinn!" she called. She reached me and extended her hand. I shook it firmly, the way my dad had taught me when I was six, and then, finally, I remembered: *Lisa*. One of the assistant coaches at UCLA. Not my primary recruit contact, another assistant coach named Wendy, but I'd met her at the camp they'd invited me to last spring.

"Hi, Lisa," I said. "Wow. I was not expecting you. I'm sorry the weather is so bad," I added, for some reason.

Lisa waved me off. "Not at all," she said. We both blinked back drizzle, and she laughed. "I mean. It is bad. But I don't mind."

But what are you doing *here?* I thought. I worried I'd said it out loud, because she continued, "Wendy wanted to be here, actually, but something came up, so she sent me."

"Ah," I said. "That's okay." I couldn't breathe.

"We wanted to let you know you're off the wait list." Lisa grinned. "We would love for you to play for us."

Much to my surprise, and Lisa's, I found myself suddenly crying. Everything I'd been feeling for months, all my doubting and dreaming and disappointment and pride, all the games I'd won and lost, the nights I went home sore and skinned and bruised, the teammates I'd watched grow up and leave and the ones who were still here, who'd been with me all along, the ones I couldn't imagine being without—all of it rushed to the surface and streamed down my face.

Lisa, looking concerned, gave me a kind pat on the shoulder.

"I'm sorry," I managed to say. "I'm really happy." Unexpectedly, I meant it. And it wasn't just relief that I'd gotten in *somewhere* (though that was part of it). Maybe UCLA wasn't my first choice, and I wasn't theirs, but that didn't mean we couldn't be great for each other. *Maybe I was wrong about what it was I wanted*, I thought. The possibility flickered through me, a series of unending question marks. It didn't scare me like I thought it would. It felt like being forgiven.

"Good," she said. "No need to apologize. This is a really stressful time for all of you. I hope this helps."

I nodded, struggling to hold back more tears. "It does. Thank you."

"Okay," said Lisa, giving me another gentle smile. "I'm off. But we'll have a formal offer to you shortly."

Not seconds after Lisa left, I felt Ronni's firm grip on my shoulders. Much of the rest of my team loitered behind her, trying and failing to look otherwise occupied.

"Was that . . . ?"

I nodded. Ronni screamed. She picked me up, and the team I loved rushed to fill every inch of space around me.

Twenty

I called my dad from the floor of my bedroom, where I wedged myself between my closet's two open doors. This was where I conducted my hardest phone calls: my coming out to Ronni; my first real fight with Jamie; all the times the love of my middle school life, Cara, called to cry about her boyfriend. With my back pressed to one door and my feet against the other, I felt solid and supported. I took a deep breath and counted each ring, hoping he wouldn't answer, hoping he would.

"Quinnie, hey!"

I exhaled. "Hey, Dad."

"I've been meaning to call you."

"Oh yeah?" *What stopped you?* I thought.

"Yeah, so listen. Good news."

I closed my eyes. *Shit.* "Wait—"

"I'm staying put. The job out there . . . I'm not gonna take it," he said. "I like it here. I'm used to it. And I want to be here for you."

He sounded so proud and so excited. He'd done the right thing and he wanted me to be grateful. I was, but not for the right reason. I didn't want him here, I realized. I felt guilty just thinking it.

"Dad," I started again. "UNC turned me down."

Silence. I ground hard against the closet door, watching my toes turn white with pressure.

"What did they say?"

"Not much."

"I'm gonna give them a call—"

"Dad, no," I said. "It's done. I don't want to go."

"What do you mean?" he asked, incredulous. "You've wanted this for ten years."

For a long time, I thought, *I did.* But when I'd started wanting it, I was a little kid, and then I kept wanting it because I'd wanted it for so long already, and soon it became part of my story. I believed it completely, and maybe that meant it was true. What was the difference between wanting something and wanting to want it? Of course I'd hoped they would want me. If they had, I'd have gone happily. But they didn't, and it felt okay. I felt happy where I was, and where I was going. It was exciting, and scary, to realize I wanted something I hadn't expected to want.

But I didn't say any of this. That was a conversation I could have with my mom, but not my dad.

"I know," I said. "I'm sorry."

I paused, waiting for him to tell me there was no need to apologize. He didn't.

"UCLA is making me an offer, and I'm going to take it," I continued.

"What about Baylor?"

Anger radiated through me. "I was never going to go to Baylor," I said evenly. "Ever."

"I understand," said my dad, softer now. "I just want you to be happy."

This was half wish, half warning, the implication—*I don't know if you can be happy if you stay in California, if you aren't on the very best team, if you don't become the person I hoped you would*—just barely below the surface. I ignored this half. I wanted to get on with my day.

"I am happy, Dad," I said. "But I've gotta go, okay?"

"Okay," he said. "Come visit me sometime?"

This was his line, meant only as much as he'd be pleased to see me if somehow I showed up without any work or disruption involved. For once, I was okay with that, and I recited my line, meaning it just as much.

"I will," I said. "I promise."

* * *

Every year on Black Friday, my mom insisted we go shopping at "the nice mall," which was fancy, and outdoors, and had rich-people stores like Prada and Rolex. It was a tradition that arose when I was a kid: my mom dragged me along on her search for deep, deep discounts, and as a form of repayment for my boredom, finished the trip in See's Candies, where I was allowed to fill a four-piece box however I wanted.

As soon as I saw the first billboard for the mall I started salivating, craving raspberry truffle and Scotchmallows. Still, I decided then and there that I wouldn't ask my mom to buy me See's, or bring it up unless she did, and I felt proud of myself for my maturity.

"So when do you think UCLA's gonna send their offer?" my mom asked. I watched as she changed the radio channel once, and then again, and then a few more times, before finally turning it off with a dismissive wave of her hand.

"I can set up music streaming for you," I said for the eighty-seventh time. "It's not hard."

"I like being surprised," she said.

"They have radio, too," I reminded her. "Like, based on music you actually like."

My mom shrugged. She didn't say what I knew she was thinking, which was *Yeah, but I like to complain.* "I asked you a question," she said.

"I don't know," I said. "Hopefully soon."

She glanced over at me. "How are you feeling about it?"

I knew she meant not just UCLA, but all of it—UNC, the dashing of my childhood dreams, having been wait-listed, et cetera.

"Good, surprisingly," I said. "Better than I thought I would."

"Have you thought more about what you might want to study?" My mom asked this question so gently I immediately stopped feeling annoyed and instead wanted to hug her. I'd been such a brat about school for so long, as if it were rude for a mother to suggest her kid might want to learn something in college. I'd taken it for granted that soccer would be my thing, and that whatever I studied hardly mattered so long as I maintained the 3.0 GPA necessary to stay on the team. The point was not the degree. The point was to be noticed by the national team. My face flushed with shame and panic as I realized, right then and there, that I might not make the national team. I turned to the window, leaned my forehead against the window's cool glass. I stared at myself in the side mirror and was comforted a little by how good I looked there. *Why don't I ever look like that straight on?*

"Quinn," my mom said.

"I'm thinking."

"I'm not saying I don't think you'll play professionally," said my mom, apparently reading my mind. "But I think it's worth exploring some other interests."

"I don't have any interests," I said.

My mom laughed. "That's not true."

"I don't know how I'm supposed to pick the right thing to get me the right job for the rest of my life when I haven't even had a job before," I said. Embarrassingly, my eyes welled with tears, sprung out of nowhere.

"You're not. Nobody gets a job in their major. You know that, right?"

I sniffed. I did not know that. "Everybody is acting like they will," I said. "Alexis is doing international business so she can be a fashion buyer for Saks Fifth Avenue." It was easy for me to remember this because she had been reminding us once a month for the last three years.

My mom snorted. "Good luck to her with that."

"Mom!"

"Sorry," she said. "I'm just saying, nobody knows what they're doing. You just pick something you like. It's great if it's something practical. I would prefer you don't pick, like, ceramic arts. But if it turns out you're really good at it, great!"

"I doubt it."

"You're going to have lots of jobs in your life. Even if soccer is the first one, it won't be the last."

"Yeah, but if it *is* the first one, I can make enough money off sponsorships to be rich forever," I said.

"Maybe that's true for the men's league, but . . ."

"Good point," I said. We both took a moment to shake our heads at systemic sexism. By then we were pulling into the mall parking lot, and we were silent while my mom circled the lanes about a dozen times until she found the perfect spot. There was something else I wanted to say, and I knew that if I let her get out of the car, I wouldn't say it. Outside, in the open air, I would feel like a traitor for speaking critically about my dad, but here in her car, my mom had cracked something open in me, and the wall of protection I kept around him fell away.

"Dad really made me feel like shit the other day," I said.

My mom froze, unbuckled seat belt still in hand.

"I mean, it wasn't *that* bad," I added reflexively.

My mom let the seat belt go and sat back. "About UNC?"

"Yeah," I said. "How'd you know?"

She gave me a look that said: *I was married to the guy, wasn't I?*

"Yeah, okay," I said. "Anyway. He pretty clearly thinks it's over for me. He even threatened to call them."

"Okay, well, that's not going to happen," said my mom. "I'll make sure of that."

I gave her a sideways glance. She looked so righteously pissed off it was hard not to smile.

"He probably wouldn't anyway," I said. "He always says he's going to start petitions for things and he never does that, either."

"He means well," my mom said. Whether she meant it or felt she had to say it because divorced parents weren't supposed to try to get their kids to take sides, I wasn't sure. Either way, it annoyed me. What I wanted more than anything was for a side to be taken: *mine.*

"Well, it didn't feel that way," I said. "He couldn't have cared less about UCLA, even though they've been very nice to me. All he heard was 'I didn't get an offer from UNC, so I'm not moving out there, because I am just a big, gay disappointment.'"

"Hey," my mom said, grabbing my wrist. "You are not a disappointment. Especially not for being gay."

"I know *you* don't think so," I muttered. *Here come the freaking tears again,* I thought. I looked down and tried to blink them back.

"Neither does your dad," she said. "He's just . . . He wanted you close by, is all. He missed you. But he made it so much about school for so long that he forgot how to express that to you in a way that doesn't make you feel bad."

I considered this for a moment.

"That's a generous interpretation," I said.

"I know," she said, which made me laugh. For a few minutes we were silent, watching other mall-goers cross in front of our parking spot, listening to their muffled chatter.

"Parents are just people, Quinn," my mom said. "And people fuck up. A lot."

I smirked. "What about you?"

"Me? I'm perfect," she said. She opened the car door and stepped out. "Let's go get some chocolate."

A few days later, I sat alone at a table at La Posta, cradling a small box of See's in my hand like a baby bird. Five minutes after my mom bought me my own, I decided I should also buy one for Ruby, seeing as our two-month anniversary was coming up. Not that either of us had called it that, or chosen a day. But I did the math, and today was two months to the day after she first kissed me. On the cheek, but still. It was the moment I knew for sure that there was something between us, and I wanted us to celebrate it. Our texting had been erratic lately, and though I knew she'd been busy with family, and I'd been preoccupied with soccer and the Save Triple Moon campaign, I still worried something was wrong. So I'd suggested a dinner date, at "our" spot, and picked up a long-stemmed rose to go with my chocolates. I offered to drive, but Ruby was granted permission to use her car, so we agreed to meet at seven, by which time I was starving. I arrived ten minutes early and ordered a horchata, and it was gone by the time Ruby walked in at 7:02. I watched her scan the restaurant for me. She found me, and smiled, and then her eyes dropped to the rose sitting on the table in front of me. I knew right then that I'd made a mistake. I dropped my hands below the table, hiding the chocolate in my lap.

"Shit," she said when she reached the table, still wincing at the rose. "What did I forget?"

"Oh, nothing," I said, laughing. "It's our 'two-month anniversary,'" I explained via air quotes, and Ruby relaxed. "This is just from Ralphs," I said, gesturing at the cellophane-enclosed rose, which now looked sad-tacky instead of cute-cheesy, the way it had looked to me in the store. Maybe it was the lighting.

"Well, thank you," said Ruby. "Happy 'anniversary.'" She leaned across the table to kiss me, perhaps out of pity, I thought. But then, no. The kiss was warm and reassuring, and just long enough to make the family two tables over stare.

"What do you want? I'll order. You can hold down the table," I said, slipping the candy box into my jean-jacket pocket.

"Let me get it this time," said Ruby. She quickly stood up, and my cheeks burned a little. I liked seeing myself as the gentleman, the one who took care of things. Jamie had put considerable effort toward coaching me out of it, but with Ruby I'd resumed the habit. She'd never stopped me, or tried to pay, until now.

She's just being egalitarian, I told myself. *That's a good thing. You're a feminist. Plus, she has more money than you. By a lot.*

"Okay," I said shakily. "I'll have the number four. Thank you."

"You got it," she said, grinning. I watched her cross back into the entryway and place our order, grateful her back was facing me so I could take a series of very deep breaths and mess with my hair in my front-facing camera. *It's fine,* I told myself. *It's fine it's fine it's fine. It was weird for a second, but you made it into a joke, and now everything is fine.*

Ruby carried our tray of food back to the table, and when she set it in front of me I searched her face for clues. She mostly looked hungry.

"I've thought about this burrito once a day since the last time," said Ruby. She took a big bite and chewed contemplatively.

"Is it still as good?" I asked.

"Almost," she said.

My shoulders slumped. "Just *almost*?"

"For me, that's really good," she said. "I usually hate going back to places I loved because it's never as good as I remember."

"Restaurants or, like, all places?"

"I meant restaurants, but I guess it's other stuff too," she said before taking another big bite. "Like, I think it's weird when families go on the same Hawaii vacation every year. Or Disneyland." Ruby made a face, and I flushed, picturing the refrigerator at home, covered with photos of my mom, my aunt, my uncle, and my cousins and me at Disneyland, when they were young teenagers and I was the eight- and nine- and ten-year old kid trying desperately to match their pace and hear everything they said.

"I don't know," I said slowly. "I think it's comforting. I know

it's for kids, but I still like Disneyland. I know where everything is and which rides to do when so the lines are shorter."

Ruby smiled. "That was just an example."

"I think I've watched *The Two Towers* at least fifty times,"
I said.

"Really?"

"Five times a year for the last ten years? Yeah. Easily."

"Isn't that movie, like, eight hours long?"

"The extended version is four," I said. "You have to watch
the extended version. The theatrical leaves a lot of important
things out."

"I guess I should watch it, then," said Ruby. "I liked the
first one."

I nodded and took another bite. I didn't know what I was
doing, but I couldn't seem to stop. I might as well have brought
my various elementary school art projects with me, worn my
retainers and zit cream, dressed in my Grinch pajama one-
sie. All I knew was that I was both tired and high on sugary
horchata, and I found that the part of my brain typically dedicated to self-restraint and self-monitoring wasn't working.
So when she asked me about soccer, and college, I told her
everything: every tiny, revealing, half-formed feeling. I told
her about my dad, and then my mom, and what my mom had
said about my dad. Ruby didn't say much, but she listened,
and that was what I needed most. When I felt close enough

to empty, I asked how *she* was feeling about everything, about school and Sweets and Stanford, and she shrugged.

"Honestly, I can't wait to go," she said.

My chest twinged, even as I realized this had also been my attitude toward college, for three years running, up until now, when it was actually about to happen. I'd never meant to hurt my friends when I told them I couldn't wait to be in college, but now, on the other side of it, I saw how it could feel. Ruby must have seen it in my face because she quickly added, "Not that I won't miss home. Or you."

I knew it was too early to say what I was about to say, but as soon as I had the thought, it was too late. It was happening.

"Would you still want to do this long distance?" I asked my burrito, too scared to look up. When what felt like a full minute passed, I had to.

"That's, like, eight months away," she said softly.

"I know," I said. "I'm jumping the shark."

"Jumping the gun," said Ruby.

"That too," I said. She laughed.

"You know I like you," she said. "A lot."

I blushed, wishing someone—the whole school?—was there to hear that part only, before the implied "but" that followed. "I like you a lot, too," I said softly.

Was it more than that? Was I falling in love with her? Two days earlier, picking out chocolates at the store, I would have said yes, definitely, I was well on the way. Thinking about her gave me butterflies, and wasn't that the primary symptom? But now, with the chocolate growing warm in my pocket, knowing Ruby would likely never love me—at least not enduringly, cross-geographically, singularly, and openly—it was harder to summon the feeling. And shouldn't it be easier to feel butterflies when the person responsible for them is right in front of you?

"I can still come over, right?" Ruby smiled at me and winked, more and more exaggeratedly until I laughed.

"I want you to," I said. Then I slipped my hand into my pocket and pulled out the box of chocolates. Ruby's dimples appeared behind the fist propping up her chin. "I may have gotten you dessert."

The recognition that this was yet another two-month anniversary gift hung between us, as did the recognition that its original meaning had changed. We both understood. We didn't have to say it.

Ruby lifted the box gently, the red print of her knuckles spread across the bottom of her face like a rash. I wanted to reach over and wipe it off, like ketchup at the corner of her lips. But it didn't work that way. I watched her open the box and select a milk chocolate caramel, then drop it into her mouth. She groaned softly. "I *love* See's," she said. She reached across the table and took my hand in hers. "Thank you." With her free hand she pushed the box back toward me, and I chose the raspberry truffle. I took the smallest bite, worried it would be ruined for me now, tainted by its involvement in an over-the-top, ill-conceived romantic gesture. But it wasn't. It tasted just as good as it always did. I licked the chocolate off my fore-finger and thumb, wishing I had twelve more.

Twenty-One

Two days later, Jamie texted me.

I got a letter from Linda Weller.

A pause.

. . . the controller? she added.

I know that now, thank you, I wrote back. I admit it had taken me a minute to remember, partly because I'd never expected we'd get a response.

What does it say?

I haven't opened it, Jamie wrote. **I'm too nervous.**

Seriously?

Meet me at Triple? We can read it together.

You're not worried they'll catch on?

It feels lucky to open it there, she wrote. **If it's good news I want to tell Dee and Gaby right away.**

OK, I wrote, growing excited in spite of myself. What if

Linda Weller really *did* save the coffee shop? What if there were some grant for small businesses that this opportunity was perfect for, and we reached her just in time? What if Dee and Gaby were so happy they cried, and named drinks after us, and maybe put up a plaque with our names on it, and left us the coffee shop after they retired? I ran upstairs to change out of my winter-break uniform of sweatpants and pit-stained T-shirt and to brush my teeth, and then I flew out the door.

When I walked into Triple Moon, Jamie was already there, seated at the table farthest from the counter, jiggling both knees so hard her iced latte shook. When she saw me she waved jerkily, and I mentally replayed so many moments in which Jamie, mid-grand plan, went haywire. When Jamie had an agenda, her brain stayed measured and sharp, but her body turned radioactive with directionless energy, causing anything from large food spills (see: the jumbo-popcorn incident at the Hillcrest movie theater sophomore year) to minor injury (see: the time she decided to run for class president and leapt triumphantly from the third-to-last stair in front of school and sprained her ankle). (She lost.)

I made a note to grab extra napkins and went to the counter, which Dee reached over to give me a one-armed, brotherly hug.

"You baby dykes get a girlfriend and fall off the face of the earth," she said, seeming more proud than annoyed. I bristled, wondering if Jamie had heard, and then wondering why I cared.

"She's not really my girlfriend," I said, shrugging. I swore I could feel eavesdropping rays extending from Jamie's ears to the back of my head, the way it looked in cartoons. I lowered my voice, just in case. "It's more of a casual thing."

Dee nodded, clearly not believing me. "Sure," she said. "Isn't it always." She started some milk under the steamer, preparing my drink. Gaby appeared from around the corner, and when she saw me she gave me a defeated wave.

"Everything okay?" I asked, even though I knew it was not.

"Everything's fine," said Dee.

"You don't have to baby them," said Gaby. She stepped in closer to me, blowing wine breath in my face as she spoke. "We're a little . . . a lot behind on some payments," she explained.

My shock was only half feigned; I hadn't expected either Gaby or Dee to confide in us so frankly, and it was clear from Dee's expression as she plunked my drink on the counter that she hadn't either.

"Gab," she warned. "Quinn has her own shit to deal with." She filled a mug with black coffee from the drip and set it on the counter, nudging it meaningfully toward Gaby. Just the sight of it seemed to straighten Gaby out.

"She's right. I'm just having a day." She looked over my

shoulder at Jamie, and my eyes followed. Jamie immediately returned to her phone, texting or pretending to. Then I felt a buzz in my back pocket and realized she was texting me. I pulled it out and read: **What's happening??**

I slid my phone back into my jeans. "This is kinda unrelated, and I definitely don't want to stress you guys out, but we were wondering if we could finally schedule that second Sweets show," I said quietly.

"What?" said Dee.

I cleared my throat and leaned closer. "Another Sweets show? We could charge more for tickets this time."

"When?" said Gaby. "We have limited hours over the holidays."

I chewed my lip. Probably I should have had a date in mind before I proposed a show. Jamie was going to kill me, for several reasons. "Let me get back to you on that," I said.

Gaby nodded distractedly and took a big sip of her black coffee. She made a face, and Dee tossed three Splenda packets onto the counter for her. Gaby grimaced gratefully. I grabbed my latte and made a beeline for Jamie, wanting to let them have their moment. It was strange, the things you learned about a person when you loved them, and how you kept that trivia always, even as that person moved in and out of your life. I could only assume I would always know that Jamie wanted her Diet Coke in bottle form, with a straw (but only if it was reusable), and while I'd found these sorts of artifacts endlessly depressing when we first broke up (because Diet Coke was everywhere, the color blue was everywhere, our songs were played everywhere), seeing Dee know Gaby that well, and that specifically, felt reassuring to me.

I sat across from Jamie, who glared at me, her lips tightly pursed.

"I know you saw my text," she hissed, trying not to move her mouth.

I laughed, like she had to know I would. Her outraged ventriloquist-dummy impression always got me. "I did. I'm sorry. I thought it could wait thirty seconds."

"So?"

I looked over my shoulder. Gaby had disappeared into the office and Dee leaned against the back counter, reading a paperback until the next customer came in. Which, on a weekday at three-thirty in the afternoon, could take a while.

"Nothing we didn't already guess," I said. "Behind on payments."

"Is Gaby . . . ?"

I nodded. "A little. Dee gave her coffee."

"I saw."

Just then I noticed the envelope from the office of Linda Weller on the table between us, turned upside down from Jamie so that I could read it.

"Am I opening this, then?" I asked. Jamie nodded. I could

feel her legs jiggling in the seat of my chair as I ripped open the envelope.

"'Dear Jamie,'" I read.

> As you may know, my husband, Greg, has owned an independently operated plumbing company for seventeen years. From him, and from many other constituents like him, I've become deeply familiar with the challenges inherent to running a small business. That's why, as a city councilmember for San Diego, I voted in favor of a "head tax" for massive corporations like Amazon, which would require those who benefit from such monopolies to give back to the city, allowing its elected officials to address vitally important local issues like small-business grants, affordable housing, and green energy.
>
> As state controller, my role is to assess those areas of government spending that can be trimmed, as well as those that need more attention. The state of California is the sixth-largest economy in the world, and, in recent years, policy decisions at the national level have presented us with a number of challenges. While I wish I could attend to the needs of every business and organization our great state has to offer, my responsibilities are limited to those funded by taxpayer money. I believe that a healthy, equitable economy begins with an accountable

government, and it is my honor to serve my constituents in that capacity.

Thank you for your interest in—and dedication to—small business, one of California's greatest assets.

Sincerely,

Linda Weller

I finished reading and brought the letter close to my face, trying to decide whether the black inked signature was real or stamped. I licked a finger and dragged it across her last name, and the *W* smeared down the page.

"At least she really signed it?" I said.

Jamie blinked at me. "She didn't even write the words *Triple Moon*," she said.

"Yeah."

"She didn't even say *coffee shop*."

"I know."

"That could have been about anything."

"I'm sorry, Jame."

She took the letter from me and gave it a once-over, maybe hoping I'd missed a paragraph or two. She even flipped it over, just in case there was a secret message on the back.

"It's not like I thought she'd send us a check," she started. "But I expected something more than this."

"I know," I said. "Me too."

"Like, I'm not 'interested in small business,' the concept," said Jamie. Her expression was so adorably disbelieving, and her tone so aggrieved, that I couldn't help but laugh. For an instant she looked angry, and then she started giggling too. "And who cares about *Greg*?"

"Not me."

Jamie picked up the letter again, pinching her fingers at the top, poised to tear it in half.

"Wait—don't," I said. "You might want that someday."

"For what?"

"Maybe in fifteen years you'll run for office, and you can use it to show people how long you've been dedicated to small business."

Jamie smiled, seemingly in spite of herself, and folded the letter in half, flattening the crease with her teal-painted thumbnail. Then she carefully placed it between the pages of her planner and pushed it aside. "Now what?"

It was obvious she was disappointed, more so than she was willing to talk about with me right now, but she was also determined, and if plan A didn't work, I knew she'd scramble to find an alternate plan B that didn't involve any suggestion of mine. Fortunately, I'd planned ahead.

"I may have asked Dee and Gaby if they'd let us do another Sweets show," I said carefully.

"When, just now?"

"Yeah."

"Before we even opened the letter," said Jamie. It wasn't a question. I realized then what I'd dug myself into.

"Well, yeah," I said. "But not—I wasn't—"

"You assumed my idea would fail," she said.

"No!" I protested. "If anything, I assumed the opposite. If anyone could have gotten the control lady to send us money, it's you."

"Controller," said Jamie.

"It's just a very menacing title for what it is."

Jamie's mouth twitched, out of what, I couldn't tell. She closed her eyes and took a deep breath: usually a bad sign.

"Did you already promise Ruby?"

"No. I swear. I don't know if they'll even be able to do it."

"Too busy recording the next album? *Gimme Glucose*?"

"I know you're joking, but that is a perfect title for them."

Jamie allowed herself a brief moment of smugness, then turned stony-faced once more.

"Anyway, you're the true Sweets fan here," I continued. "Remember?"

"Not so much anymore." Jamie's eyes dropped when she said this, and my stomach flipped. This was no longer about a benefit concert, or Triple Moon. She was leading me somewhere I hadn't planned to go, and in fact had been avoiding for months, but I couldn't not follow her there now, and it seemed like she knew that.

"Because of me?" I asked.

Jamie looked at me but did not answer.

"You broke up with me," I said. "I'm not sure what right you think you have to be mad about this."

"You basically didn't give me a choice," she said softly, her eyes darting to the counter to make sure Dee wasn't looking our way. Mine followed, but Dee was still deep in her book.

"Are you suggesting I asked you to dump me?"

"Indirectly." Jamie shrugged. "Yeah."

I thought I might pass out, even hoped I would, so I could wake up hours from now, in a hospital, on some soothing IV drip with endless Jell-O on a tray at my side, this conversation forgotten and everyone I knew just relieved to see me alive. A dizzying wave did pass over me, as if summoned, but I didn't fall. I was still there and so was Jamie and it was my turn to say something but my mouth was too dry and I couldn't think. Jamie suddenly stood up and went to get me a glass of water from the dispenser by the milk and sugar. She returned and placed it in front of me.

"I'm sorry," she said. "Drink this. Take a breath."

As much as I wanted to refuse, cover my mouth or make a scene if I had to—anything to avoid doing what Jamie told me to do—I took the glass and drank, because I didn't want to feel like this anymore and I knew Jamie was right. Since I'd known her, she'd seen me through a half dozen panic attacks and even more low-grade anxious episodes, and by now she was as close to an expert in Quinn Ryan freak-outs as someone without a therapist's license could be.

"Put your forehead on the table and breathe," Jamie instructed. I hesitated, and she gave me her signature *just do as I say* look. I lowered my head to the table and was instantly comforted by the cool, hard Formica.

"I'm going to touch the back of your neck, okay?" Jamie's voice came to me from above, and I could feel her leaning closer to me. I knew we might look crazy, and if Dee saw us she might call over to ask what was wrong. I knew that to let Jamie touch me that way was to give in to a kind of intimacy we hadn't shared since we broke up. I didn't know if that was allowed. I didn't know if Ruby would care. I knew that once Jamie offered, it was the only thing I wanted.

"Okay," I said, and Jamie's palm was smooth and cool and firm, reminding me I was alive, in a safe place, with someone I loved.

I do still love her, I thought. *Maybe I always will.* Maybe the love would change shape and maybe someday it would be much smaller, a marble I rolled around in my mind when I was old and hadn't seen her in years. I didn't know if I believed in God or destiny, but knowing Jamie, having this exact person in my life at this exact time, felt like more than lucky coincidence.

"Tell me what you meant," I said. Jamie's hand tensed on

my neck and then lifted. I sat up again, faintly surprised the sun was still out.

Jamie cleared her throat and took a sip of watered-down coffee, all the while avoiding my eyes. She was silent for what felt like ten full minutes, and just as I was about to prod her, she looked at me and spoke.

"You were always going to leave me," she said. "From the minute we got together, or maybe even before—and I just didn't notice because I liked you so much—you were fixated on the future. And in your future, you moved across the country and became a national soccer star, and it was clear I wasn't there."

I felt a knot form in my chest and descend to my stomach. My face got hot and my ears rang. All the signs were there: I'd been called out, caught doing something wrong even if I hadn't fully realized I was doing it. Though part of me had known. I had to have known. Because I knew instantly that Jamie wasn't wrong to have felt that way. I'd looked so far ahead for so long that I'd forgotten she was there with me, then, in the present. Now past. First I was too early and now I was too late.

"It wasn't like I planned to break up with you right before college," I said. "It wasn't, like, oh, I can't wait to meet a different girl at school."

"I know," said Jamie.

"Do you?"

She shifted in her seat. "I think putting it that way trivializes my point. You're making it out to sound like I was just this jealous, insecure girlfriend."

The knot kicked around my stomach, called out once more.

"I'm sorry," I said. "I didn't mean it like that. But it's not like it didn't occur to me that *you* might meet someone else at school."

"Like who?" Jamie looked at me incredulously, as if it were impossible there could ever be anyone else, and a warm, buzzing electricity shot through to my toes.

"We're not always gonna be the only queer girls we know," I said. "We already aren't."

Jamie flushed, and I knew we were both thinking of Ruby, and Natalie, too. All the things we did and didn't want to know. "You think that's why we got together? Just, we're both gay? That's a little homophobic."

"Is it really homophobic, or is it more heteropatriarchal? Something-normative?"

"You're being a brat," she said.

I was quiet because I knew she was right, but I wasn't about to let her know that.

"Okay," she sighed. "I'm gonna move past that, because I know that's not really what you think. I know you loved me."

I noted the past tense, and a small but insistent part of me cried out, wanting to correct it, but I was petrified. You don't tell the girl who dumped you that you still love her four months later. That's not how you retain the little dignity you have left. It wasn't fair of her to put me in the position to correct her, and it wouldn't be fair to Ruby if I did. So instead I said nothing.

"All I meant," Jamie started again, "was that we always had an expiration date, as girlfriends. And if you know that, why wait around for it?"

I looked down at my lap just in time to pretend Jamie couldn't see the tears sliding down my face. As embarrassed as I was to be crying here in public, in front of her, I was also relieved. The thing I'd most wanted to avoid doing in front of Jamie post-breakup was happening. It couldn't get any worse. And knowing *that* made me free. I wiped my cheeks with my sleeve and looked up.

"I was planning trips," I said. "I was gonna meet you in New York so we could take a bus to DC and see all the government buildings and statues and stuff." It was Jamie's turn to look away, dropping her gaze to her favorite clicky pen. We both watched her thumb wedge its way under the pocket clip and turn red.

"Quinn," she said. "I didn't even apply to NYU. I haven't wanted to go there for more than a year."

"What?" I said dumbly. "Since when?"

"I just told you—"

"Yeah, okay," I said. "I got it."

I ran through my memory, certain it was full of Jamie-made

proclamations like "Next year at NYU" or "When I'm a fresh-man at NYU, not long from now" or "I, a seventeen-year-old, can't wait to go to college in New York." But I couldn't find one. How was this possible?

"We talked about this," I said. "We were both going to be on the East Coast."

"*You* talked about it," Jamie countered. "If I agreed with you once in a while it was vaguely, and it was only because I didn't know what I was going to do, and it was easier to go along with your imagination than to tell you mine was blank."

"So you just let me believe something that wasn't true."

Up until that point I'd felt mostly sorry, and confused. I was willing to admit I'd spent too much time in my head, but at least I'd been honest about where I thought I was going. How was that so much worse than what Jamie had done, pretend-ing that what I imagined for us was still possible? Suddenly it all felt like her fault: not just the dumping-me part, but me not getting into UNC, and me failing to properly move on with Ruby. In that moment even Triple Moon's money problems fell under Jamie's terrible, dream-killing reign.

"It wasn't *un*true," Jamie said gently. "I just wasn't as sure of everything as you seemed to be."

"I get it," I snapped. "I'm delusional."

Jamie sighed, giving me a look I couldn't quite read. "You're a romantic."

I felt my face reddening, but I pressed on, determined not to let her lessen my anger. "And that's a bad thing?"

"It's not inherently bad or good," said Jamie. "It's just a thing about you."

A dull throbbing had started on the right side of my head, and I pressed uselessly at it with my fingers. *Maybe I* am *starting to get migraines,* I thought. *Great.* I dug in my bag for my travel-sized aspirin bottle and swallowed two with what remained of my water.

"I'm not feeling very well, so maybe we can talk about this later," I said.

"Oh," said Jamie. "Uh, okay. Are you okay driving home?"

"Yeah, I'm fine. It's just a headache." I got up to put my water glass in the dirty-dish bin and returned to the table, not sitting but standing over it, willing myself to say what I knew I needed to. Jamie watched me expectantly.

"I'm sorry I didn't listen," I started. My voice shook a little, and I hoped that somehow Jamie didn't notice. But of course she did. "I'm sorry I didn't make it clear that you mattered more to me than UNC did, or soccer in general. Because you did. I mean, you do." As I corrected myself, Jamie's eyes dropped to her hands, fidgeting with her pen. "I'm sorry I held on too tight to something that didn't make sense for you," I continued. "I didn't know there was more than one way for things to turn out okay, in the end."

"It's okay," Jamie whispered. Finally she looked up from her pen. "Thank you."

"Well, I'm gonna go, but we'll talk later," I said. I turned to leave and then turned back. "Where *are* you hoping to go next year?"

"Berkeley," said Jamie. "I should find out next month."

I nodded. It wasn't the first time she'd mentioned it as a possibility, but Berkeley had long been background noise for Jamie, the school to which her AP US History teacher had suggested she eventually apply based on her very evident interest in political science. At the time, we'd rolled our eyes, mortified at the idea of staying in state. Or at least that was how I remembered it. The idea had stuck with her, clearly, turning over and over until it fit just right.

"I'm sure they want you," I said. She looked up at me, her expression inscrutable. I stared back, trying to figure it out, until she broke, and looked away. I turned, and with a quick goodbye to Dee and Gaby, I was gone.

The next morning, I got the official offer from UCLA. They offered to cover half my tuition and all my textbooks, and they said I had two weeks to decide. But I didn't need it. There was nothing else to wait for, and, finally, nothing I wanted more. I signed my letter of intent and sent it back. Three and a half years I'd waited, and it was over in twenty minutes.

Twenty-Two

Over the next week, Jamie and I worked out our Triple Moon plan over text and FaceTime. It was Jamie, surprisingly, who insisted we go forward with the Sweets show, and so I looped in Ruby, feeling very much like a band manager, and I wondered if this was the feeling Jamie got from starting clubs: the mild thrill of creating an event dependent entirely on you, having ungraded administrative tasks to perform and calendars to coordinate. Because the show would fall in December, it was Jamie's idea to give it a Krampusnacht theme. Krampusnacht, Wikipedia taught us, was a European pre-Christmas holiday on which a "wicked, hairy devil" appears in the streets to give bad kids coal. This idea seemed very much in line with Sweets's vibe, and when we texted Ruby the idea, she proclaimed it *dope*. (Somehow, when Ruby said it, it worked.) We convinced Dee and Gaby that we could charge thirty dollars a head—six times as much as last time—of which the band would keep just eight (two per member), leaving the coffee shop with twenty-two.

I immediately started doing calculations: If fifty people came, Triple Moon would earn eleven hundred dollars. If a hundred people came, twenty-two hundred. If two hundred people came . . . but then Jamie interrupted me over text, reminding me that the coffee shop couldn't even fit that many people inside.

Jamie also texted me to tell me she'd biked to the LGBT Community Center in Hillcrest and convinced them to put out a donation box for the holiday season, agreeing to split any profits between the center and Triple Moon. This inspired me to ask my mom if she knew any young queer reporters who could write a story about the coffee shop's impact on queer teenagers and twenty-somethings who lived here, and simultaneously advertise for the show, and she put me in touch with a college grad named Davey, who promptly emailed to ask about setting up phone interviews with me, Jamie, Dee, and Gaby. If you didn't know Jamie like I did, it would've been easy to miss how impressed she was with me when I told her what I'd done, and she texted back **Wow.** Period. But I knew. That *wow* was everything.

Over the same few days, Ruby and I had texted back and forth, trying to decide on a time to hang out before the show. It shouldn't have been any harder than usual, but I noticed we were slow to respond to one another, and vague when we did. Ruby bailed on the first afternoon I suggested, and when she counter-offered the following night, I ended up canceling with the excuse that I had a migraine, which was only half true. I didn't know why, exactly, but I was nervous to see her again. It had only been about a week since I had, but it felt like twenty. At night when I couldn't sleep I tried to replay our hookups in my head, but I found they didn't rush to me like they used to. I squeezed my eyes tighter, trying to concentrate, but that only made it less sexy, and more like a fact I was trying to remember for an exam. *The Fourth Amendment is the right to security from unreasonable search and seizure. Carbon has four valence electrons. First I kissed Ruby there, and then she put her hand here.* Or was it the reverse? I gave up.

The obvious solution was to see her again, and do it again, but part of the reason I put off seeing her was because I was worried I wouldn't want to. I was also worried that I would want to but she wouldn't. But as the date of the show crept up on us and I texted her more and more about those logistics, it got weirder and weirder that we weren't hanging out, so finally, on the first of the month, we met up at Balboa Park. It was my suggestion, offered because it felt romantic, a throwback to before we kissed but clearly wanted to. But also, maybe, I suggested it because it was neutral territory, a public place not particularly close to either of our beds.

At the moment the calendar flipped to December, Balboa

Park was lit with strands of green and red and white lights, strung across the main plaza and draped from flagpoles in the shape of Christmas trees. Those trees that weren't covered in bulbs were lit by rainbow lamps dug into the ground, and little kids and their parents lined up outside Casa de Balboa, waiting to meet Santa Claus, who was set up inside for photos and present requests. Another Santa, this one made of wood, sat in his sleigh, just beginning to take flight between the Plaza de Panama and the Organ Pavilion. This part had been my favorite as a kid, and was even now, because I loved the reindeer's long painted lashes, and the shiny wrapped presents, which looked poised to spill off the back of the sleigh. The effect was best at night, when you couldn't quite see all the wires and stands holding the displays together.

It was warmer than usual that night, but Ruby and I had planned to meet at the concession stand for hot chocolate, and because it was almost Christmas, we went ahead with it. I paid for us both, and we carried our steaming cups to the nearest open table, pausing to watch a woman pull her wailing four-year-old boy toward the line for Santa. The boy went limp, collapsing to the ground as if being led to his death, and rather than pick him up, she waved goodbye and walked ahead, pretending to leave him there. Seconds later he got up, hiccuping, and ran after her.

"I feel for him," said Ruby. "I never wanted to sit on Santa's lap. I always knew it was just some creepy guy."

I laughed. "Always?!"

"By age five, yeah. My older brother told me Santa wasn't real, and I was like, that makes sense."

"Wow. That's young."

Ruby smirked. "Why, how old were you?"

"Umm," I said. "A little older."

"How old."

I picked up my cocoa, knowing full well it was still too hot. "Ten or eleven?" I murmured quickly before taking a scalding sip.

Ruby's astonished laughter made me feel warm and bashful.

"I don't have any older siblings!" I exclaimed.

"Didn't you have friends?!"

"Yeah, mainly Ronni. She conspired with our other friends to keep it a secret," I said. "She didn't want to ruin it for me."

Ruby shook, holding her fingers under her eyes to catch any trailing mascara, and though my later-than-average credulity had previously been a sore spot for me, I finally agreed. It was really funny.

"That's true friendship, right there," said Ruby.

"I know," I said. "I'm really gonna miss her. Maybe you guys can be friends at Stanford."

"Maybe." Ruby smiled politely.

We took cautious sips of cocoa and looked around at the lights, each of us struggling to come up with something to say next. I watched Ruby press her thumbnail, currently painted white, into her cup, leaving a little half-moon pattern around the rim. After a nearly interminable silence I settled on a question I'd already asked her, in varying forms, three times at least: "Are you excited for your show?"

"Yeah," said Ruby. "It'll be fun. I hope it helps."

"Me too."

"I was gonna say, actually—they can keep my share. Dee and Gaby."

My heart sank a little. "You really don't have to do that," I said.

"I want to."

I quickly ran the math in my head. "Are you sure? That's, like, probably more than a hundred bucks," I said.

"I don't need it," said Ruby. "Honestly. They've been really cool to us, and I want them to have it."

Suddenly I was so sad I almost couldn't speak. I tried to thank her, but it came out like a whisper. Ruby reached across the sticky table and brushed away a tear I didn't feel until it was gone.

"I'm sorry," I said. "I don't know why I'm so emotional."

"It's Christmas, it's senior year, you aren't going to school where you thought, you're trying to help some friends in trouble?" Ruby guessed. "PMS, maybe?"

I laughed. "All of the above, yeah."

"We synched up," said Ruby, looking so fond of me I had to look away.

"Jamie told me that's a myth," I said. "But I don't believe her."

"I like that you want to believe in things," said Ruby. "It's a really good way to be."

My vision clouded with tears again, because I could feel it: we were breaking up. Only I couldn't call it that, because we hadn't been girlfriends in the first place. A year or two from now, when I wanted to describe to someone what Ruby Ocampo had meant to me, what would I call her? Not a friend. Not an ex-girlfriend. *My former lover,* I thought, and snorted involuntarily. Nothing fit. Nothing would do our brief, informal, up-and-down, exciting, stressful, thrilling time together justice. It would be too much and too weird to tell anyone I didn't know very well that she was the person who'd made me believe in love again, but she had.

"Why are you crying?" Ruby asked gently.

"Because you're not in love with me," I said. I laughed, embarrassed and astonished by what I was willing to say out loud.

For a moment Ruby looked like she might cry too. "I mean, are you in love with me?"

I had wondered, but as soon as she asked, I knew. "No," I admitted. "But I think I could have been, eventually."

Ruby smiled. She pulled at her rubbery mint-green phone case, suddenly shy. "I don't think I've ever felt that way about anyone."

Even though I was the one being dumped (or whatever), I felt sorry for Ruby then. Before her, I thought that quote about it being "better to have loved and lost than never to have loved at all" was bullshit. The losing hurt too much. I would have given anything not to feel it.

Ruby was watching me now, I realized. "You have," she said.

It was a question, but it wasn't.

"Yeah," I said. "Just the once."

It was impossible to explain, and somehow, simultaneously, it was as simple as everyone said: when you were in love, you knew. What surprised me most was the way the feeling morphed and faded and brightened again, reliable only in its unreliability. When I told Jamie I loved her for the first time, it meant something different from the last time I told her I loved her. But both times, and every time in between, it was true. I felt it in my bones. Sometimes I felt that love still knocking around my body. It was like a fish, once granted an entire ocean to swim in, now restricted to a tiny bowl. Still, it moved within me.

"Are you a Cancer?" Ruby asked suddenly, her eyes narrowing suspiciously.

"Aquarius."

"That's why."

"Why what?"

"Your feelings are so . . . big," she said.

I laughed. "Would you have said that explained it no matter what I said?"

"Maybe," Ruby admitted. "Unless you said Capricorn, and then no."

Unsure what else to do, I reached for my cocoa and took a sip. I grimaced—too cold—and was once again mystified by my inability to catch hot chocolate at the correct temperature.

"What do we do now?" said Ruby.

"Can we be friends?"

"Of course."

"Can I still come to your show?"

Ruby threw her head back. "Ha! No, Quinn. You're banned from your own event you planned."

I smiled, squashing the tiny part of me that hoped she'd ask me not to come, just so I could feel justified in my woundedness. If our conclusion were more dramatic, and Ruby properly dumped me, or I properly dumped her, and we refused to speak to one another ever again, at least people would know I mattered to her.

"What did Mikey and them think? About us, I mean," I said.

She rolled her eyes. "Mikey was whatever, but David and Ben were big fans."

"Ew," I said.

"I know. I had to give them a lecture on, like, the fetishizing male gaze."

"I bet they *loved* that."

We smiled at each other, and in that moment, something in my chest unlocked. I realized then that I did not care, really, what Mikey or David or Ben thought of me, or of me and Ruby. Neither did I care what any of the other ruler-straight so-called popular kids thought. Their long and horrible reign was ending. Soon we would all be starting over. There would be a new social order in college and, if my mom was to be believed, at every job I ever had, but nobody could make me care if I didn't want to. The way those people lived their lives didn't have to have anything to do with the way I lived mine. And the truth was, nobody was thinking about me and my decisions and my feelings as much as I was. Ruby had shown me that, in a nice way. Maybe the thought should have scared me, or depressed me, and months earlier, it definitely would have. But I didn't feel that now. I felt light. I felt free. *Nobody cares!* I thought, and it made me laugh.

Twenty-Three

I awoke on December 7 to an anxious ache in my stomach. Though Jamie and Ruby both assured me that attendance would be good, we'd only been able to get verbal or social media confirmation from thirty-three people. *(Thirty-three times twenty-two is seven hundred twenty-six, plus sixty-six if Ruby waives her share, making . . . seven hundred ninety-two dollars.)* I rolled over in bed to find the article Davey had written, which was supposed to go up late last night or early this morning. I'd given up refreshing the page around one a.m. When it loaded, and I saw the headline—LOCAL COFFEE SHOP PROVIDES SAFE SPACE FOR SAN DIEGO'S QUEER YOUTH—I shimmied excitedly. I texted it to Jamie, who'd probably already read it five times through, and then skimmed it quickly for mention of my name.

"Without Triple Moon, I don't think I would've been brave enough to come out when I did. Dee and Gaby are like gay guardian angels," says Quinn Ryan, a senior at Westville High School and organizer of tonight's event.

I smiled and searched next for Jamie.

"The most important books I've ever read, the most meaningful discussions I've had, the most amazing person I know—all of that happened here," says Jamie Rudawski, also a senior at Westville High School and Ryan's co-organizer.

First I only noticed that "Ryan's co-organizer" part, which thrilled me even as—okay, maybe because—I knew how much Jamie would stew over it, because it made it sound like I was the one in charge. I planned a little consolatory speech: I would tell her it was just a matter of clarity, and I only came first because I'd said the coffee shop's name. Her quote was better, more moving. Her quote was . . . wait. I reread it, then read it again. Was I that most amazing person? I had to be. Right? Unless it was Gaby. I knew they had a special connection. But that didn't fit quite right. Had she said *inspirational*, maybe, but *amazing* sounded like someone she once loved. Or was it *still* loved? I stared at the present tense of *I know*, squinting as if I might find a clue in the space between the words.

Just then Jamie texted me back, a string of nervous fragments.

I saw!!!! It's good

When should we head over

I want to help them clean and stuff

Is 10 too early

I laughed.

Haha. I love you

I bolted upright in bed. I'd sent the text reflexively, before I knew what I was typing, before I could think through its implications. I had to bury it with other texts before Jamie could wonder what kind of love I meant.

Yes I think 10 am is too early

How about 5?

I just got up, I added pointlessly.

I watched the bubble appear and disappear and reappear again. I knew she knew that that bubble meant as much as whatever she ended up sending. We'd talked about this. We'd argued about it once, and I'd accused her of puppeteering my emotions via text bubble. I didn't remember if either of us apologized. I only remember that it became a joke, both of us typing gibberish into our phones to keep a bubble on the other's screen for as long as possible before finally texting a one- or two-word good-night.

5 works! she wrote.

I breathed a sigh of relief.

Cool. See you then.

The mood at Triple Moon when I got there was—how do I say this?—funereal. Instead of the usual riot grrrl soundtrack, Sarah McLachlan cooed over the speakers. Dee leaned against the back counter, staring into space, and Gaby sat at a table nearby, reading glasses on, hunched over a laptop. They both perked up when they saw me, but it was too late. My heart sank.

"What's up?" I asked, trying to sound cheerful and instead sounding a little manic.

"Hey, Q," said Dee. "You're here early."

"I'll have you know, Jamie wanted to get here at ten. In the morning."

Dee snorted. "I'd have killed you both."

"I know." I glanced at Gaby, but she was still absorbed in whatever was on her screen. When I looked at Dee again, she gave a sad sort of shrug. Morale was treacherously low. Sarah, goddess love her, wasn't helping. I had to do something.

"Can I?" I pointed to Dee's phone. "It sounds like a commercial for dying animals in here."

"The ASPCA is very important to Sarah," Dee said, handing it over.

I scrolled until I found the set of playlists I'd shared with Dee in an attempt to modernize the coffee shop's music selection, and tapped the one I'd called *Screw Everybody*. The Yeah Yeah Yeahs' "Black Tongue" burst through the speakers, defiant and dirty. Dee bit her lip and raised rock hands above her head. She looked so dorky, and about a million years old, and I loved her for it. I pulled the extra *Union-Tribune* copy my mom had brought me out of my tote bag and opened it to the Triple Moon story.

"Did you guys see the article?"

Dee took the paper gently, mouthing the headline as she read, and Gaby got up and joined her behind the counter. "Oh, wow," said Gaby.

"You didn't look it up online?"

"I didn't—did you, Dee?" said Gaby.

"I forgot," Dee murmured. I gave them a minute to read the story, drumming the counter to the beat while I waited. I was stunned to see that when Gaby finished, and looked up, she had tears in her eyes. Dee took a few moments longer, but she placed a hand on Gaby's shoulder, somehow knowing she needed it. *Please don't cry*, I thought. Gaby was bad enough, but if Dee cried, I feared I might never recover.

Finally she looked up, clearing her throat. "This is incredible, Q. Thank you. This means a lot to us."

I blushed. "I didn't write it."

"But you made it happen," said Gaby.

I shook my head. "No, you did." Dee was watching me but I couldn't look at her. Mercifully, the door whooshed open, and we turned to see Jamie stop in her tracks just inside.

"What's happening?"

"Come in here," said Gaby. She and Dee looped their arms over each other's shoulders and together they pulled us into a hug over the counter. Jamie's hand burned hot against my back, and I pictured its pink print still there, hours from now.

"They just read the story," I explained.

"Ah, got it," said Jamie. She paused. "Have you guys ever heard of the internet?"

The next hour flew by in a frenzied rush, Jamie and me inventing tasks just to complete them. I wiped down tables while Jamie neatened the bookshelf, stopping periodically to remove a novel from a shelf and reread a favorite passage. Jamie took out the trash while I swept the bathroom floor. When it finally seemed reasonable to begin decorating in earnest, we hung strings of red lights over the "stage," taping them to the corners of the back wall and connecting the end to a bright orange extension cord Dee dug up from somewhere in the office. We put lumps of charcoal in disposable aluminum ashtrays on every table as centerpieces, and hung swaths of torn black gauze from every available surface. Finally, on the front door, we taped up the truly terrifying Krampus concert poster

Alexis had drawn for us in Advanced 2-D Art. The effect was just right: spooky but not Halloween-y, thoughtful but not try-hard. Jamie and I took a step back to evaluate our efforts, and clinked our iced lattes together in self-congratulations. I pulled out my phone to check the time, and realized we still had an hour to kill.

Later, I was removing old, out-of-date notices and ads from the community corkboard when I saw a neon-pink notice for something called QU33RZ for JUSTICE, signed by a name I thought I recognized. I called Jamie over to look.

"Do we know this person? Jess?" I pointed.

"Yeah! They're a sophomore. Really good trumpet player," said Jamie.

"They're starting an LGBTQ club at Westville," I said, re-reading and marveling over this information as Jamie leaned in closer to get a look.

"Wow," she said. "I can't believe they put *queer* right in the name. That's so cool."

"Yeah," I agreed. We exchanged a look, and I knew we were both thinking of our own little GSA, feeling overwhelmed by just how much had changed in two years.

A little after seven, Ronni and Alexis showed up with a bag of sandwiches and chips, and we inhaled them standing over the counter, watching the door for early arrivals. When seven-fifteen rolled around and it was still just us, I was able to tamp down the nerves rising into my throat. At seven-thirty, a trio of freshman girls walked in, looked at us looking at them, and retreated into the parking lot to stare at their phones, pretending to wait for someone else they knew.

"Sooo many people I've talked to are coming," said Alexis, reading my mind. "Like. So many."

I glanced at Jamie, trying to read on her face whether one of those people might be Natalie. I got nothing.

"Well, the show starts at eight," I said. "It's seven-thirty-six."

"Everybody knows eight means nine," said Ronni.

Jamie and I exchanged wide-eyed looks. "What?"

"I'm sorry, but that's insane," I said.

"If I'd meant nine, I'd have put nine!" Jamie shrieked.

Ronni shrugged. "The band isn't even here yet."

"Yeah, but that's because they have to, like, be cool," I said. "And Ruby said they're on the way."

Alexis gave me a knowing smile, and I realized she hadn't yet heard the news. For once, I wished Ronni *had* just passed my secrets on to Alexis.

"It's not like that," I said. "We're not together anymore." I glanced at Jamie just in time to catch her looking at me.

"Oh my God, are you okay? Did she say why?" Alexis rushed to me, a hand on my shoulder, furrowed brow inches from my face.

I shook her off me. "Um, *I* ended it, thank you very much."

Another sidelong glance at Jamie. This time she didn't look away. Alexis called me back. "But. Why?" she said.

I thought about what to say. I could tell her something was missing. I could tell her that Ruby didn't want to be in a serious relationship, and that I didn't know how not to be serious. I could say it was practical, that high school would be over soon, and neither of us wanted to do long distance, though that was only sort of accurate, because there'd been a period of time in which I would have done anything to keep her. I could say Ruby and I never quite made it off the ground and I didn't know why, but that wasn't quite true either. I did know why. We didn't love each other. As it happened, I loved someone else. I'd never really stopped.

The air around me grew thick and charged. Maybe Ronni felt it too, and that's why she changed the subject.

"Look," she said, pointing over my shoulder. I turned and saw a small horde of juniors parking and climbing out of their cars, the freshman trio slipping in just behind them.

"Thank God," I whispered.

I felt my phone vibrate and pulled it from my back pocket: a text from Ruby.

We're here! Just parking

"Um. Ruby's here, so—"

"Should we go help?" said Jamie.

"You and me?" I asked dumbly.

"Y-yeah?"

"Yeah, okay," I said. "They're parking out back. Make sure everyone pays," I told Ronni and Alexis, and handed them the large plastic Cheez Balls bucket we'd converted for tonight's event. Unlike the first show, for which Dee and Gaby had handled the money, we claimed treasurer duties this time around, wanting the amount we collected to be a surprise.

"Yes, sir," said Ronni, and we laughed to see Alexis, hugging the bucket close to her body, eyes gleaming with power.

Jamie and I went out through the back entrance and found Mikey and Ben unloading equipment from the back of David's van. Ruby stood behind them, supervising. When she saw us, she rushed over to give me a hug, and then Jamie.

"Sorry we're late," she said. "*Someone* couldn't find his 'lucky pick.'" She rolled her eyes.

"You're fine." Jamie's voice, cheerful and reassuring, surprised me. "People are just starting to get here."

"Good," said Ruby. "Or . . . bad?"

My face must have conveyed my concern. "No, it's good," I said. "I'm just nervous."

"How do you think I feel?" Ruby gave me a playful shove. Maybe it was my imagination, but I thought I could feel Jamie bristling beside me.

"You'll be great," I said.

Ruby grinned. "I know."

When we shuffled into the shop minutes later, all of us struggling under the weight of guitars and guitar stands and various pieces of electronic drum kit, Jamie and me bringing up the rear, we were not prepared for what we saw. My mouth fell open, and Jamie and I exchanged a look of wide-eyed excitement. The place was very nearly full, and by a quick mathematical estimate I deduced there were fifty-five people or more. We sped up, rushing to deposit Sweets's equipment on the stage, and I yelled "Break a leg!" to Ruby. She waved her thanks, but she was already in rock-star mode, surveying her crowd of adoring fans. Jamie and I weaved our way through them back to Ronni, at our table by the counter.

"What happened?" I marveled.

"Where's Alexis?" asked Jamie.

Ronni held up her hand to calm us.

"Alexis is doing her job ruthlessly," she said, pointing to the door. Alexis stood outside, half bouncer, half bodyguard. No one got past her without dropping cash in the bucket. "As for how it got this packed, I do not know. I swear I looked at my phone for two seconds, and when I looked up it was like this."

I held up my hand for Jamie to high-five, which I regretted as soon as her hand met mine. I felt hot and sick and alive with nerves. It was a horrible kind of ecstasy, being in love and not knowing what exactly was going to happen, or when, but certain *something* would. And there I was, feeling it again, for someone I'd already loved and lost.

Ronni, perhaps sensing the vibe, or just as embarrassed by our awkward high five as I was, stood up. "I see Janelle and Kate," she said. "I'm gonna go say hi."

With Ronni gone I was painfully aware of the precise distance between Jamie's arm and mine, her leg and mine. The band was starting to warm up now, tuning their instruments while Ruby sang them notes off mic. I was desperate for them to get started and drown out my thoughts. Jamie, too, seemed to be scanning the room for anything to look at that wasn't me, but that could have meant two very different things. I tried to make eye contact with Dee, but she was busy making lattes and espresso shots, and I noted the overstuffed tip jar with pride. I checked my phone, but everyone who ever texted me was here. Finally, there was nothing left I could think of to do but the thing I wanted to do most: talk to Jamie.

"Do you think it'll be enough?" I asked. We watched three more people stream through the door, and then another four. There had to be at least eighty people here, and surely at least a few more would show up late, after the show had begun.

Jamie smiled at me sadly. "I don't know. But I think we've raised more than they hoped for, and that has to count for something."

I had a sinking feeling Jamie was right. As enormous a sum as two or three thousand dollars seemed to us, two people who had previously had zero, it might be like trying to stop the *Titanic* from sinking with a cork. For some twisted reason, this mental image made me laugh. Jamie always said I tried to compare too many things to the *Titanic*.

"What?"

I shook my head. "Can you imagine not having this place?"

Jamie appeared to give it an honest effort before answering. "No. I can't."

"What are the gay kids after us going to do?"

"There's always the internet?" Jamie said, sounding unconvinced.

"I should have come here more," I said. My voice came out thick and garbled. "I should have been here every day."

Jamie and I looked at each other, and I knew that she knew it wasn't just Triple Moon I regretted taking for granted.

Feedback pierced through the speakers, and we winced and turned to the stage.

"Hellooooooo, San Diego!" Ruby cried. We whooped and clapped, and she bent over laughing. "Sorry. Pandering. We don't even play anywhere else."

"YET!" yelled someone in the crowd.

Ruby grinned, and everyone else cheered.

"I wanna thank y'all for coming out to support this establishment," she said. "Most of tonight's proceeds will go to Triple Moon and its owners, Dee and Gaby, who've been extremely cool to us." She waited while people clapped politely. "I also wanna thank Jamie Rudawski and Quinn Ryan for organizing this thing. Where are they?"

She raised a hand to her brow, as if the crowd went on for acres and not forty or so feet. Half the audience turned to look for the people they were being made to clap for, so I gave a little wave and Jamie followed suit.

"Quinn," said Ruby. My heart stopped. "This one's for you."

The noise was immediate, silence to pop-punk explosion in the blink of an eye. Drums, bass, guitar, and Ruby's voice, above them, scream-singing about a girl who everyone knew was me. I was so cemented to the spot, trying to make out the lyrics and scanning the audience to see who was looking at me, that I didn't notice Jamie had slipped away until the chorus.

Ruby, smiling at me, singing: "Big feelings / you've got / big feelings / and I'm not / big feelings / but it's cool." I smiled back, relief and affection coursing through my veins. It wasn't a love song, and it wasn't a fuck-you song either. It was a song about almosts. It was about me, and her, and the unnamed but not unimportant thing we'd been to each other. Standing at the back of the crowd, aware of all the curious, envious looks directed my way, I felt like I'd lived this moment before. Certainly, I'd imagined it. In the fantasy version, though, Ruby sang about how much she loved me. In the fantasy, I loved her too. We left the show together. We became prom queens. We dated throughout my freshman year at UNC. The fantasy got blurry for a bit; I skipped ahead: I became famous and beloved and I married a woman who loved me exactly as much as I loved her. There were no surprises, and I was never wrong.

But I'd been wrong so many times already this year. I'd been wrong and I'd lost and I'd been rejected and dumped. My dreams had been crushed, and my heart broken. I did not particularly recommend either, but I survived both. People had changed, done unexpected things, deviated from the course I imagined for them. I had, too. We were still here. I didn't know what would happen to me or to any of us, but I knew what I wanted to do now.

I smiled at Ruby, so widely my cheeks hurt. I waited until I was sure she understood everything I was trying to say with that smile. And then I ducked out.

I found her by the dumpsters out back, and when she saw me she lifted her phone to her ear, evidently pretending to be on a call. I laughed, and she scowled.

"Okay, fine."

"What are you doing out here?"

My heart raced. I knew the answer. She wasn't waiting for anyone else. I took a step closer.

"Nothing, I just—" She cut herself short. She stared at her feet. "She wrote you a *song*?" she blurted out.

"Did you listen to it?"

She paused. "She wrote you a *song.*"

"Yeah." I nodded. "And I'm out here."

Jamie blinked at me. "That's actually a little rude."

"Very," I said. Another step.

Jamie wouldn't look me in the eyes, speaking instead to my right shoulder. "Natalie and I are just friends," she said hurriedly.

I froze. "Oh?"

"I mean, we sort of hooked up. But then—" Finally she looked me in the eyes.

"What?"

"I cried on her."

I only barely managed not to laugh out loud, instead making a weird, choking throat noise. "You cried—"

"On her. Yeah." Jamie's eyes twinkled. She looked like she could cry or laugh or maybe both. "It was after . . ." She trailed off. I finished her sentence in my head: *After Ruby and I slept together.*

Poor Natalie freaking Reid, I thought.

"Blagh," said Jamie, shaking her curls at the ground. "Sorry. I'm just— I don't know what my problem is. I'm the one who—"

"Dumped me?"

She looked up and saw me smiling. "Yeah."

"Maybe I deserved it." Half a step. Just 7.75 inches between her chest and mine.

Jamie shook her head. "No." She paused. "Well, kind of."

"I never pictured us not together," I said. "For the record."

"It's okay if you did," she said. "I was the first girlfriend you ever had. How often does that work out?"

"Probably not very often," I said. We stood so close now I could feel her breath on my neck. "But second girlfriends are different."

Jamie's face dropped, head sinking into her chest. I hooked a finger under her chin and lifted her back up.

"I mean *you*, dummy."

Then we were kissing, and it was just how I remembered it, but better for having thought I'd never get to kiss her again. *From now on,* I promised myself, *I will think about how lucky I am every time we kiss. I will treat every kiss as the possible last.* Because someday, if we were together until college or until we graduated or until we grew old together and died, the last kiss would come. Being apart from her had made me understand that in a way I'd only abstractly known before. I understood now that there was a lot about my future and hers I couldn't predict. Already things were so different than I'd imagined. My year so far had been full of rejection. But I lived. I was still worthy, and good. Kissing Jamie, I still felt like the luckiest girl in the world.

Just then, Jamie pulled back and looked around.

"We're making out, like, *in* the garbage," she said.

"Jamie," I said. "You're the love of my life."

Her eyes grew wide as the moon, but she quickly recovered.

"*So far*," she said. "We're seventeen. I'm the love of your life *so far*."

I rolled my eyes. "Isn't that all anyone can say?"

Jamie thought this over. "Yeah, I guess you're right."

"Thank you," I said.

"I guess we should go back inside."

I was still afraid. I was afraid our friends would think we were making a mistake. I was afraid the show wouldn't be enough, and Triple Moon would close. I was afraid we'd go to college and lose touch with Dee and Gaby. I was afraid to leave Ronni and my team and be part of a new one, full of strangers. I was afraid the five-hour-and-forty-eight-minute drive between Jamie's school and mine (without traffic—ha) would be too much.

But Jamie was right. We couldn't stay there forever. So I took her hand, and we went forward, together.

Acknowledgments

Back when writing this book was just a vague idea, Marisa DiNovis, my wonderful editor, emailed me to ask if I'd ever considered writing YA. We exchanged a number of frantic, excited emails in which it soon became clear to me that the book I was starting to work on belonged with her. Marisa, you reached me at a time when I was feeling frustrated and a little lost, and reminded me of what's important, and what I want to do. Thank you so much for making this book what it is, and thanks to the rest of the wonderful team at Knopf Books for Young Readers for their support and enthusiasm.

Immense thanks to Allison Hunter, my incredible, superstar agent (and part-time therapist). You were the first to see something in my work, and I will never forget that. Thanks also to Clare Mao for her promptness, insights, and honesty. Thank you to Josephine Rais, for creating the beautiful art for this book.

I also want to thank my dear friend Chiara Atik, who tells me what I need to do whenever I feel stuck, which is often just "keep writing." There's nobody whose storytelling instincts or taste I trust more.

Thank you to my family, both old and new. Irene, you raised an amazing woman. I didn't know little fifteen-year-old Lydia, but I would have liked to. Thank you to my wife, Lydia: for loving me, supporting me, and inspiring me. I love you.

MARY TRIES. IT'S WHAT SHE DOES.

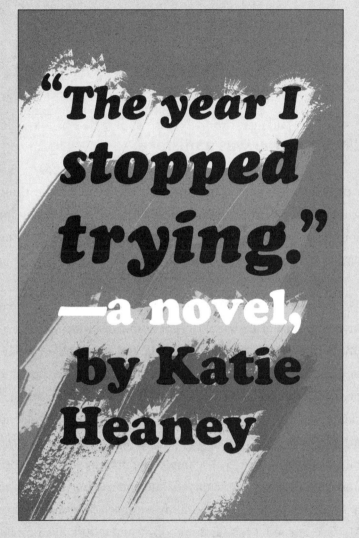

"The year I stopped trying." —a novel, by Katie Heaney

But when she finally realizes she isn't going to find the meaning of life in a 4.0 GPA, she asks herself: *What if I stopped trying so hard?*

The first time was a mistake.

I don't like to admit that, because I think this whole thing would be cooler if I'd meant to do it from the beginning for some good reason, or even *a* reason. But the truth is that one day, after ten years without incident, I just forgot.

There wasn't anything unusual going on that week. I worked my usual shift at La Baguette, got home, did what was left of my homework, watched a little TV, and went to sleep. The next morning I got up, ate the same breakfast, made the same peanut butter and jelly sandwich and put the same chips and carrots in little plastic bags, and drove my brother, Peter, and me the same way to school. I walked into first period three minutes before the bell, completely prepared for another normal day. Then class started, and the teacher asked us to hand in our homework . . . and my stomach fell into my feet. My face burned. I felt faint and dizzy and a little like I might throw up. Because I had not done my AP U.S. history homework. Somehow, in the list of things I had to do the night before, this one had gotten lost. As everyone around me dug through their bags for their short essays on Manifest Destiny, I flipped through my planner and scanned yesterday's to-do items. And there it was, with a line drawn through it, like everything else on the page. But I had not written that essay. I looked through my folder, just in case, but I knew there was nothing to find.

I sat there, sweating, for the rest of class, planning what I'd say to Mr. Delaney to let him know I knew I'd made a mistake and I'd never do it again if somehow he could find it in him to forgive me. I could offer to do a make-up assignment, a five- or ten-page paper on a topic of his choosing. Or I could pretend I *had* done the homework but had packed my bag wrong because of unspecified stressors at home. I could say I'd gotten home late from work and set a 4:00 a.m. alarm to finish, but then my phone died, and I was almost late for school. He might believe me and offer me half credit to bring it in tomorrow. I weighed whether the damage to my dignity would be worth it if he did.

Maybe I would just run.

Class ended. I hovered for a few moments over my desk, slowly gathering my belongings, waiting for Mr. Delaney to call me over to explain myself. He had his shirt sleeves rolled up just slightly, revealing powerful-looking wrists and the merest glimpse of a tattoo faded navy. He was a former marine, and the rumor was that under his shirt and slacks he was covered from neck to ankle in tattoos. He loved pop quizzes and had a particular knack for calling on people exactly when they'd decided it was safe to zone out. Once, allegedly, he'd even offered an open-book final, only to retract the open-book part on the day of the exam. Mr. Delaney was not a teacher who could be counted on for grace.

Finally he looked up and saw me there, watching him as the next class's students started filtering into the classroom. "Yes, Mary?" he said. "Did you have a question?"

"No," I said automatically. "Sorry."

"See you tomorrow," he said firmly, and a little patronizingly. So I turned, and I walked out.

And that was it. After forty-seven minutes of agony and anxiety, my heart rate up and my head woozy and hot, it was over? I wasn't relieved; I was furious. I consoled myself by thinking he'd hold me after class the next day, after he'd had a chance to go through the essays, but he never handed them back. He just talked about the themes he'd seen, our collective mistakes. At the beginning of class, my shoulders were tensed up near my ears, but the more time passed, the lower they fell, until it felt safe to confirm: I'd gotten away with it.

The Year I Stopped Trying excerpt text copyright © 2021 by Katie Heaney.
Cover design by Casey Moses. Published by Alfred A. Knopf,
an imprint of Random House Children's Books, a division of
Penguin Random House LLC, New York.

through their bags for their short essays on Manifest Destiny, I flipped through my planner and scanned yesterday's to-do items. And there it was, with a line drawn through it, like everything else on the page. But I had not written that essay. I looked through my folder, just in case, but I knew there was nothing to find.

I sat there, sweating, for the rest of class, planning what I'd say to Mr. Delaney to let him know I knew I'd made a mistake and I'd never do it again if somehow he could find it in him to forgive me. I could offer to do a make-up assignment, a five- or ten-page paper on a topic of his choosing. Or I could pretend I *had* done the homework but had packed my bag wrong because of unspecified stressors at home. I could say I'd gotten home late from work and set a 4:00 a.m. alarm to finish, but then my phone died, and I was almost late for school. He might believe me and offer me half credit to bring it in tomorrow. I weighed whether the damage to my dignity would be worth it if he did.

Maybe I would just run.

Class ended. I hovered for a few moments over my desk, slowly gathering my belongings, waiting for Mr. Delaney to call me over to explain myself. He had his shirt sleeves rolled up just slightly, revealing powerful-looking wrists and the merest glimpse of a tattoo faded navy. He was a former marine, and the rumor was that under his shirt and slacks he was covered from neck to ankle in tattoos. He loved pop quizzes and had a particular knack for calling on people exactly when they'd decided it was safe to zone out. Once, allegedly, he'd even offered an open-book final, only to retract the open-book part on the day of the exam. Mr. Delaney was not a teacher who could be counted on for grace.

Finally he looked up and saw me there, watching him as the next class's students started filtering into the classroom. "Yes, Mary?" he said. "Did you have a question?"

"No," I said automatically. "Sorry."

"See you tomorrow," he said firmly, and a little patronizingly. So I turned, and I walked out.

And that was it. After forty-seven minutes of agony and anxiety, my heart rate up and my head woozy and hot, it was over? I wasn't relieved; I was furious. I consoled myself by thinking he'd hold me after class the next day, after he'd had a chance to go through the essays, but he never handed them back. He just talked about the themes he'd seen, our collective mistakes. At the beginning of class, my shoulders were tensed up near my ears, but the more time passed, the lower they fell, until it felt safe to confirm: I'd gotten away with it.